Emma Styles writes contemporary Australian noir about young women taking on the patriarchy. She grew up on Whadjuk Noongar country in Perth, Western Australia and now lives in London where she was born. Emma loves a road trip and once sat out a cyclone on the north-west coast of WA in a LandCruiser Troop Carrier. She is less afraid of great white sharks than she should be, and hopeless at surfing.

Emma has an MA in crime fiction from the University of East Anglia. *No Country for Girls* is her debut novel; it won the Little, Brown UEA Crime Fiction Award 2020.

NO COUNTRY FOR GIRLS

EMMA STYLES

SPHERE

SPHERE

First published in Great Britain in 2022 by Sphere
This paperback edition published by Sphere in 2023

1 3 5 7 9 10 8 6 4 2

A CIP catalogue record for this book
is available from the British Library.

ISBN 978-0-7515-8386-1

Typeset in Caslon by M Rules
Printed and bound in Great Britain by
Clays Ltd, Elcograf S.p.A.

Papers used by Sphere are from well-managed forests
and other responsible sources.

Sphere
An imprint of
Little, Brown Book Group
Carmelite House
50 Victoria Embankment
London EC4Y 0DZ

An Hachette UK Company
www.hachette.co.uk

www.littlebrown.co.uk

For Mum and Dad,
and the place I grew up

The author acknowledges the Traditional Owners and Custodians of the lands, waters and skies where this story is set, and pays her respects to Elders past, present and emerging. She supports the Uluru Statement from the Heart and recognises that sovereignty has never been ceded and this always was, and always will be, Aboriginal land.

The highway is long and flat and arrow-straight, running into the setting sun, and that is how he gets into difficulty. That, and his too-frequent glances between the rearview mirror and the holdall on the passenger seat. A ghost-limbed tree out of blackened scrub, half a painted truck tyre, and a steer, outlined in gold, standing across the centre white line. These things appear suddenly, as static objects, as if he has blinked too long and leapfrogged a section of road.

He brakes, swerves, slews from this lane across into the other.

A lucky escape, to be told loud and with relief to strangers at the pub, the steer moving only its eyes as he passes. Had it not been for the other car.

Later, in the immediate aftermath of the accident and throughout the years that unfold from it, he continues to think of the treasure as his. The risk is worthwhile. This not entirely honest bounty is the making of him as a man.

Here is a country that is there for the taking, after all.

SUNDAY

1

Charlie

Dickhead Daryl

It's past eight at night when I get near to home, full dark except for a half-arsed moon. My feet hurt from walking and there's a strong euc smell coming off the trees like summer's already here. I take the cut through Shenton Bushland and Karrakatta Cemetery in case he's out in the ute and come after me.

Course he's come after me. Dickhead. Haven't seen him, but.

The track through the cemo is dead straight, dead flat, bare dirt around the graves and gumnuts everywhere, rows of head-stones like white teeth. Creepy as fuck. I've got my headphones round my neck, music off – I'm not stupid, Geena – my thongs going *scrape*, *slap*, *scrape*, *slap* on warm bitumen and a bunch of noisy parrots in the trees overhead. Daryl's bit of gold in my hand and I feel the weight of it, how it fits exact in my fist when I close my fingers.

My phone vibrates in my shorts pocket. Geen, about her twentieth go at getting a hold of me tonight. This time I look behind to check no one's there, slide the gold into my pocket and pick up. 'I'm not giving it back, so you can get fucked.'

I can see her face, imagine it, trying to smile and keep her shit together. I talk quiet but she talks loud back.

'Howdy, Sis! How's it going with ya?' she says. 'Where are you?'

'Shh, keep it down, can't ya? As if I'm gunna tell you that. Dickhead there with you, is he? Given up 'cause he can't find me?'

'No.'

'Got me on speaker so he can listen in?'

'No, I do not. He's not back yet.'

I rub my neck and check behind again, but there's nothing there, no headlights. Dunno if the gates are shut at the far end and I pick up the pace. I'd hear the ute's engine growl, anyhow.

'You could bring it back while he's still out?' she says.

'No way.'

'Chrissakes, Charlie. It's not yours.'

'Fucksakes, Geen! You're not Mum.'

'And you're not twelve years old no more!'

I roll my eyes at the screen. What does it matter to her, that I took it off him? I only did it to piss him off. My thumb's ready to end the call when she says sorry for yelling.

'Come back here, okay?' she says, softer. 'Get the bus and bring that gold bar back. I'll tell him you didn't mean to take it.'

'I did mean to take it. Shoulda been more careful with it, shouldn't he? Got no cash for the bus, anyhow.'

'Shit.' She takes a drag of her smoke. She thinks I can't tell

6

over the phone when she's smoking but I can. 'Payday tomorrow, okay?' she says. 'I can get some dollars to you, for food and stuff.'

I keep walking, cross another path. The birds follow me, dropping euc flowers and gumnuts out the trees like a bunch of kids.

'What's going on, Geen?'

'I'm trying to get you to bring Daryl's—'

'No, I mean, whatcha doing at his place all the time? When are you coming home?'

Another drag of her smoke. 'Soon.'

Takes her too long to say it and my fingers tighten around the phone. I kick at a gumnut and stub my bare toe on the ground. She's been staying over at Daryl's all week, ever since the thing with school.

I stop at the main gates, shut and locked up. I hang back and stick in the shadows. A pool of yellow streetlight out on the footpath and some traffic noise off Thomas Street. No green ute waiting for me out on Smyth Road. He could be anywhere, but.

'I've gotta go, Geen.'

'Where are you?' she says. 'Is that cockatoos?'

'Karrakatta. I'm almost—'

'The cemetery? How many times have I told you not to—'

'Keep yer head on. I'm nearly home, aren't I?'

A car goes past on the street but it's not him.

'Just be careful, okay?' She takes another drag and her voice goes quiet. 'You haven't shown that bar to anyone, have you? Because—'

'Course not.'

'You can't try and sell it or anything.'

''Cause Dickhead Daryl stole it, ya mean? I'm not stupid.

7

How'd he get a hold of it, anyhow? Did he take it from the shop?'

'No! Hell, no. Nothing like that.' I hear it in her voice, but. How big it is, whatever the thing is she's not telling me.

I slide the gold out my pocket and it gleams in the light from the street. Long as my thumb and sits perfect in the palm of my hand. Like an icy-pole with no stick, except smaller. 'You reckon it's fake?' I ask. I like the feel of it, heavier than a rock, flat smooth with some letters and numbers engraved on one side.

'Fake?' Soon as she says it, I know it's not.

'A scam,' I say. 'That'd be more like Daryl.' Except now I'm only saying that. Now I know it's real.

Either way, he's not getting it back off me.

'Do us a favour?' Geen says. 'Can you not wind Daryl up any more than you already have? He's not some Year Eleven kid at school you can punch in the mouth.'

Yep, there it is. Every conversation since Monday.

'Listen, Charlie. If Daryl comes around—'

'If he comes around, I'm not gunna let him in. I'm gunna tell him where to stick his fat head.'

'Just be careful, okay? And don't show it to anyone. I'll see you tomorrow. I'll come around after work.'

She ends the call too quick and I stare at the busted screen of my phone before I ram it back in my pocket.

Fucksakes, what is it she's not telling me? What if she doesn't come home?

I climb out the cemo next to the main gate and cross the street in the shadows. No traffic, no green ute. I stick on the back streets until I get onto ours, click my music and pull my headphones back on. 'Reckless', one of Mum's favourites. It's a shit song, but – too slow – so I skip to the next. 'Say Goodbye', Hunters and Collectors.

I get halfway along the street before I see the fat girl outside our place. Stood underneath a streetlight, bent over like she's run a race, leaning on the top of the gate. She's got messy black hair in a plait with half a bottlebrush in it, staring at the busted mailbox, the upside-down number seven. I yank my headphones off when I get up to her. 'Who the fuck are you?'

She jerks upright and spins around. Not much older than me, eighteen tops. She's got a swollen cheek on one side like someone's smacked her in the face and she's puffing from her run, her boobs like a bouncy castle. Her eyes slide up and down me, across the brown lawn I haven't watered, to our front door. Place looks dead with no lights in the windows. 'This ... number ... twenty-seven?' she says.

'What if it is?' The big square villas either side are blazing out light like they're trying to make our shit house disappear up its own backside. My face burns the same as when Sass came to pick me up that very first time. 'There's zero stuff in there to take, if you're planning on robbing it.'

Her mouth opens and nothing comes out and she shuts it. She's got these hooded eyes so I can't see her, not properly. She's not white, either – she's Aboriginal, a bit or a lot I can't tell. I wrap my hand around the smoothness of the gold, ram it deeper into my pocket, past my phone.

Don't know her, do I? She could be anyone.

I check the street, both directions. No headlights. She keeps up her puffing, head down like she's gunna spew.

The music out my headphones sounds tinny and piss-weak and I click it off. 'Not being funny, but I gotta get inside. You asthmatic or some shit? Not gunna die on me, are ya?'

She shakes her head, frowns at my feet in my thongs. She's no better – got no shoes, has she? Designer denim skirt, cream silky top and a new suede jacket, plus half the local bushland in her hair. Scratched up her feet, too – prickles, glass, rocks, the works. She straightens up again, taller than I thought she was. Hitches her bag up her shoulder. One of those messenger bags, suede to match her jacket. 'You do live here?' she says.

'What do you care?'

She frowns like it's a whole big effort. 'Do I know you?'

'No, mate. You don't know me.'

What is she, a few brain cells short the full set? Doesn't look it, but. There's something about her, like a queen, someone flash. So, what's she doing here? Why's she got no shoes?

She limps a step and her eyes slide past me, searching for someone, up and down the street. My neck twitches and I rub the back of it. Take a look behind me. Nothing.

A siren cracks the dark along Railway Road and she jumps so high I do too. She spins her head and follows the sound, her eyes big and round. The siren dies and she stares at our mailbox again. 'I think ... I need to get inside somewhere.'

'Not here, you don't. Not being funny. Like I said—'

'Seriously,' she says. 'I can't stay out here.' She puts a hand up to her head. There's blood there, a smear like black paint. Another dark patch on the hem of her jacket. Fucksakes, I'm not babysitting a fat injured person.

'You on the run or what?' I say.

She blinks. 'I can't explain right now.'

I try to get around except she's blocking the gate. I nod my head up the street. 'Hospital's up there. You know the way?'

'No.'

'Yeah you do,' I say. 'Thomas Street. You want me to call someone? I can call someone.'

Her eyes shoot open. 'No! Like, I had an accident. In my car. I need to rest, that's all.' She pulls the twigs and shit out her hair and tries to smooth it down. 'Not the hospital. I'm fine.'

There's a Band-Aid on the side of her hand, blood soaking through that too. She's not fine.

'All I want is a couch. Is that so hard?' She smiles like she's making a real big effort, except it only half works. Talks flash, too, considering what she looks like. I don't trust it.

'What, crash at mine? Why can't ya go home?'

'Too far to walk.' Her eyes skitter away like two bugs.

She's lying, it's written all over. Takes one to know one. 'You need to move,' I say. 'I gotta get inside.'

She steps in front of me, looks at my feet again, over her shoulder at the house. 'I can pay you.'

Like she knows I've got no cash. And she'd be right, 'cause I can't do nothing with Daryl's bit of gold, can I? Not right now. Plus I dunno if Geen'll come tomorrow like she said she would. It takes me about two seconds to decide.

'Orright,' I say. 'Forty bucks for the couch, one night.'

She stares at me hard, presses her lips together. I reckon she'll haggle but she lifts the flap of her bag and rakes around. 'Fine.' She hands over two new twenties, stands back for me to get the gate open.

Shit. Should've asked her for more.

I push the twenties into my pocket next to my phone. Scrape open the gate and she follows me up the path to the front door.

I go to stick the key in the lock and I stop. 'How'd ya cut your hand?'

'I told you. I had a car accident.'

'Where is it then?'

'Sorry?'

'The car you stacked?' I nod past her at the street. 'You're meant to stay with it. Not leave the scene, yeah?'

She blinks in the light from next door. 'I don't remember. I might have hit my head.'

Fucksakes, I'm getting this knot in my stomach. 'If you're gunna be on my couch I reckon I've got the right.'

'Right?'

'To the full story.'

She presses her lips together.

'I do,' I say. 'It's my place and Geen's, except she's away. That's my sister. Don't wanna be axe-murdered in my bed, do I?'

She holds out a hand. 'I'm too tired for axe-murdering, but if you want to give me that forty dollars back—'

Bitch.

'Orright.' I get the door open. I'm not gunna think about where she got the forty bucks, what kind of trouble she's in. In the morning she's gunna be gone.

She tells me her name's Nao, says it like Nay-oh. Doesn't mean shit, anyhow – it's probably fake. I give her my real one, don't even think. She follows me inside and down the passage to the back. I can smell burnt toast from this morning and it makes my stomach growl. 'You can take the couch in the sleep-out,' I say. 'Not Geen's room.'

Before we get across the kitchen the light in the sleep-out snaps on and I stop, my eyes out on stalks and my heart going hell for leather.

It's Daryl, the big ugly bastard. 'G'day, Charlize. You took your time. Been out on the town, have we, you thieving little cunt?'

He's sat in Mum's chair like he owns the place. The back door's wide open and whanging the shit outta Geen's wind-chimes, Freo sea breeze blasting through the flyscreen. 'You're breaking and entering, Daryl. You can get outta that chair, too.'

He doesn't shift, course he doesn't. He's got BO and Bundaberg rum coming off him like kerosene, and the lampshade above him is swinging like it knows how mad he makes me, the light reflecting off the top of his shaved fat head. I feel it start in my fingertips, the massive epi tantrum I'm gunna chuck if he doesn't get out.

It's not as if I'm scared of the dickhead. I'm not. Geen pretends like she's not scared of him when she is. 'Where's my sister?' I say. 'When's she coming back home?'

'She'll be making my dinner, making herself fragrant.' He stretches his thick neck like he's been practising at the gym. 'You want my opinion, she won't be back here anytime soon. Where's my piece of gold, Charlize?'

My fingers twitch towards my pocket but I stop them short. 'It's Charlie, you deadshit.' A shift of air behind me. Nao, hanging back in the kitchen. She better stay outta this. 'How'd you get in? Better not have busted that door.' I cross the room and pull it shut, stop the wind-chime noise. The fridge in the kitchen clicks on and starts to rattle.

He opens one hand to show me the keys dangling there. Geen's keys, the Surfers Paradise keyring I gave her. My hands ball into fists and I have to blink. Can't believe she's sent him round here.

He smiles. 'All I want's the gold and I'll be out your way.'

'Dunno what you're on about.'

'Don't even try, Charlize.'

'Get outta that chair! You know full well that was Mum's.'

He waggles pink fingers. 'You first.'

The gold burns in my pocket. Nao calls from the kitchen. 'Where did you say the couch was? I can just—'

'Hold on,' I say to her. 'I'm sorting it.'

Daryl clocks Nao through the doorway, propped against the kitchen bench like she's gunna fall down. He checks her out like the perv that he is. 'Who's your mate?'

'She's not my mate,' I say. 'She needs somewhere to crash.'

He laughs. 'Must be fucken desperate.' He raises his voice to Nao. 'Can't trust this one as far as you can dropkick her. I'd get out while you can.'

It keeps building, running up my arms and into my shoulders – how bad I want to punch his lights out. 'I'll dropkick you if you don't get out my house.'

'I mean it, you little bitch. Where is it?'

'Musta lost it.'

He stands up and I take two steps back. Across the kitchen, Nao straightens up.

'Don't shit me, Charlize,' he says. 'I hear you got expelled from school for fighting, Monday. Three strikes and you're out. Shame.'

'Shut it, Daryl.'

I slide my hand in my pocket, real casual. Get my fingers round the gold and push it past my phone, into the bottom corner where that hole's been getting bigger. Push again and feel the drop as it slips into the lining of my shorts. He's not getting it off me. He can piss off home.

'No one likes a fighter,' he says. 'Not in a girl.' He takes one step and another one, backing me into the kitchen. He's head and thick neck taller, like the aggro makes him bigger. The Bundy fumes would flatten a camel. 'I hear your best mate won't talk to you, either. That you punched out her boyfriend. Like her a bit too much, is that it?'

'Shut it!' What's Geen been saying to him? He doesn't know shit. I try to count to ten but my eyes are pricking.

'No wonder your sister's left you—'

'She's not left me!' I fly at him. It's like hitting a Mack truck with BO.

He grabs the collar of my shirt and slams me into the fridge, the back of my head ringing. 'Don't try that shit with me, Charlize!' The fridge magnets scatter and Geen's keys go flying.

'Ow, you dick! Watch my headphones.'

'Give me the gold.' His face red, his hand at my neck, twisting my shirt. His other hand groping me down one side.

Nao's frozen, blinking behind him.

'Daryl, you perv!' I've got my left arm caught behind me and his hand at my neck is like a clamp. Can't pull my right arm back for the punch. I kick his shin but it does fuck-all. I go for his face with my nails.

'Bitch!' He squeals and backhands me. I taste blood, but there's a nice werewolf scratch down his cheek. He pins my right arm up to the fridge with a fat forearm, tightening his grip on my shirt. He digs in the pocket of my shorts with the other hand, pulls out Nao's twenties. 'What's this? Where is it?'

I smile 'cause he won't find it, but he's twisting the shirt so I can't get air. I'm on tiptoe, fighting for breath, the stuff on the fridge clanking like it's gunna come down on us. 'Sold it,' I gasp.

'Bulldust.'

Nao. 'You're choking her.' Useless.

My feet leave the floor and my mouth opens. Can't breathe. I grab the top of the fridge with the arm he's got pinned there, kick up at his nuts and miss.

'Put her down. Please.' Nao grabs his arm. He shakes her off but his grip loosens. I get my left arm free, scrape at the neck of my shirt. Too tight.

'I'll put her down, all right.'

I grope the top of the fridge with my right hand. What's up there? Wok, bread board, baking stuff. I hit something – smooth, a long handle.

Nao yanks on his T-shirt. 'Stop! Look at her face.'

The T-shirt rips and she falls backwards. Daryl rolls his neck and keeps digging, the other pocket now – wrong again, except he won't let go. This pressure in my head like there's too much blood in it.

My lips go numb. Black spots start up in front my eyes and I can't see Nao. My heart's bashing away like a Melbourne Cup loser but I'm fucked if he's gunna kill me. I get one hand round the thing on the fridge and then the other one. It's stuck underneath something, won't shift. I yank harder and it does, swinging out and down, too quick. Daryl rears backwards and his eyes go massive.

There's a shit-awful crunch and we go down hard, a twist of

arms and slippery sweat and Daryl's big bastard legs. The black spots do ballet in my face until I get my fingers to my neck and pull the shirt away, and I choke and cough and try to get my breath until I can. The banging of blood in my head getting less and the gold digging my thigh where I've landed on it. 'Fuck, Daryl,' I say. 'You fucking bastarding fuck.'

It's only then I hear Nao. 'Oh God. Oh Jesus. Oh God,' over and over.

I lift a hand off the floor and get why. The slippery wet is hot dark red, pooling under Daryl and soaking the top of my shirt.

It's not sweat.

'You could have, like, tried to knock him out with something,' Nao says. 'Not chop his head in half.'

'As if I meant to!' I'm leant over the sink, coughing and retching, except there's nothing coming out – only spit. My voice rough as guts and my throat aching. 'Didn't know what was up top of the fridge, did I? How about you? No use to anyone.'

She's bent over in the doorway to the sleep-out, near his legs. I'm not gunna look.

'Not . . .' I swallow. 'Is he?'

'I'd say so. Come and see.'

I shake my head. It hurts like a bastard. 'No way.' I stay at the sink and keep one hand around my throat. Shivering, the flanno shirt sticking to me, my blood slowing down, after—

Fuck. Daryl. Geen. Fuck. *Don't think about it.* I go for the phone on the kitchen bench and punch in the numbers. 'You have dialled emergency triple zero. Your call is being connected . . .'

'Recorded message,' I say to Nao. 'Triple zero, you'd think they'd—'

She's across the room in two steps. Smashes the phone onto the floor and the case cracks open. 'Are you crazy?'

'I was talking on that!'

'You just—'

'Yeah and I didn't mean to! And he might not be . . . He might need a hospital.'

'Wait.' She sticks a palm in my face. 'There could still be someone—' She picks up the front part of the phone and listens. 'Okay,' she says. 'Dead.'

She looks at me and her eyes go big and she looks at Daryl. I do too and my mouth fills up with spit. It's like Stephen King . . . Daryl on the floor with Geen's meat cleaver rammed into the front part of his head. Dad gave her that cleaver.

'Thought it was the wok,' I say.

Did too, 'cause I was panicking. And that's what I'll tell the cops. But are they gunna—

There's a choking sound from Nao and I look up. She's got half a fist in her mouth like she's trying not to laugh. Fucken fruitloop.

I rip the phone off her and get the back part of it off the floor and try to fit them together. 'You've wrecked this. Geen'll be spewing.' I keep trying but it's no good – a bit's cracked off the side and my hands are shaking.

What's she gunna say? He's a dickhead but he's still her boy-friend. 'How can you tell if someone's dead or not?'

'You want to check?'

'No! But what if he's not?'

'I'll do it.'

I stay hunched over the phone while she does it.

She comes back. 'He's dead. No breathing, no pulse.'

If I didn't know better, I'd reckon she was relieved. 'For real?'

'For real.' She climbs onto a stool at the breakfast bar, her good hand wrapped around the cut one. Musta hurt it, bashing the phone out my hand like she did.

'Still have to call the cops, but, don't I?'

Nao doesn't answer. She's got her lips pressed together. I see Geen's keys, on the floor by the oven. I imagine telling her, what it's gunna mean for us, the heap of shit I'm in when it wasn't even my fault.

Geen thought it was bad I got expelled from school this week. 'Not thinking, Charlie!' she said. But I am thinking, I'm thinking all this crap. I'm thinking about Mum and Dad, and everything going to shit, and what it's like in jail when you're only seventeen.

'Why don't ya want me to call?' I say to Nao. 'What the fuck's going on?'

2

Nao

Corellas

The feral white girl glares at me, her chin lifted and pointy. *Charlize*, he called her. Battler. I'm not a snob, but she is – the cut-off denim shorts, the once-white singlet under the checked flannel shirt, the bitten-down nails. She has a set of house keys in one bloody hand, the keys the bloke dropped in the fight.

There's a rushing in my ears and the room smells of blood – coppery and too warm. I breathe through my mouth so I won't throw up and curl my body forwards so the edge of her kitchen worktop presses in above the waistband of my skirt. I lean hard until it hurts. I don't look at the bloke again, but I don't need to; I'll remember that object sticking out from his forehead for ever. It made a sound like someone chopping into a pumpkin.

'Why don't ya want me to?' she says again. Her eyes are narrow slits, Indian Ocean blue in the light from the next room. Her voice is hoarse but persistent, her mouth open to show the gap between her two front teeth. She's not going to let this go.

She's not.

I keep my breathing steady and my face smooth and I look down at my throbbing feet, perched on the metal rung of the stool – the smears and streaks of drying blood. It dawns on me that I have tracked this through her house. We've gone way beyond forty-dollars-to-sleep-on-the-couch and I'm not sure how it has happened, at exactly what point I made the wrong choice. I can't be a witness for her, can I? They'd ask questions. They'd want my address, want to call Mum and Warren and drive me back to the house. And then what?

I can't think about my stepfather right now.

'You don't have a cigarette, do you?' I say.

She looks up from the keys. 'Course not. Smoking's shit for ya.'

I could go out for a pack and not come back. That would be smart, in the circumstances, except how far would I get, the state I'm in? She'd call the police, anyway, like she wanted. She'd give them my description, point out the blood I've left on her floor. She might even blame the whole incident on me. I don't know her, after all.

Plus there's her address. The address Warren had on his phone. I don't know yet if that was a mistake.

'That emergency call you made,' I say. 'Was there ... did someone answer it?'

'Recorded message,' she says. 'Told ya.' She's shivering, her skinny neck marked and blotched where he choked her. The flannel shirt is wet through, the front part of it stuck to her and red. All that for a piece of gold – I hope it was a flaming big one. 'Can't leave him in the middle of the floor,' she says.

'No.' I watch the dark window and listen out but there's nothing – no sirens, no flashing lights. No one knows I'm here. Still, there could be a record of the call.

'Who is he?' I say. 'I mean—'

'Bastard. I'm not sorry.' She shoots the bloke's legs a look that would incinerate a small town. 'Geen.' She licks her bottom lip. 'Geen's—'

He must have a car. Must have got here in one. The keys will be in one of his pockets. 'Your mum and dad,' I say. 'Are they likely to—?'

'My mum's dead. My dad don't live 'ere.'

'Oh. Okay. Well, I'm sorry.'

She sniffs and doesn't answer. Both her hands are clamped around the keyring, a cheap plastic square. I can see she does it to stop her hands from shaking but it doesn't work.

It's delicate, this, like talking a jumper down from a roof. I'm not having her take me down too. 'Look, it was self-defence. No doubt about it,' I say. 'But let's think it through. That ... chopper ... what if the police don't believe you?'

Her head snaps up. 'Cleaver! I didn't know that was up there.'

'Oh, I'd back you on that, no question—'

'Good, 'cause you haven't told me shit. How'd ya cut yourself? Who ya running from? How'd ya get that blood on your jacket?'

A breath catches half-in and half-out and I want to pull my jacket around to take a look. A smudge from the cut on my hand, surely, but it might be more than that.

'Need another Band-Aid on that cut,' she says.

She's right, the plaster is wet through like her shirt, the cut throbbing, *boom*, *boom*, like a drumbeat. All the while I feel her sharp eyes, a match for the pricking in my feet. How come she has so much to say about everything? Doesn't she ever stop?

'So, what we gunna do?' She's shivering harder. 'What do I tell Geen?'

'Nothing. I mean, obviously.'

'Nothing? Don't be thick.'

'Do you want to tell her about this? Really, Charlize? You're not thinking it through.'

'My name's Charlie! And I am thinking. She's my sister.'

'And how do you think she's going to take it? You attacked her boyfriend—'

'He went for me!'

'You provoked him. Look at that chopper—'

'You can't pin this on me. It wasn't even my fault!' Her mouth stays open and she looks at the blood on her shirt like she's seeing it for the first time. She opens her hands and stares at the keyring and drops it. It takes a moment for me to see she's hyperventilating, her skinny ribs sucking in and out.

'Hey.' I get down off the stool and grab her shoulders. 'You need to calm down. Okay?'

She shakes her head, hard. The breathing gets faster. The headphones she's still got around her neck jerk up and down, her shoulders fluttering under my fingers.

Panic attacks – what do you do? I turn her, walk her between the dead feet and the fridge and into the hallway, away from him, away from the smell. 'It's okay,' I say. 'We'll figure it out. We'll think it through.' If anyone should be having a panic attack, it's me, but I find a light switch, a brown tiled floor, the bathroom, and I sit her down on the closed lid of the toilet. There's a paper bag full of cotton balls. I scatter them, put the bag to her face and she doesn't fight me. She puffs the bag in and out, her face slick with sweat, the heaving of her chest slowing down.

'That's good,' I say. 'Breathe.'

It takes a while, and when it stops, she lowers the bag but keeps hold of it. She takes a slow breath, in and out, like a test. She looks down at her shirt and makes a face, but it doesn't start her up again. She blinks at me. 'Thanks.'

'No problem. It's fine.'

It's way off fine.

I get up from the edge of the bath and I stagger a step because my bum's numb from sitting there. I've left bloody smears on the cracked brown tiles and we both stare at them.

Accessory after the fact to an indictable offence. A definition from my second semester Criminal Law class, not to mention countless TV crime dramas. There's a long moment of wavering, the possible courses of action lining up in front of the blood-smeared tiles before I blink them all away.

'You know what we need to do, don't you?' I say. 'If you don't want your sister to find out?'

She clamps her jaw but she nods.

'Find his car. Clean up. Dispose of the body,' I say. 'Pretend he was never here. That.'

Charlie is wiped out after the adrenaline dump of her panic attack, but she showers and changes into an almost identical set of clothes and goes to find the bloke's car. This at least gets her out of the kitchen so she doesn't start hyperventilating again.

My adrenaline from before is gone too and I am bone dead tired. I've washed my feet and smoothed my hair, pulled the prickles out of both and tried to tame my hair back into its braid. My feet aren't too bad, only a couple of cuts doing most of the bleeding, but I'm sure to have a black eye by tomorrow and every inch of me feels off, like it will never go back to the way it was.

I haul cleaning stuff out from under Charlie's sink – yellow washing up gloves, three different surface sprays, a mountain of Chux. I pull on the gloves, the edge catching my cut hand so I wince, and I fill a bucket with hot water and bleach. It's what they use in films, but does it work?

Charlie's given me clean Band-Aids for my feet and my hand. I've put two on the side of my hand but the cut won't stop bleeding. I trail up the hallway and into the bathroom, cleaning up the smudges I left there – my DNA alongside hers. I go over and over the same few tiles, trying to remove every trace when there's no way I can, putting off the job that's waiting in the back room.

When I can't stall any longer, I lug the bucket in there. The bloke is a slab of colour at the edges of my vision and a sweet clammy smell. His legs are in the kitchen, his upper body in the doorway. The room beyond is empty apart from a frayed cane armchair and a matching couch against one wall. I look everywhere except directly at him. A yellow rug under his top half has taken up most of the blood.

Charlize. The kind of person you least want to run into on a night like the one I'm having and wammo! I have. An undernourished kid who kills a man twice her size. Bruised knuckles from the fight he said she'd had at school, and that hair – like she's plugged those headphones into the mains. Or her fingers. It would be one finger, though, wouldn't it? One finger up at anyone and everything.

I didn't run into her, either, did I? Warren had her address, although I'm starting to think he was wrong about it. I can't see this girl stealing Warren's safe; she's way too chaotic for that.

At least she's stopped with the questions. My car is in the driveway at home, crumpled against the gatepost. For all I know the front door is still open, the lights of the house blazing full. How soon before someone . . . ?

Bile presses upwards and I slop water out of the bucket onto the floor. I kneel next to it and swallow hard. Panicking is a non-starter. Can't have the two of us doing it.

I'll do the things we agreed, one thing and then the next.

The worst is the cleaver, and I do that first. I find a white towel under the sink and put it down to catch the blood, turn my head away and grab the handle. I don't know which way to pull. I think it'll be stuck deep in the bone between his eyes but it falls away with no effort, just a sucking sound like the ocean, followed by an extra heave of nausea.

I can't believe I laughed. I didn't, not really. It was what she said about the wok. It was the shock of it.

There are bloody bits of something stuck to the blade. I close my eyes and wipe them on his shirt, take the cleaver and wash and scrub and rinse it in the sink until it gleams. I put it back on top of the fridge although we haven't discussed this, and the fridge clicks off as I do which makes me jump. I wrap the bloke's head in the white towel but the blood comes straight through it, the same as the Band-Aid on my hand.

There are moments I think I'm dreaming. That I'm going to

wake up on my bed and it will still be afternoon, the square of sun on my back and the only bad thing the last question I was sure I'd stuffed up on Friday's exam. But my face gets tight when I think about these things, and what's underneath the tightness is worse.

Because whatever Charlie might think about what's happened here tonight, whatever the story with her parents or her fears about her sister, she has not ripped the guts out of her life as spectacularly as I have mine.

I roll the body inside the rug and mop the blood from the old floorboards. It's hopeless, down between the cracks and I picture it creeping along under the floor, but I do what I can and then switch off the light. This is not a forensic clean up. This is: *there's a body on the floor and in the morning the neighbours will see it through the windows*. Perhaps they already have; there are no curtains, and watery moonlight spills through the louvres on three sides. But the backyards on either side are Sunday-evening quiet and dark.

The bloke weighs a ton and I don't know how we're going to lift him.

Charlie takes too long. I put the cleaning cloths I've used into the wash along with her clothes and another load of bleach. The washing machine fills, washes, rinses and spins as the worry climbs inside me. The clock on the oven says 11:18 p.m. She said she'd find something to wrap the body, so where is she? I start to imagine she's changed her mind, that she's panicked again. She's cracked and called the police or the sister. She's done a runner. I shouldn't have let her go. I listen for sirens, ready to bolt, but I won't get far without the car.

I need that car.

The bloke's keys are in the back pocket of his jeans, wedged down behind his phone. The phone is sticking out but I have trouble pulling it the whole way. The screen is shattered in one corner and there are five missed calls and three voicemails – the last one twenty minutes ago. Two different callers – Geena K and Lee A.

The sister, then, and someone else. God, he said Geena was back at his place, didn't he? Cooking dinner. How long before she looks for him here?

Do I turn the phone off? No, I push it back. I think of mine and feel the shape of it, tight against my leg in the pocket of my skirt. I want to pull it out to check the screen and at the same time I don't, and then I realise.

Holy crap, I can't keep my phone. I have to get rid of it.

The back door opens and I jump away from the bloke, heart pounding. For a second it could be anyone – police, neighbours, the sister – but it's her.

'What took you so long?' I hear the wobble in my voice.

Charlie throws a look at the body and keeps her distance. She's pale in the moonlight, the freckles on her nose standing out like someone has dotted them with a pen. Scared. I was right to worry. But she tells me the bloke's car is in the back lane behind the houses. She's carrying a tangle of rope and a blue tarpaulin, streaked with red dirt. 'Had to scout a few sheds. This orright?' She unfolds the tarpaulin like a map, too big for the tiny space.

'Fine,' I say.

We wait until two a.m. before setting out in the bloke's car. I drive, although Charlie kicked off about this, reminding me I crashed my car and am a liability. I didn't argue – she needs to keep thinking that – but I wasn't going to let her drive. Apparently, she's seventeen and has her licence but she's so small I find this hard to believe. She's a liability herself. She's been jumpy since the panic attack and in the enclosed space of the car her skin has a hot smell, as if she's lit a match and blown it out.

She directs me out of the lane and the first few streets. 'Left here. Right at the end. Go straight.' Apart from this we don't talk.

The car is a metallic-green Holden dual cab ute with leather seats, not new but insanely clean. A laminated photo of a girl hangs from the rearview mirror – Lana Del Rey hair and dramatic eyes, the same freckles and gap between her teeth as Charlie – and behind it a pale-yellow Magic Tree that smells of lemons. There's a set of weights and what looks like a gym bag on the floor in the back, both of which alarmingly remind me of Warren. I'm trying not to think about this when I brake too hard coming up to Railway Road.

'Watch it!' Charlie says. 'Got whiplash off Daryl, don't want it twice.'

'I don't think you can get it twice.'

'How would you know?'

I don't answer, I just take the corner slowly into Railway Road. There's no traffic, no one out on the street at all and very few lights in windows; the inhabitants of suburbia safely inside their homes. The rumble of the ute's engine is conspicuously loud, the blood rushing in my head still there but softer. I think about when it will stop, when everything will be done and over and go back to normal.

If.

The bloke, Daryl, is in the tray of his ute behind us and looks exactly like what he is – a dead body wrapped in a tarp criss-crossed with rope. He is solid muscle, going to fat, and inching him down Charlie's backyard to the dark lane and up into the tray, the constant dread of a shout from next door or the sudden glare of a security light, is something I never want to think about again.

My hands sweat and I can't stop looking in the rearview mirror. What do I think, that he's going to climb back out?

So far, we've agreed on one thing: the body is going in the ocean, down at Woodman Point, weighed down with a sack of gravel Charlie found in a neighbour's shed. All I need to do before we get there is get rid of my phone, and I know exactly the place. I asked Charlie about hers once we'd got him in the tray and the two of us were huffing and sweating, leant up against the side of the car. She looked cagey and told me she doesn't need one. Most likely this was a lie, and she can't afford one.

It's not the same for her, anyway. It doesn't matter so much. She's going home, back to her life and her sister. She doesn't have to know I'm throwing my phone. She'll only want to know why. I can pretend I'm carsick and I need to get out at the lake.

After that, we dump the body, I drop her back at her place and we are done. I've told her I'll abandon the ute somewhere south of the river before I go home, but the fuel gauge tells me I have practically a full tank of petrol, far enough for a start. I won't be going home.

My hands tighten on the wheel as I turn under the railway.

Charlie's head jerks up, she doesn't miss a trick. 'Where ya going? We said Woodman's.'

'I'm heading for the highway.'

'No, yer not.'

'West Coast.'

She sniffs. 'Fucken long way around.' Her face is pinched in the light from the dash, her eyes raking the display. She's scratching the back of one hand; I can hear the sand-papery sound above the engine. 'Just get us there. Don't speed, but. Don't get us pulled over.'

'Keep calm and I won't.' I make another turn, no traffic. I drop my hand from the wheel to the shape of my phone against my leg. There's a no-through-road to the lake and I take it, down towards the car park. 'I need to stop,' I say.

Charlie grabs the door handle as I swerve around a pothole. 'What? Not got the time.'

'I'm going to throw up.'

'Fuck, pull over,' she says. 'Here!'

'Not yet. You need to keep calm.'

'I am fucken calm!'

I jerk on the handbrake at the end of the track. There are no other cars in the car park. I spill out of the car towards the water, into the trees, head down. I make like I'm retching, make the right sounds.

'Don't be too long!' Charlie yells.

The lake is a dense wash of dark with no lights. A circle of dead trees spears out of the water, black against black. There are layers of frog sounds, the smell of tea tree over the stink of mud, and the wet sand sucks at my feet. Something invisible flaps across in front of me and lifts the hairs on my arms – a crow or a black cockatoo.

I shiver and pull my phone out of my pocket, but I forget not to look and the screen is crammed with messages.

The ground lurches under me – Mum. Someone has called Mum in Bali. But I read the first two messages and see it's not that. The Sunday session last-exam drinks – Jessica, Ertan and Mel, wondering why I didn't show. Commiserating, debriefing, celebrating even when you think you've screwed up.

My throat clogs and I want to call each one of them back.

I throw the phone and it spins end on end until I hear the splash. I'm close enough to home to have lost it here, for it not to seem strange if someone checks.

I wipe my eyes and I'm wiping my mouth as I come out of the scrub near the car. I see Charlie and get a flapping rush of panic. 'What are you doing?'

'What d'ya reckon?'

The back of the ute is down, the interior light spilling out of the rear window. She's backed it up to the water on a short square of jetty and got the body half out. 'No.' I rush and grab the end she's pulling and try to push it back. 'We had a plan.'

'So? I changed it. He can go in the lake – we're here orright? We'll weigh it down like we said.'

'No. You can't do that.' I lift and push but she's stronger. How can she be stronger? 'We have to get him back in, stick to the plan. The lake's too small.' There's not enough jetty between me and the water. The body shifts, awkward and heavy, and the head part lolls off the end of the ute as I let it go.

She climbs up into the tray. 'You got eyes in yer head? See how dark it is. We can do it here.'

I look at the trees against the sky, the outline of stars. 'It's dark everywhere.'

'Not down the beach! There'll be lights. And fishing. They'll be fishing down at Woodman's, we shoulda thought of that.' She drags the other end of the body around and then the bag of gravel, scraping against the metal tray.

'Not in the middle of the night.'

'Yes, tomorrow morning! Monday. You don't know everything. Why d'ya think ya do?'

I lean against the end of the ute and press the heels of my hands into my eyes. When I pull them away she's still there. 'Why couldn't you have waited for me? It's not far to the beach. Even the river is better.'

'No, it's not,' Charlie says. 'You don't know every fucken thing. People out in boats, fishing, surfing, fucken surf lifesaving. Here there's gunna be no one – a coupla dog walkers, if that.' She gets the bag of gravel to the edge of the ute.

I think of my phone, all those messages, a few metres away. I can't tell her this. I can't tell her what happened at home. The whole thing will unravel. 'We can't put him in there,' I say. 'I've just thrown up in the water. My DNA is in there.'

She plants her fists on her hips. 'I don't care if your whole fucken dinner is in there. Both our fingerprints are all over this tarp in case you hadn't noticed. Now either fucken help me or get out the way.' She puts a foot on top of the bag of gravel.

'No, I will not do either of those things.' I brace myself against the gravel, glance behind at the water. 'Do you have to, like, say eff every second sentence? Can't you think of anything else?'

She goes quiet and there's a moment I think we're in for a

fight. I should probably be scared of her. Why aren't I scared of her? But she barks a laugh. 'Can't ya say fuck? Too posh?'

'Don't be ridiculous.' My face hot.

'Stand back.' She shoves with her foot and the bag of gravel lurches and I can't stop it.

'Charlie, no! My phone.' I scramble to the side. 'My bloody phone is in there.'

She stares at me, too late. I wince as the bag hits the jetty, the body dragging after it. She's tied the two things together.

Crunch, jerk, slither. The rope looping and tightening, and all of it gone off the edge. Two splashes. A sickening silence.

A flock of corellas wheels out of the dark.

Charlie sulks in the car on the way back, curled up on the passenger seat like a shelter puppy. Which is flaming unfair when she's the one who got her own way.

She lifts her head as we pass under a streetlight. 'Coulda told me you'd chucked your phone in there. Whatcha do it for, anyhow?'

I look sideways at her, the checked shirt and denim shorts. 'It doesn't matter.' She shrugs and tucks her head back into her shoulder.

I am trying very bloody hard not to think about it – the smell of the lake and the circle of dead trees, the corellas like ghost birds. How the frog sounds stopped and the body floated before the bag of gravel pulled it all the way under.

My phone in the lake practically alongside a dead body.

I take us back the same way; quiet dark streets, the occasional car. Charlie is right about our fingerprints on the tarp. I should have kept the gloves on, after cleaning up the blood. We haven't thought about CCTV. We haven't thought of everything. I am very aware of this.

These things go with the rest, pushed down and under while I keep both hands on the wheel and watch the road ahead.

None of it matters as long as no one finds him.

When we get close, I say, 'You'll have to direct me.' Charlie's eyes spring open and she yawns. I feel how tired I am too. 'The last few streets. I can't remember.'

She does, and as I turn the last corner I realise this is it: we won't see each other again. I wonder if she's thinking the same.

Probably not.

'Here,' she says.

I pull in two cars past on the opposite side of the street.

She stretches. 'Be okay with the ute?'

'Of course. I'll wipe it down like we said.' And I will, but not yet. I check the petrol – still almost a full tank – and straighten my back. 'Listen, I'm sorry if I lost it a bit, back there. I had a fight with someone, earlier tonight.'

She looks at the cut on my hand, up at my face. 'Bastard. He hit ya?'

My breath snags. If only.

'That how come you didn't stay with the car?' she says.

'Car?'

'After you stacked it?'

'Oh. Yes, exactly.'

'Bastard,' she says again. 'Dickhead Daryl hit Geen. Four times, maybe more. Needed stitches, once. She lied about it but he did.'

I tighten my lips and nod. 'Well, he won't do it again. Remember what to tell her?'

'That I never seen him.'

'Good.' I haven't told her about the missed calls on his phone. It doesn't matter now, it's at the bottom of the lake. 'And we've never met.'

'Okay.' She unclicks her seatbelt and puts a hand to the door but she stops. 'What the fuck?' Her eyes are on her front gate. Her hand finds my sleeve and grips it.

A man in a dark hooded jacket peels himself from the shadows next to Charlie's front door. He strides down the path towards the low gate, slow at first and then faster. 'Who's that?'

'Dunno,' she says.

He vaults the fence next to her gate. Dark jeans and white sneakers. Head up, looking our way.

'You don't know him? Are you sure?' I'm whispering, the rushing in my ears louder than it's been all night.

'No, I do not.' Her grip tightens.

'Is he looking for Daryl?' I'm trying to make sense of it. If he saw us, after all, through the windows, or struggling with the body. If despite all our efforts, here it is, the end of the line.

But where are the police?

'Charlie, that hurts.' She lets go and refastens her seatbelt.

He steps between two cars into the street. 'Do you think he's seen us?' I say. She punches me hard in the arm. 'Ow!'

'Course he's seen us,' she says. 'He's headed straight for us. Drive!'

'What if he—'

'Go!'

I jerk the handbrake off, shoot out of the space too fast and stop. The angle's all wrong and he's still coming. I reverse back, fumble the lever into drive. Charlie yells, 'Fucksakes, go!' He gets an outstretched hand on the back corner of the ute as I wrench the wheel and floor it.

He rocks to a stop as our tyres squeal away.

'I don't know which way to go,' I say. 'I don't know what to—'

'Anywhere! Drive.' She's glued to the rearview mirror. 'Shit, he's going back for his car.'

MONDAY

3

Charlie

Cherry Ripe

The sun wakes me, too hot and too bright. Gotta be a dream, a real shit one, 'cause all I see is highway, flat orange dirt and blue sky.

Fuck, it's not a dream. 'What happened to the city?' I sit up and look at Nao, blink again at the windscreen. There's not even paddocks or fences, just spiky grey bushes and dead brown grass, a few crook-looking trees chucking shadows across the dirt.

Nao doesn't answer. She's eyes front with the windscreen visor pulled down, this big pair of sunnies on her face. Where'd she get them from? She's driving like an old woman, like there's a Violet Crumble up her arse. Got her window cracked open – a blast of hot air and bitumen and the sound of tyres rubbing on the highway.

She's dead on the speed limit, not a k over.

I clock the fake lemon smell and the yellow Magic Tree, Geen's photo hanging from the rearview, and I get a pinch of cold on my neck. Daryl, the pisshead dickhead. I'm still not sorry. Don't feel no different, do I? Dunno if I should or not. Feels like a thing that happened to me, not the other way around.

Not gunna think about it. Doesn't matter, anyhow. Long as he stays where he is.

I blink and pull the visor down. Wipe the spit off my face where I dribbled – chuck a look at Nao but she doesn't see me – and stick my hand in the pocket of my shorts to check the gold is still there, that she didn't take it while I was out.

'What time is it?' I say. 'Where are we? Thought you wanted to go to your aunty's place.'

'I do.'

'Northern suburbs, you said.'

'I didn't say anything about suburbs.'

No way. Better not be some place in the bush. Who am I kidding? It already is. The highway dead straight and totally flat, one lane each way through empty scrub. One set of white lines on grey bitumen, the same out the back window as the front. There's nothing else between us and the horizon. There's zero. The sky bigger than I've ever seen it and makes my brain hurt.

I remember the tall dude in the street outside our place. Zig-zagging blocks before we lost him. 'I need to call Geen.'

She side-eyes me. 'You can't tell her anything. I thought we agreed.'

'She's gunna worry. Doesn't know where I am.' I check my phone under my shirt so Nao can't see it. Six thirty-four in the morning, three missed calls from Geen – last night, one before and two after Daryl happened. Got that forty bucks tucked into the case, my headphones in my lap. 'Coulda woken me.'

'You fell asleep before we crossed the river.'

'So? I got tired. Not every day shit like that happens.' I stretch my neck and my arms. In one piece, no thanks to Daryl, except my throat still hurts like I've been eating gravel. The back of my hand pricking and I give it a scratch.

Nao looks in the rearview. 'It's not exactly how I imagined the week starting, either. An accessory to murder, on the run in the victim's vehicle—'

'Hardly murder! Accident. Self-defence. Manslaughter, tops.'

She huffs out a breath. 'And we're about to run out of petrol.'

'Shit, are we?' I clock the yellow dashboard light.

'There's a roadhouse in forty kilometres. We'll make it.'

'What road are we even on? How far to your aunty's?'

'A couple of hundred kilometres. We're on Great Northern Highway, a bit over halfway.' She looks across at me. 'The main road north. You don't know that?'

'Why would I know that?'

She tucks a chunk of hair behind her ear. Got the rest of it back in that plait last night and washed her face. Not much of a cut on her head but the one on her hand's still bleeding. She keeps pressing on it, that's why. She's got one of them nail jobs, too, where they paint your fingernails to look like fingernails. Can't see the point.

'You wanted to come,' she says.

'Only 'cause it wasn't safe to go back home. Didn't know we were going out bush, did I?' I check the empty highway in front and behind, rub the back of my neck. We pass a heap of something that looks like prime mince with a tail. 'What was that?'

She flares a nostril. 'Roadkill. Kangaroo.'

I watch it suck backwards in the wing mirror. Dead meat. 'When can we go back?'

'I thought you were worried about that man outside your house.' She checks the rearview again. 'You should be. He recognised the ute. He was looking for your bloke, Daryl.'

'Not *my* bloke!'

'Whatever. But who was he? Is he going to report him missing? Will your sister?'

'How should I know? That's why I need to call her.' I pull my phone out my pocket and Nao near enough chucks a handbrake turn.

'You can't use that!'

Big blast of horn. 'Watch the fuck out!'

She swerves us back into the left lane as a truck sucks past and overtakes, one of them big road trains with two trailers on the back of it. Rattles the teeth in my head.

'Fucksakes,' I say. 'Get your licence out a Weetie packet?'

'Your phone. It's trackable. You can't keep it.' She keeps turning her head to look at me.

'Watch the road, orright?'

'That's why I got rid of mine.'

'Coulda told me that was why.'

'I am telling you. I'm telling you now. You said you didn't have one.'

'So? You were dumb enough to believe it.' Didn't want her to see it, did I? Geen's hand-me-down phone with the screen cracked to shit.

'Well, you can't keep it; the police can track it.' She slows the car. 'It's a precaution, that's all. In case they find him. Throw it,' she says. 'Chuck it out the window.'

'No way.' I unlock the screen. 'How am I gunna call Geen?'

'Just do it.' She reaches across.

I slap her hand away. 'No! Give us a second. Got all my music on it.'

'It's better if you don't think about it,' she says.

'That what you did?'

Our eyes meet, a patch of cloud in hers that slides away. What's her story? She still hasn't told me it. 'Here.' She digs a hand in her messenger bag, between the seats, waves a pen at me. 'Write her number down.'

I biro Geen's number onto the inside of my arm, pull the SIM out the phone and stare at it before I crunch it between my teeth.

'What's that for?' Nao says.

'Watch the road. The SIM – you destroy it, yeah? Like they do on TV. That what you did with yours?'

She doesn't answer, just shifts her eyes front while I let the SIM and the phone case go out the window. I watch them flip off the bitumen onto the dirt, the little puffs of dust. The flat country stretching out forever and the sun and everything else making my eyes sting. The phone I slide into my pocket so she can't see.

Got all my music on it – Mum's music. I can keep it turned off. Nao doesn't have to know. Feels like nothing's gunna be the same ever again as it is.

We pull into the roadhouse a bit before seven a.m. – a dusty white place with a tin roof, middle of nowhere in a stretch of dirt – and it's only then I get a shot of the nerves. I mean, it's people, yeah? It's public. And Nao and me have killed a dude. Well, I have, basically.

What if I look different? What if people can tell?

The engine does that clicking/cooling thing. Out front of the building is a cracked concrete forecourt with two fuel pumps. Two wooden picnic tables at the side with no one sat there, a bunch of noisy black parrots in the one tree and sharp-edged shadows on the ground. Nao pulls the key out the ignition and looks at her feet. The Band-Aids I gave her have sweated off but they're scabbed to buggery. That's gotta hurt, driving with feet like that. I glance up at her face. Tougher than she looks, maybe. 'You need shoes,' I say.

She's grabbed her bag and got the door open when I yank on the sleeve of her jacket. 'Wait. Not gunna tell anyone, are ya?'

She shakes her head. 'Of course not.' Pushes the door except I've still got a hold of her.

'Wait,' I say. 'I wanna say something. Explain something.'

She pulls her leg back in and looks at me. 'Okay.'

I stick my hand in my pocket around the gold, turning it over, feeling the ridges of the letters under my thumb. It's always warm, that bit of gold. Even in my pocket and out the way of the sun it's warm.

'It's about Daryl,' I say. I glance out past her. No one at the fuel pumps, a truck pulling back out onto the highway. No one else.

'Okay,' Nao says again.

'You're not gunna dob me in.'

'No.'

'How do I know you're not?'

She huffs. 'Because if I was going to, I'd have done it back there, wouldn't I? Like, not helped you. Not waited until now.'

'Why did you?' I say.

'What?'

'Why do it? Why drive outta town to your aunty's? Not for me, is it?'

She's got a hand up to her face against the sun, staring straight ahead. Her lips pressed down tight, that thing she does. 'I thought you wanted to talk about Daryl.'

She's not fooling me. Dunno if she thinks she is. 'Daryl hit Geen,' I say.

'I know that. You told me that.'

The ute's warmer by the second, got that hot car smell. Hot and prickly inside my shirt. 'It's not like I wanted him dead, but she's better off with him gone. I clocked the bruises – her arm, her wrist, her jaw, two times a black eye.' I reckon Nao's got one herself by now, underneath the big sunnies. 'One time she had a patch of hair missing, size of a dollar coin. Shoulda stood up for herself.'

Nao's real still. I can't see her eyes through the sunnies. 'Sometimes that makes it worse.'

'What, so it's not okay to fight back if someone goes for ya? Like I did with Daryl?'

'That's not what I meant, but you went for him first, didn't you? And he said you'd hit someone, at school, you'd got expelled—'

'That kid deserved it. He wasn't respecting my mate.' Except I can still see the way Sass looked at me, after. I feel my head and up under my ribs getting hot. Same as last Monday, same as last night.

'You don't just go around attacking people,' Nao says. 'You talk to them.'

'Like that helps! You don't know shit. You coulda helped

47

me, last night. Coulda done something, instead of standing there. Then maybe we wouldn't be in this situation. Maybe he wouldn't be dead.'

And she's out the car, slams the door, rattling at the fuel cap like she's trying to throttle it, and I want to punch myself in the face for not explaining it right and her in the face for not getting it. I head around the side of the building instead and bash my fist into the door to the ladies' toilet. The door slams inwards but it still hurts, opens up the cuts on my knuckles.

Feels better, but. Stops me thinking. I stick my bleeding hand in my armpit and go in the shop, which is pumping out cold from too many fridges and cools my skin. I get barbecue shapes and a Cherry Ripe and choc milk and it sets me back nearly ten bucks. Fuck. I get change from the woman for the payphone and call Geen but it goes to voicemail. Dunno what to say to her so I hang up but it still takes my money. There's a hot breeze lifting dust, getting it everywhere, and the parrot noise is hurting my brain. Geen's number's rubbing off my arm already in the heat so I write it on the receipt from the shop and stick it in my pocket.

I don't wanna get back in the ute with Nao, except where else is there?

She goes inside to pay – still limping, can't tell if she's faking it – and I get back in the ute and open the choc milk. In two seconds flat she's back at the door of the shop with her sunnies in one hand and her head stuck forwards. 'Charlie? Charlie! Can you come back in here?' I make like I can't hear her for half the choc milk but she doesn't give it a rest.

'What?' I say.

'Can you come in here? *Please.*'

Fucksakes. I get in there and she's bright red, which I didn't expect with her face but there you go. 'Have you got that cash I gave you?' she says.

She must be dreamin'. 'What cash?'

The woman behind the counter's got a face like a smashed potato. 'The money I gave you,' Nao says, smoothing down the end of her plait. 'We need to pay for the petrol.'

'How come I have to pay for it?'

The woman pipes up. 'I don't care which of youse pays but one of youse better.' She looks Nao up and down like she's the cat's vomited-up dinner.

Nao mouths, *See?* She's got a credit card between two fingers, her bare toes scrunched against the floor. She's got money, course she has. The flash clothes. A gold chain around her neck and studs in her ears to match.

'What's wrong with your card?'

'I don't know,' she says. 'But I used the last of my cash and we're still short.'

'Declined,' the woman says. 'Thirty for the balance of the fuel and another thirty-eight fifty for these and the water.' She's got a hand on top of a packet of smokes and a Cherry Ripe on the counter. She stares at my cut knuckles and Nao's cut feet, rude as.

'Ya don't have to be such a bitch about it,' I say to her.

'Charlie, don't,' Nao says.

The woman's jaw's going like I've already smacked her. 'She is,' I say to Nao. 'Try it again. You over your limit, or what?'

'I don't want to do that.' Nao's got her arms around the big bottle of water like the woman's gunna try and take it off her. Which she is.

'All I've got's thirty dollars and sixty cents,' I say.

The woman slides the smokes and the Cherry Ripe to the back of the counter, twists her mouth at me. I square up to her but Nao edges in front. 'Please, Charlie, just pay the money, okay? We need to go.' She looks out at the highway the same way she's always looking in the rearview mirror. The same way she was looking over her shoulder in front of our mailbox last night.

Fucksakes. I rip the dollars out my pocket and slam them down. Keep the sixty cents change. We don't have enough for the water.

Nao goes around the side to the toilets but it smelled feral in there so I hold it and get back in the ute. I watch this dude load up his LandCruiser with cartons of beer and bottles of water and Coke. Big party or big beer gut. Both. He's talking on his phone the whole time with it up between his shoulder and his ear. His dog eyeballs me, head stuck out the passenger window, and I give it the finger.

I've finished the choc milk and half the barbecue shapes when Nao gets back in. Her face is wet like she's had a good scrub at it, all the stray bits of her hair back in the plait. She's taken her jacket off and rolled up the sleeves of her silky top to the exact same length. She's a neat freak, isn't she? I drop the Cherry Ripe into the door, my side, save it for later. Not as if Nao needs it, the size of her.

'What happened to your hand?' she says.

'Nothing.' I stick it back under my arm. 'You should make some calls, about your card.'

'I'll deal with it at Aunty Mar's. It's fine.'

It's not fine. She's upset about it. Takes her three goes to get the key in the ignition.

'Wait.' I get the door open. 'Give us a second.'

'What are you doing? We need to go.'

I step out into the hot wind. Beer Gut Dude's washing splatted bugs off his windscreen. His dog distracted, snapping at the squeegee from inside the cab. Dude's left a five-litre bottle of water by his back wheel. I open the door behind my seat, ignore the faces Nao's making at me and load up the bottle, smooth as.

'What did you just do?' Nao, twisted around in her seat. 'Charlie?'

I'm about to slam the door when I see the bag.

It's squished half-under my seat where it's hard to spot, next to the weights Daryl shows off with every chance he gets. Except he can't now, can he? 'Cause he's dead. The bag's a holdall with a zip, stiff black leather, two handles. Gotta be his, a gym bag or something, might have some cash in it. I check the dude – still busy. Lean in and unzip the top.

I stick a hand inside, cop a feel and then another feel. Little packages of something, hard and flat. I dig with my fingers, get my hand in one of the packages – smooth on one side, ridges on the other – and yank it out fast. Shit, it's not a gym bag.

When I get back in my seat my hands are in fists. *Bitch*.

She grips the wheel. 'I saw that.'

'Yeah? Weren't gunna tell me, were ya?'

'About what? You need to give that bottle of water back.'

'Don't bullshit me. Daryl's holdall.' She knows what's in it already. It's the whole reason she drove out here, how come she never got rid of the ute. 'When did you get a look in it?'

'A look in what?' She pulls her big sunnies off, cranes her neck between the seats. 'I don't know what you—'

'Don't shit me!' I don't buy it, the big eyes and blank face. 'You clocked it, last night, didn't ya? You got a look in it. You were gunna leave me – out here, up shit creek with no money.' My heart's doing crazy stuff, feels all slippery and weird. 'When were you gunna do it? When I went to the dunny?'

'No.' She frowns, sticks her sunnies back on. 'I don't know what—'

'You were gunna keep it for yourself.'

It's what I woulda done.

'I don't know what you're talking about,' she says. 'But if you don't give that water back, I will.' Beer Gut Dude looks at his back wheel, scratches his head.

'You can't. We haven't got any.'

'Jesus, Charlie.' She hauls it between the seats, slams out the car and drops it at the dude's feet. I see her say sorry, his head snap up, the dog watching and panting.

She gets back in and clicks her seatbelt. 'We need to not draw attention to ourselves.'

'Orright, drive,' I say. 'But pull over first chance you get. There's a fuck-off bag full of gold bars on the floor in the back, same as this.' I pull out the one in my pocket. 'As if you didn't know.'

She drives us down the highway with her hands tight on the wheel and parks at a picnic spot – a stretch of dirt with a coupla tables and trees. Turns off the ignition and looks at the gold in my fist. 'I didn't know.'

'Pig's arse you didn't.'

'You were supposed to dump that piece of gold with the body, Charlie. It was his. You said you would.'

'Yeah, and you were s'posed to dump the ute. Now I know why ya didn't. You were gunna drive out here, offload the gold and pocket the cash. Except ya got stuck with me.'

'I told you. I didn't know about it.' She sucks one side of her mouth in. Dunno if she's acting or not, can't tell behind the sunnies. 'Can I see it?'

I hesitate a second, shrug and drop it into her palm. 'Go for your life.'

I don't take my eyes off the bar. She lifts it up to the light and it glows in the sun through the windscreen, brighter than the dirt outside. Looks smaller in her hand than mine. She bends her head over it. 'There are letters on it, a logo,' she says.

'I know that.'

'Heavy, isn't it? A hundred grams, it says.' She frowns. 'Are they all like this?' Maybe she's not acting. Still can't tell.

She hands it back to me and stretches between the seats and unzips the holdall, doesn't even ask before she does it. She's got one hand gripping the back of my seat and the other in the bag. 'Oh God,' she says. 'Holy crap. There are lots.'

'Yeah, we should count 'em.' I get antsy, watching her dig in the bag. Empty scrub outside the windows, the whole way to the horizon, the highway with no traffic on it. Where the fuck are we? Does she even have an aunty?

She says, 'Oh God,' two more times and zips the bag shut and sits upright, dead straight with her hands back on the wheel. Her mouth set in a weird line like she might spew, except I can see her brain working.

'What?'

'There are dozens of them. There's nothing else in the bag.' She's breathing funny.

Orright, maybe she didn't know it was there. 'Told you there was. Working out how to get shot of me, are ya?'

She starts the engine and pulls back out onto the highway, no traffic in either direction. Gets us up to speed and cuts her eyes at me. 'Your bloke, Daryl—'

'Not *my* bloke.'

'What does he do? I'm guessing he doesn't buy and sell gold.'

'Bouncer. Works at this club in Northbridge.'

'So . . . he's not a thief?'

'What? Nah.'

Sells a bit of speed on the side, most likely. Except, I think of that call with Geen, how cagey she was about the gold. What if she knew there was more? I've gotta talk to her, ask her about it, except how can I?

'Maybe he won Lotto,' I say.

The hot wind off the highway is flipping the picture of Geen around and lifting Nao's hair off her face. 'That bloke outside your house,' she says. 'This is what he was after.'

'You don't know that. Mighta been waiting for Daryl.'

'Yes, but why? It was three a.m. and—' She looks in the rearview. 'Oh, crap.'

I look where she's looking. Big police LandCruiser behind, red and blue lights flipping us the finger. No one else on the road. 'Where did he come from? He's pulling us over? No way.'

She's already braking, indicating. My mouth like the bottom of a budgie cage.

'What did you do?' I say. 'Did you zip that bag up?' She

nods, her face tight. Pulls onto the shoulder and stops, shuts the engine off.

Dipshit, why didn't I shift the holdall? Put it in the back? 'This is your fault,' I say. 'You gave that water back.'

'You think it'd be better if we'd stolen it?'

Just the one cop. Blue stockman's hat to match his uniform, little blond beard, mirror sunnies. He parks directly behind and does the slow cowboy walk up to Nao's window like he's watched too much TV.

'You've got your licence, yeah?' I say. 'Don't tell him shit. Don't let him see your feet. And don't let him check in the bag, not even if he pulls a gun.'

'Why would he pull a gun? Jesus, Charlie.' She wipes her hands off her skirt and puts them back on the wheel. The cop steps up and she fumbles the button, shimmies the window all the way down.

'Morning, ladies,' he says. 'Hot enough for you? Where are you all headed today?' Like there's ten of us.

Nao swallows like a pelican sucking down a fish. Doesn't say shit. I wait but she doesn't. I didn't mean it literally. She's gunna mess this up big time.

'We're going to her aunty's place.' I look at her. 'That right?' She frowns but she nods.

The cop smiles. Can't see his eyes behind the sunnies. 'Come up from the city?'

How can he tell that? 'Yep.' I sit on my hands and stare out at the highway. Want to rip the door open and do a runner with the holdall, except how far would I get?

'Not used to country driving, am I right?' He nods towards the front of the ute. 'No bull bar. You want to keep safe, two young ladies alone. There'll be livestock on the road for the next few hundred k.'

'Yeah?' He can't book us for that, can he? The bull bar thing? Nao stares straight ahead. He scans the back seat next: Daryl's weights on the floor, the leather bag. Fuck. Beer Gut Dude musta called him, or the woman in the shop. Is Nao gunna dob me in? Is she gunna give him the gold, tell him about Daryl? I pinch my fingers into my legs and try to breathe.

'Are you aware your passenger is not wearing a seatbelt?' he says to Nao.

I look down. Shit. See Nao's jaw set. 'No, officer, I was not aware of that,' she says.

He steps back and scans the windscreen. 'No P plates?'

'I'm off my P plates, officer.'

'That'll be an infringement notice, for the seatbelt. I'll issue that now. I'll need your licence.'

He looks a bit sorry. Might be I'm imagining that or might be he's not used to people who look like Nao being so polite. He's not sorry enough to let her off the ticket, but. She says she's forgotten her licence and he nods, concentrating on writing on the green notepad he's got. He asks her name and address and date of birth, and she tells him and he writes it on the pad. He rips off the top sheet and gives it to her, tells her she's got forty-eight hours to show her licence at a station.

He walks away, no joke. He gets in his car and pulls back out onto the highway. For a second I'm that relieved I don't give a shit about everything else, and then I stare at the side of Nao's face until it gets red.

'What was that?' I say. 'Since when is your name Cherry Ripley?'

Her face stays red and she tells me to do my seatbelt up, and she starts the ute and slams it into drive.

'Where'd that even come from?' I lift the Cherry Ripe out the door pocket where the top of it is sticking out. 'Seriously?'

Nao cracks a sad after the seatbelt episode and drives the whole rest of the way without talking to me. We're even, but. She lied to that cop. I reckon it might come in useful down the track so I keep quiet about it for now.

I'm distracted, anyhow, thinking about Geen and the gold. Where Daryl got it. If Geen knew about it. How I'm gunna keep it for the two of us without letting on to her that he's dead.

The more I think on it, the more I reckon she did know. Those bars in the holdall are in single black bags with a drawstring, like something out of a jewellery shop, like the shop Geen works in. She said it wasn't to do with the shop but what if it was? I press my fingers around her keyring, in my pocket next to my sixty cents change, all I got left of Nao's cash. Got the gold and my phone in the other pocket.

What if Geen did give Daryl her keys, to come around and get that bar back off me? What if she wasn't even gunna tell me, just piss off with him and the gold and never come back? Except now I've gone and killed him.

The further down the highway we get, the more shit I feel about Geen. Nao doesn't look too crash hot herself, driving more like a granny with every kilometre, so I figure it's not exactly gunna be a happy reunion with her aunty.

As we come into town it gets flatter, which can't be possible but is. The few big trees look like they can't hack how hot it is and, no shit, the highway is the main street, like one of them Wild West towns on TV. We pass one servo, two pubs and a bakery and that's our lot. Every building's made out of corrugated metal.

Nao gets a bit of paper out her bag, looks like a map she's printed off the internet, and turns off the main street. The aunty's place is one block over and another block back the way we came, and when we get there the house is even crappier than Geen's and mine. A tiny fibro place with a tin roof sloping down into a veranda like it's frowning at us, like it's pissed off we've even showed up. There's a low mesh falling-down fence, a bare dirt yard and a stringy-barked tree, and next to the house is more bare dirt the whole way to the horizon. Gives me a headache to look at it.

Nao pulls up in the drive behind a rusty yellow hatchback and cuts the engine. Everything too quiet after the growl of the ute. 'She still lives here,' she says. 'It's the same car.' She's staring at the house the same way I am, and she hasn't let go the wheel.

'You didn't know that?'

'I haven't been here for a long time.' She folds the map back into her bag, takes her sunnies off and pushes them in there too. Yanks that bit of hair behind her ear, the bit that's always falling in her face. 'Right. We won't mention the gold to my aunty.'

'Good.'

'Or your bloke Daryl.'

'*Not my* . . . I fucken hope not.'

'Fine. And my name's not Cherry.'

'No shit.'

She gets out, slams the driver door and goes up the path to

the veranda steps. I lag behind with the gold. It's heavy as, like a dead dog in a bag, but I'm not leaving it in the car. Nao side-eyes it on the doorstep and says, 'I don't like lying, as a rule. So it might be better if you don't—'

The door opens and we both jump. It's an Aboriginal woman with a cowboy hat made out of straw on her head. She's so tiny she can't be related to Nao in a million years, except the way she double-takes Nao you can tell she recognises her. Nao says, 'Aunty. Hi. Um, can we come inside?' The aunty's eyes come past her to me and I see she does the exact same thing with her lips as Nao does. I step back off the doorstep but Nao sticks her arm through mine – the one I'm holding onto the bag with – and pulls it tight.

Like we're best mates all of a sudden, when all I wanna do is take the gold and leave her for dust.

4

Geena

Reckless

Geena's phone died in the night and she lights up a ciggie and makes a coffee while she waits for it to charge. She drinks the coffee looking out of Daryl's kitchen window in the anaemic light, at the black sand yard where nothing ever grows and his brand-new Colourbond shed. She's going to have to go down there. He never came back last night after he went out after Charlie.

He took Geena's keys, too. Rifled her bag and just took them, and she only clocked it this morning. That's the third time he's done that.

She knows there's no point panicking but it's there under her ribs, waiting for its moment alongside the guilt. She only put her head down on that couch for two minutes. She'd been trying Charlie's phone but she wasn't picking up.

When her screen lights up, there are three missed call notifications and a voicemail from Lee. She tries Charlie first and gets her voicemail message without it even ringing. That's different from last night and she doesn't know what it means. Out of charge, most likely, but she tries Daryl too and gets the same, the panic drawing crop circles on her insides.

Lee picks up first ring. 'Babe, I've been trying to—'

'My phone died,' she says. 'I'm still at Daryl's place.'

'Can you talk? Did you get my voicemail?'

'I haven't listened to it. I don't think we should talk on the phone, Lee.'

'Is Daryl there?'

'He never came back last night.'

'Babe, you don't think he's done a—'

'We're not talking about it on the phone, remember? Can you come and pick me up for work? I need to check on Charlie before my shift.'

'Where's your wheels?'

'He's taken my keys.'

'What did he do that for? Okay, but listen to my message. You can delete it, after.'

Geena finishes her ciggie with Daryl's shed key in her other hand. She breathes deep in the hopes the smoke will warm her up, her eyes narrowed against each exhale, steeling herself. She's had a bad feeling about the day ever since she woke up on the couch, like everything's about to go to shit but hasn't started to yet. Except maybe it already has.

She tries Charlie again but gets the same, runs the butt of the cigarette under the kitchen tap and slam-dunks it into the trash.

There's warm air and cicada sound in the yard already as she takes the key down the brick-paved path to the shed, tripping in her work heels. Summer creeping out from behind cloud cover and magpies warbling in the lemon-scented gum that towers over the back fence, too big for the yard there and she doesn't know what the neighbours were thinking, planting a tree like that in a suburban backyard.

Her heels *tap, tap* the pavers to match her heartbeat, too fast and then faster, ramping up by the door to the shed as she slides the key into the padlock. For a second it sticks but the lock clunks open and she rips a nail. Bugger, she'll have to fix that before work.

She's expecting Daryl's fingers in her hair or pinched into her upper arm, ready to spin her around and ask what the actual fuck she's doing in his shed. But, chill. He's not here. She tilts her head and listens out but there's nothing, no sound of the ute in the drive, no front door slamming shut. She's not one hundred per cent relieved about that, either. She'd be happier knowing where he was.

Geena scrapes the door over the poured concrete floor and steps into the shed. The interior is dimly lit from the back-corner window and the smell of burning metal lingers. It's stuffy with heat already and in no way suitable as the home gym and man-cave Daryl wanted it for. Not that he'd ever admit that.

The safe is a metal box on its side with a neat black square where the door hangs open, smaller than how she imagined it. Lee's welding gear is stacked on the floor behind it: the Darth Vader mask and his tools and cables, everything neatly coiled and packed away. He should have taken the lot of that back to the workshop yesterday, as soon as they got into the safe.

It makes it real, seeing it. Holy hell, what has she started? A tune starts up, the neighbour's music from over the back – Australian Crawl, 'Reckless' – too early in the morning for it. As if Mum is haunting her, a tune from the playlist Charlie listens to on a loop, and the hairs on Geena's arms stand up. She gets the bad feeling again and thinks, not for the first time, that she's surrounded by highly incompetent people. The fact Daryl and Lee managed to steal the safe at all from the big Mount Claremont house without being apprehended right there on the doorstep has the quality of a miracle about it.

She *tap, taps* towards the metal box, slowing down and bending as she gets close, peering into the black empty space.

Where's the bag? The leather holdall Daryl said was inside? She scouts his shelves of weights and eBay junk and the floor around the gym machines and it takes her a way-too-long moment to realise it's not anywhere, that the dark inside of the safe is empty.

That he took it with him last night.

Shit a brick. She lights up another cigarette and smokes it right there in the shed, trickling the smoke out of her nose the way he hates – *not ladylike, darl* – because she doesn't imagine for one moment now that he's coming back.

Not ladylike, darl, most definitely includes having a brain and using it. She thought he hadn't figured that part out, the double cross, but clearly he has, and she wonders how. Unless this is all to do with Charlie.

Geena is fair bloody furious with Charlie – her radar for drama, her sun in Leo and Aries rising, all played out in the exit from school last week, and now this. Swiping that tiny gold bar when Daryl was only showing it off, only wanted to show Geena how good they'd done after Lee got the safe open and confirmed what Daryl had said would be inside.

Either way, he took the rest of the bars with him when he went out after Charlie last night.

And just like that, the plan falls apart, in the oh so ordinary suburban space of his giant bloody shed.

She grinds the dead ciggie under the toe of her shoe and pops a strip of spearmint gum as Lee's car guns and grumbles into the driveway. She rips the passenger door open before he's fully stopped and tips herself into the seat. 'Howdy,' she says. 'Shit, these shoes.'

Lee's rocking his gangster sportswear and smells of that coconut hair wax he uses. He gives her a George Michael pout and she kisses him. There's loud eighties hip-hop coming out of the car stereo – Grandmaster Flash giving them the message, and not one they need to hear right now. She slides off her shoes and turns the volume down.

'Thought you were giving up the cigarettes, babe,' he says.

'I'm stressed, Lee. Our place, quick as. I can't be late for work today.'

Lee frowns at Daryl's empty carport. His hand hovering over the handbrake and his forehead creased above his aviators. 'Did you listen to the voicemail?'

'I deleted it. I didn't listen to it.'

He gawps at her. 'What did you do that for?'

'I felt weird about it. I feel weird about a lot of stuff today, Lee. Can we talk on the way? I'm real antsy about Charlie.'

He checks his hair in the mirror and reverses out. 'What if I'd stacked on the way and got in a coma and you never got to talk to me?'

'Then I guess I'd never have found out what was in the message.'

He straightens the car and drives one-handed through the early morning streets with the low sun bronzing up his tan. His left hand resting light and warm on Geena's thigh through her work skirt. 'Would you have got over it? Me being in a coma?' he says.

'In time.' His bottom lip juts out at that and she adds, 'You're right, by the way. He has.'

'He has what?'

'Done a runner.'

Lee's mouth is a perfect 'O' as he changes down for a school zone, picks up speed again at the end of it. 'With the stash?'

'Don't call it that, you make it sound like drugs. It's not as bad as drugs.' She pulls the visor down and checks her makeup in the mirror. 'But yeah, he's taken it. It's not in the shed and I searched the house too.' She snaps the visor back up and tells him about the empty safe, the one gold bar Charlie took and Daryl's paranoia. 'He must have twigged something, to take the whole lot with him. He went out looking for Charlie. That's what I'm mostly antsy about. I can't get either of them on their phones.'

'Shit, babe.' He slows for a stop sign and takes off again, lifting his hand from Geena's skirt each time he changes gear. 'I saw him last night, too, in the ute.'

'Daryl? You saw Daryl last night?'

'Outside your place. This morning, early.'

'Why didn't you say that! But he went out hours before. What was he doing all that time?'

'Don't know.' He turns into Geena's street and she slides on her shoes. 'You said to act normal so I went to the poker game,' he says. 'Daryl wasn't at the game and he wasn't picking up his calls. He owes a couple of the guys and I couldn't get a hold of him or you. I got rattled.'

'My phone died, I told you.' She hopes she's over-dramatizing and Daryl took her keys just to ground her at his place like he's done before. That he wouldn't have come after Charlie, not seriously, and Charlie wouldn't have mouthed off at him if he did. That nothing bad has happened apart from Daryl taking off with the gold out of the safe.

Lee parks out front and the two of them pile out, Geena in her heels and tight skirt and Lee with his white trainers and tracksuit. 'I checked his place and then your place,' he says, 'straight after the game.' He opens the gate for her and follows her up the path. 'It didn't look right. The front of the house was too dark.'

She presses her face to the hallway window. She can't see anything but a rectangle of light at the far end. 'What time was it?'

'Three a.m. The ute pulled in across the street and drove right off again.'

She trips across to Charlie's bedroom window. The room looks like a laundry-basket explosion, completely normal, but Lee's right – Charlie keeps the hallway light on all night when she's in the house. And what was Daryl doing still out in the ute at three o'clock in the morning?

'Shit a brick, Lee. I'm going around the back.'

He follows her around and through the side gate. She levers

open the right-hand back window and starts lifting out louvres, stacking them on the step.

'What you doing, babe? Where's your keys?'

'Daryl took 'em, I told you that,' she says. 'I'm breaking in, Lee. I've got a real bad feeling about this.'

Charlie's not anywhere in the house. The fridge magnets have been rearranged and the yellow rug on the floor in the sleep-out is gone. Charlie always hated that rug.

Lee's Ian Thorpe shoulders fill the back doorway, Geena's wind-chimes clamouring behind him where he's failed to duck his head. He's got his aviators in one hand, raking the other one through his hair. 'Maybe she left for school already.'

'She got expelled from school last Monday, Lee, right before the final exams, and don't ask.' Geena's panic is full-on letting rip. She's scrutinising the fridge magnets like there's some message in the way they've been put back, but that's a crazy idea. 'Does the place seem extra-clean, to you?' She's expecting a few toast crumbs at the very least, but the kitchen is spotless. She can see her face in the bottom of the sink, and that smell itching her nostrils is bleach. 'Can't you feel it?' she says. 'The negative energy? Something fair bloody terrible has happened in here.'

There's a half-load of wet washing in the machine, too – Charlie's clothes from yesterday – when she's got a bedroom floor covered in dirty laundry. Maybe she spilled something incriminating on her shirt and the rug, but she's not into booze, is she? She's bloody puritanical about booze. And anyhow, the rug's not in the wash with her clothes. Geena steps back into the sleep-out, the patch of floor where the rug was. The bleach smell is stronger here and is it the light, or is that a stain?

'Is this my bad?' Lee rubs his stubble, frowning at the patch of floor she's looking at. 'I should have come looking earlier. I should have left the poker game when he didn't show.'

'No, Lee. This is my bad for getting the safe-burgling bright idea in the first place and talking Daryl into it. I am fully responsible for this.'

There's something down between the floorboards, a thread of white cotton. She gets down on her knees and slips a nail into the crack and teases it out. Lee steps closer and the light shifts and she sees half the strand is stained pink. 'Hell, there's blood here, Lee.' There's a red-brown rind of it under her nail.

The room tilts, everything in it suddenly too bright. She can visualise exactly how it happened: Daryl, over the limit and aggro. Charlie, no sense of self-preservation or control what-soever, giving it back to him despite being half his size. Him hitting her just that bit too hard.

She puts a hand flat on the scrubbed-clean floor and stares at Lee. 'I think they got into a fight and Daryl hurt her. I think he might . . . I think . . . ' She hears the tremor in her voice and feels the thing that's been waiting all day tighten around her heart. 'Jeezus, what if he used the rug to roll her body in? What if he's taken her out bush and scraped a shallow grave and put her in it?'

'I reckon you might be jumping the gun, babe.' Lee rubs his face some more, not quite meeting her eye. 'There was two people in the ute.'

'*What?* Daryl and Charlie, together?'

'Don't know. Two people. That's all I could see in the head-lights when I followed it.'

'You didn't say you'd followed it, Lee! Which way did they go?'

5

Nao

Magnet

Aunty makes me think of a kookaburra – her quick eyes, the way she holds her head pushed a little way forward. She hangs her straw cowboy hat on a hook next to the back door and washes her hands at the sink. I remember her house as bigger, not so dark, but how old was I? Five or six? The house smells the same, of eucalyptus oil – she must use it for something. There's an all-pervading shimmering sound of cicadas from outside in the yard and the tin roof holds the heat like the lid on a locked metal box.

It was Mel who first asked me about Dad's family at the start of uni this year and why wasn't I in touch with Aunty? It was only when things got more difficult at home that I started to listen, looked for Aunty's address in Mum's contacts and printed out the map. I never expected I'd use it, though, not seriously. And not like this.

Coming to Aunty's place was a thing to say to Charlie, that's all, after we lost the bloke following us and she didn't want to go home. It only became something different last night during the drive. Traveling the dark highway with Charlie sleeping next to me, trying to keep awake and outrun the storm of thoughts. I decided then that I could spill everything to Aunty – she'd take it out of my hands and tell the police and it would all be over.

But that was then. Now I'm here, I don't want to do it. I don't know Aunty. We don't know each other. She's nothing apart from a name and address in a list of contacts. And there's a pull through the floor into my bare feet that itches, that makes me want to get back on the road.

'Can we have some water, Aunty?' I say. 'A glass? We've been driving a bit.'

She dries her hands on her skirt, an olive-green sundress. She hasn't asked me what I'm doing here but she must be thinking it. I washed the blood out of my jacket back at Charlie's house. I washed my feet, my face and my hands and re-braided my hair. But the makeup keeps sweating from around my eye, the bruise that's come up this morning and probably looks worse than it is, and there's the Band-Aid on my hand, the blood soaking through it but not so fast now. I see her take in these things but I wonder if there's any more to it; if she knows something, if someone has called her. Not Mum. Mum would never call her. The police, though?

Aunty's lips are dry, her hair clipped back off her face in the heat. Her bird eyes don't leave Charlie while she gets us tall glasses – she doesn't trust the white girl in her house. I wonder when I can ask her for money, if she'll give me any.

Charlie watches too, her gaze raking everything – the couch, the table and one chair, the TV and house plants on metal shelves, the blinds leaking yellow light. She keeps hold of the black leather bag with the gold inside and it's obvious how heavy it is, that it's not normal stuff in there. I whisper at her to put it down on the floor but she grips it harder and curls her lip.

Charlie doesn't miss a thing. Did she notice my tsunami at the roadhouse – floods of tears in the toilets and trying to pull my hair out at the roots? I bloody hope not. It was that woman in the shop, the way she looked at me. The way Charlie looked too when I asked her for that money back. What it means that my credit card that has always worked has stopped working, today of all days.

That the police have put some kind of stop on it.

The water's out of the tap and warm but I say thanks and drink it down while Aunty waits to take the glass. 'This heat,' I say. 'And still early morning. How do you stand it?'

But I've said the wrong thing and she doesn't answer.

Charlie's still got her headphones round her neck, the cord dangling into nothing like a stray bit of thread. She holds the water glass like it's an explosive device, her knuckles scabbed and swollen. She's opened up the cuts there, doing whatever she did back at the roadhouse.

The bag of gold drags so hard on Charlie's arm I feel the ache in my own. It alarms me, her carrying it everywhere. It pulls my eyes down along the hallway towards the front door and the street, expecting sirens or the bloke from last night, the one who followed us. I don't know which might be worse.

That gold came out of Warren's safe. The bag is a twin of the one he takes to the gym, the exact size and shape and brand of soft black leather, except the bag Charlie won't let go of isn't oiled and well-used but stiff and inflexible, a darker black like it's been sitting under glass. It's been sitting in Warren's safe, that's why. It's what was stolen, why he had Charlie's address on his phone. It's the only explanation that fits.

But how did he know it was there?

I realise with a jab of pain that I'm pressing on the cut and the Band-Aid is wet again. It hurts more now than it did at the time, but I was flooded with adrenaline, wasn't I? I didn't know I'd cut myself.

I scan the wall and stop at a pinned-up photo above Aunty's TV: two teenagers, the girl grinning, the boy younger and serious, red rocks and dark water at the back of them. I remember a story, from school: they call this place Magnet because of the hill out of town – some white explorer bloke and his compass. It's true: that's the pull I can feel in my feet through the floor.

Aunty takes us to a room halfway along the hallway where there's more thick heat and a set of bunks. 'That one,' Aunty says. 'Two beds in there. That okay?'

'Thank you,' I say. 'It's great. Isn't it, Charlie?' Charlie says nothing. I hope she doesn't expect me to get up top. 'Thanks, Aunty,' I say again.

'There's towels in the wardrobe. Bathroom next door. Not this one.' She raps on the closed door opposite. 'A snake in there. Don't frighten that fulla.' She turns her eyes on me, almost accusing, before she disappears towards the kitchen.

'Snake?' Charlie says. 'In the *house*?' She glares at the bunk.

'Fuck. Not gunna sleep, now, not with that … anyhow, it's morning. Do we have to crash here? Can't we keep going?'

'Like, where? I don't know about you but I have to sleep.' Does she think we have options? It's like she doesn't think at all.

She grumbles something, pushes the bag onto the top bunk ahead of her and climbs up.

I shut the door and ease onto the bottom bunk, the whole thing creaking and cracking like it's going to come apart at the joints. 'Stop shifting yer fat arse,' Charlie says. There was a time I'd have been embarrassed by this, bloody mortified, but now it feels like nothing, like that person no longer exists. I lie still and so does the bed.

The sheets are cool despite the heat, the eucalyptus smell penetrating here too. I'm shaken by Aunty, how unhappy she is that we're here. I didn't expect it, didn't factor it into my thinking about her, and I wonder again if she knows something. Still, I can sleep, check the news, ask her for some money, whatever she'll give me. Keep driving north and lose Charlie along the way. North feels like space, room to breathe, although I know this isn't rational. Lawless, is that what I mean? The word makes my eyes prick.

Last night, on the drive, a line kept repeating in my head on a loop, about needing to be a person *of good fame and character* in order to practice the law. Break it and you don't get to have a career in it, in other words. I don't even know if that came from a lecture. Mostly what I remember from those early lectures was an overwhelming urge to get up and run out of the room. I stayed for Dad, because he never got that far. And to prove Warren wrong and make a go of it.

The law is there to protect people, but only if you stay on the right side of it, especially if you look like me.

'I've gotta call Geen,' Charlie says. 'You reckon I can use the phone?'

Jesus. No. 'That's not a good idea. I thought you wanted to stay away for a few days?'

'That was your idea.'

Was it? I don't remember.

'Gotta tell Geen I'm okay,' she says.

'I don't think Aunty has one; a phone. She didn't used to, and I don't have a number for her.'

'Fucksakes, who doesn't have a phone?' She breathes for a bit, loud, through her mouth. She'll give up and fall asleep. 'She really your aunty?'

I keep my eyes shut.

'She doesn't like me,' she says.

So what? I'm not sure she likes me either. This is not about liking; it's about getting through the next few days. 'I need to sleep, Charlie. I've driven six hours straight.'

'And whose fault's that? I woulda done if you'd let me.'

And driven us off the road, quite possibly. 'You don't look old enough.'

'Bullshit – told you I was. Is she, but? Your aunty?'

'Yes, she's my aunty. Now—'

'Ya don't look like her. Don't sound like her, neither. How come you talk like you do? Posh. Western suburbs?'

'What do you mean? You live in Shenton Park.'

She sniffs. 'You saw the house.' She turns over and the bunk creaks. 'You don't even look that Aboriginal. I mean, you do, except . . . I mean, how Aboriginal are ya? A quarter, less, or what?'

74

My jaw clenches. Are we really doing this? Are we really doing this now, in the middle of an insane scenario where people have died?

I think of the countless times I've had that look from people, the one where their eyes skip from Mum and Warren to me and back again, trying to work us out. How every fight between the two of them felt like my fault for being different. 'We're either too Black or we're not Black enough,' is what Mel says. I picture her rolling her eyes as she says it and I feel a tiny bit better, until I think of Dad again and how much I've let him down. Tears threaten but I swallow them. I'm not showing Charlie that. 'You should really say what you mean, you know, not hold back?'

'All I said was—'

'I heard what you said. Now give it a rest.'

'Can't even ask one question.'

For about thirty seconds she's quiet.

'How come you get to tell me nothing when I've told you shitloads?'

'That's your problem. You should talk less. I'm going to sleep now.'

'No way I'm gunna sleep with a snake in the house. Might as well try to crash under a tree.' More noisy breathing. A blowfly is banging up against the window. 'What if I tell your aunty what you said to that cop? How you gave him a fake name. Or is Nao not your name, neither?'

She can't be serious. I glare at the underside of her, the mattress bulging between the slats. The one three from the top is cracked right through. 'One question,' I say.

'Where are your parents? Why didn't ya call them after that fight with your boyfriend? After you stacked your car?'

'That's two questions.' Does she not know how exhausting it is, listening to her, hour after hour? Trying not to tell her anything?

I can half answer them. I can make something up.

'They dead?' she says.

Why would she think that? How is she always two steps ahead? 'My mum's in Bali. She's collecting an award. Mother of the year.'

'Still coulda called her . . . is that a joke?'

'She's away, for work. I don't want to talk about her.'

She goes quiet. God, she said her mum died, didn't she? Last night at the house? I think I've upset her, been bloody insensitive, until she starts again.

'Yer dad? Where's he?'

I fix my eyes on the broken slat. It can't hurt, telling her this. It's the most straightforward question of any she's asked me. 'He's dead, Charlie. In a car accident.'

'Shit, I didn't—'

'It's fine. It was a long time ago, twelve years. I haven't seen Aunty since. And I'm sorry. You said your mum died too. I forgot.'

She sniffs. 'S'orright.' For a second I think she's stopped. 'Runs in the family, yeah?' she says. 'Car accidents? Coulda warned me about that.'

I roll my eyes and stay quiet. It's not a real question, anyway.

'Last one,' she says. 'Your boyfriend – the one you were running from. Did you do something to him? That why you lied to that cop and got covered in blood? You bash his head in or something?'

The air sucks out of the room. The magnet pull throbs in my

limbs. I shouldn't have told her anything, shouldn't have started. I say, 'No, I didn't bash anybody,' and, 'Go to sleep, Charlie,' too low and too quiet for it to shut her up, but it does.

Next thing I know she's sleep-breathing, snake or no snake. I watch the broken slat and try not to shift on the bed. I won't sleep now, not until I've talked to Aunty and checked the news. Not until I know if someone's found him.

Warren.

Warren's body, slumped at the bottom of the stairs.

Better to face facts. Easier, now there's some distance between us.

It's sweat-hot in the kitchen, the sun not yet down and the blinds now open, the back of the house hazy with light and the cicadas outside grown sluggish. I've showered and covered my black eye with more makeup, but I see Aunty take it in as I enter the room. She's made us dinner – baked potatoes and sausages off the grill, and a salad. I haven't told her I don't eat meat and I don't want to get into it. I ask for one sausage and when she's not looking I fork it onto Charlie's plate. She screws her face into a question but eats it. She eats the whole lot like she hasn't for a month.

Aunty tells us the snake story, talking more than she has the whole time we've been here. It's like she's covering something – nerves, maybe – or she doesn't know what to say to me with Charlie here. 'King brown,' she says. 'And no one to help me catch him. All scared.'

'Pest control, that's what ya need.' Charlie's got her mouth full. Don't say it, spray it. It's the first thing she's said and she goes bright red.

'Nah, leave him be,' Aunty says. After that it's like there's nothing more to say on it except a big awkward silence. Aunty shifts her eyes sideways at Charlie and then me – that trace of accusation again – and that's when I get it. It's not only Charlie she doesn't trust in her house. Aunty has put me in that camp too.

My face gets warm, seeing this. I don't know what to do with it. I want to leave right away but how rude would that be, straight after dinner?

Charlie's fingers pick at her headphone cord, her swollen knuckles standing out in the light. She darts looks between me and the door to the bedroom and Aunty watches her do it. Charlie's left the gold bag under the sheet on her bunk. What does she think – I'm going to run in there and out the front door with it? She needs to calm down.

I can't sit any longer. I thank Aunty for dinner, get up and clear dishes until she muscles in and tells me to sit back down. When I turn back to the table Charlie's gone.

For a second I think she's done a runner with the gold. Does it even matter? Yes, it flaming well matters. I haven't worked out what to do about it. It could lead straight back to Warren if one of us gets caught with it. But the bedroom door shuts with a click and I hear the creak as she climbs onto the bed.

I step up to the shelves of house plants and catch sight of the photo above the TV again – Dad and Aunty as teenagers, at least I think that's who it is. I recognise Aunty in the girl, and they're clearly related, despite Dad being taller. I don't have memories of my dad, not really, only a sense of safety that disappears as I turn towards it. Dad is always just outside the frame, as if he's there but I can't get to him.

I have no pictures of Dad, either. Warren would never allow

it; he told Mum it would only confuse me – one of his arbitrary rules. I get a wash of shame about this, the same as at dinner. It's not like I wasn't curious about Dad and his family, growing up, but it was easiest to do what Warren wanted, easiest to keep my head down and keep the peace.

'You've got your father's face,' Aunty says, and I drop my hand from the photo as she turns back to the dishes; there's a hard outline to her words as if she's read my mind. In the picture she's older than Dad, pointing at him and grinning – a softer, different Aunty. Dad looks the same age I am now, in jeans and a T-shirt. There's a crease beneath his lower lip I recognise and I touch two fingers to it. His eyes are set wider apart than Aunty's in a way that seems to take in the whole of the scene. She is right about our faces. I realise those eyes are mine too.

The dark stretch of water behind the two of them has a natural rock jetty extending out into it, the red walls of a gorge further back and above it a sun-pale sky. The ridge and sky seem to shimmer as I look, and I step back too fast into Aunty's couch, bashing my heel against the wood.

I see the sign in the bottom corner of the picture, part of it disappearing out of the frame: MINE SITE. AUTHORISED ACCESS ONLY. SALTWATER GOLD CORPORATION.

The same as the letters on the gold bars we found. *SGC.* Isn't it? I glance at Aunty's back, go to the bedroom door, knock once and slip inside.

Charlie's on her knees on the top bunk, her face red and shiny with the heat in the room, the tip of her tongue in the gap between her teeth. She's got the leather bag unzipped and the little bagged-up gold bars lined up like cars on a freeway.

'What are you doing?'

She jumps and bangs her head on the ceiling. 'Ow! Coulda knocked.'

'I did knock. What are you doing with them?'

'Counting.'

She's taken one of the bars out of its bag and placed it on top. The logo is the same as in the photo, *SGC,* I see as I step up close. How is that possible? How did this gold end up in Warren's safe?

'How many are there?'

She frowns. 'There's ninety-nine.'

'Not counting the one in your pocket,' I say, and she looks at me sharply. 'That's ten kilos in total.'

'What's that come to?' she says. 'What's each one worth?'

'I don't know.'

'Bet it's a lot. Can't believe loser Daryl stole this. It's way outta his league.'

'So you admit he stole it?'

'He didn't fucken save up for it, that's for sure.' Her eyes are like blue marbles in the half-light. One hand grips the handle of the bag and the other hovers over the bed.

'We should get rid of it,' I say. 'Dump it. It doesn't belong to us.'

She glares at me. 'You lost it, or what? Bet you never needed cash real bad.'

'It's stolen. We don't even know who from.'

This isn't completely a lie. I don't know how Warren got hold of it.

'Who cares?' she says. 'Some rich bastards.'

'And that bloke is after it, the one from last night.'

I have the dizzying thought that this man is connected to Warren and has the same information Warren had on his phone. But we got away from him, didn't we? He hasn't followed us.

Charlie repacks the bag and zips it up, lifts it like she's testing the weight and places it up near her pillow, between her body and the window. I watch this with a kind of horror. She doesn't know what she's dealing with. She's like a loose cannon transporting an unexploded bomb. She thumps the pillow twice with a fist and lies down on her back with one arm looped through the handle of the bag.

'Dunno what you're looking at,' she says. 'You don't even want it.'

But someone will. Associates of Warren's, whoever else knows about it. We won't stand a chance against people like that, not when they come looking.

I'm going to have to get it away from her. I'm going to have to dump it.

She blinks, the blue of her eyes winking out and reappearing. 'Seen that snake of your aunty's yet?'

'Twelve years,' Aunty says. She's made us tea and cornered me on the couch. 'Twelve years, no cards, no letters, no nothing.'

I stare at the steam off my tea and shift on the couch. 'Is it that long?' But I know it is.

'And now you bring trouble with you, like your mother.'

I jerk and slop the tea. I put the mug on the floor. 'Did she call you?'

'There's no phone here, girl. Next door's got one.'

'But did she? A message from next door?'

She lifts one eyebrow. 'You expecting a phone call? Come a long way for that.'

Right. Not yet. So they haven't found him, or the police have called Mum and she's flying back. She won't expect me to be up here. I put a hand up to my forehead. It's radiating heat, but so is everything. 'You get the news up here, Aunty?'

'What? Nah. Too far out in the sticks for news.'

'Really? Oh.' I get it, her joke. 'Can I . . . can we watch it?'

Her eyes narrow at me. *What for?* But she picks up the remote and clicks channels until it comes up. It's regional, but they have news from the city, they must do. I watch with my hands knotted in my lap and Aunty's eyes on me the whole time. Jesus, people watch the news, don't they? But my heart is too high up in my chest like it's floated there on a swell, and it only drops back down when the weather comes on. We missed the first few minutes, so I can't be sure, but—

'Happy now?' Aunty says. 'No news on the weather, only more of this heat.' She clicks the TV off and sips her tea.

It's no relief, that no one's phoned, that there's nothing about Warren on the news. Because there will be; they will find him. I think of going next door and calling Mum myself, the first time I've seriously considered it, but all that does is suck the air out of my lungs. Mum can't help me. She made her choice when she went away on this last work trip. There's no going back.

Aunty pushes her face forwards over the top of her mug. 'What have you come here for, Nomi?'

The name shocks me – what Mum and Dad used to call me when I was small – but of course she'd call me that. I look at my tea on the floor. Rude, not to have drunk it. 'I don't know.' Now is the moment to ask her for money, but the shame is pricking and I can't do it.

'A long way to come for nothing,' Aunty says. 'Long way to come to watch news on TV.'

'Yes.' My eyes go to the photo – Dad and Aunty Mar. 'That picture,' I say. 'What is that place? Is it around here?'

She flicks her eyes sideways. 'That's up on country. Saltwater country, in the Kimberley. Never you mind about that.' She lifts her chin at the bedroom door. 'Are you friends with that girl?'

'Who, Charlie?' I glance at the door. Quiet now.

'She's not like you. You want to listen to your liyan, Nomi. Pay attention to it.'

'My what?'

'She's trouble.'

'Oh, she's not . . .' I think of Charlie's bruised knuckles and bitten nails, her clutching the leather bag, and how she looked when I first saw her. 'She's okay. She's not as bad as you might—'

'What have you come here for, Nomi?' That's three times now. 'Finished up school, have you? At the uni now?' Her voice dropping low, soothing. It would be so easy to tell her everything. 'Just passing by, is it?'

'I don't know, Aunty. I thought . . . I was looking for—'

'You're not looking. You're running.' The words make me flinch. They hang in the air. I wonder if Charlie's awake and can hear them.

But Aunty's right, and I keep staring at the photo – the dark water behind the two of them, the rock walls and pale sky. Kimberley, she said. Far north. I think of the distance I need to put between myself and Warren's body. The gold, inside the room with Charlie, that I have to get rid of.

'I could go to that place,' I say.

'What place?'

'In the picture.'

'You want to do that now?'

'Well, yes. I mean, maybe.'

She frowns. 'What and leave your friend? That's not thinking.'

'No, it's fine.' I lower my voice. 'She's not my friend. I mean . . .'

'You fight with your mother? That what this is about?' Her eyes skim my face and the cut on my hand.

'No. She's away. It's not that.'

But the mention of Mum has pressed me back into the couch. Mum and Aunty – the arguments before Dad's funeral and the silence after. Aunty blaming Mum for Dad's accident.

'You want to go back down south,' she says. 'To your mother.'

She can't still be angry after twelve years, can she? About Dad? I sit straight and look at the picture. 'What if I want to go there instead?'

'Nothing there for you. I sent letters, you know that?'

'Did you? Well I didn't—'

'Nah, she didn't want you to. Didn't get 'em, did you?' She swings herself off the couch and picks up my mug.

'I'm sorry,' I say. 'About the letters.' She purses her lips. 'I was only six when the accident happened.' I get why she blames Mum but it's not fair to blame me too. The shame is back in my face and that's not fair either.

She straightens up, all five foot nothing of her. 'Accident, is that what you call it? Remember it good, do you?' A darkness in her eye that isn't like a bird anymore. A stillness that scares me.

'No, I don't remember it at all. I was only a little kid. You know that, Aunty.'

'You want to know what's what? Why she stole those let-ters off you?'

'She didn't *steal* them. She's my mother.' I get to my feet, my head swimming and my mouth like dust. 'She was ... I don't know. Protecting me.'

Aunty puffs air through her lips and turns towards the sink.

'Tell me where it is,' I say. 'Please? The place in the photo. I'd like to go there.'

She clatters our mugs into the sink. 'And who would want you up there, Nomi? Who are you to them? You've got your father's face but you're a white girl now too. Go back down south to your studies. Go back to your mother.'

I wake from a dream where someone is screaming, drowning in the lake where we put the bloke's body, except it's not the lake, it's the waterhole in the photo. Black water swirling, and my shirt heavy and wet. I crash out of bed onto hard, gritty floor. It's sweat soaking my shirt, not water, and I grab lungfuls of air and try to slow my heart. It's not me screaming but the sound doesn't stop, and I've touched Charlie's shoulder before I see she's still asleep.

I pull on my skirt and lurch from the room. The screaming is louder in the dark hallway and I think of Aunty, Warren, and then the snake. But it's birds, cockatoos, having a shrieking fight in Aunty's backyard. How does she sleep through that?

I push the back door wide but the birds don't quit. I hear their feet scraping, footsteps on the tin roof between the squabbling, the only sounds in the quiet. It's still dark out, still night, and I can't see them, they're black and invisible against the sky. I smell eucalyptus again and realise there's an entire native garden out here, ground covers and small trees between the house and the back fence. You'd never guess it was there from the front.

Back inside the house, the heat is solid slabs you could cut. I click one light on in a corner of the kitchen to make tea. I pull down the photo of Dad and Aunty and slip it into a pocket. The door to the snake room is open and I don't think it's supposed to be.

The dream has gone, is not important. They'll find Warren before they find the bloke in the lake. I feel that pull in my feet, the same as when we arrived here, the itch to leave mirrored in the cockatoos scratching above my head. I'll get as far as I can in the ute and then sell it for money. Get shot of Charlie and dump the gold on the way north. Cut the connection with Warren.

I'm curious, though, about how he got hold of it. About the place in the photo and why Aunty doesn't want me to go there. That word comes back to me, from last night: *liyan*. She never told me what it meant.

I'll wait to check the news before I go. One last look before the road. That would be the smart thing to do.

6

Geena

Confide in Me

Back home after her shift Geena lights up and paces the rooms. The emptiness and the smell of bleach mess with her head, like something that should be on Netflix instead of happening in her own home. The place is silent apart from a family of kookaburras, echoing one another out in the backyard. She can't eat, won't sleep, ignores Lee's calls.

She imagines Charlie telling her off for these things, except for the part about Lee because Charlie hasn't met Lee yet, and now they might never get that chance. The plan to take off to the Gold Coast, to get as far as they can get from Daryl, out of the state and across to the other side of the country, can't happen without the gold. Geena knows how badly she's screwed up here. She can't plant it all at Charlie's feet. Charlie didn't know about the plan.

She's called Charlie's phone on her breaks all day only to get the same every time – no ringtone, straight to her voicemail. She's left a shitload of messages.

Lee said he followed the ute last night until he lost it in traffic on Kings Park Road. She's spent the whole day angsting that Charlie's been abducted by Daryl, not knowing what parallel universe that might happen in when they hate each other's guts. He had the rest of the gold in the ute with him already, why would he need Charlie? She only took that one piece.

Neither does this explain the missing rug or the bleach, the clothes in the wash or the blood. She's expecting the cops any second now. That knock on the door you get, with their hats off, when someone has died.

It's after nine p.m. when her phone rings. The caller ID on the screen says *private*. She freezes, sits down in Mum's chair, stands up again and answers the call.

'Geen?'

'What the fuck, Charlie? I've been tearing my hair out with worry here.' The tension of the day blooms into a bubble and pops, like something made of soap.

'About Daryl?'

'About you, numbat! I didn't know where you'd got to.'

'Yeah, that's why I'm ringing you.'

Geena sighs, nothing left in her but a softness and tiredness. 'Where are you? Are you okay?'

'I'm orright. I wanted to let ya know. Are you still at Daryl's?'

'I'm at our place. Daryl never came home last night. Charlie, what the hell is—'

'Geen, I'm on a payphone. I've only got fifty cents.'

'Why? What's happened to your phone? I've left all these messages.'

'Remember that plan we had? Surfers Paradise?' She's talking low and fast, her words running together. Charlie always talks fast but this is extreme, the sounds distorting like her mouth is too near the phone or she's trying not to be overheard.

'You sound weird,' Geena says. 'What's going on? Are you injured?'

'Geen, you're not listening!' That's more like Charlie. 'The Gold Coast. Remember it? We can do it.'

Geena drops her head and pinches the bridge of her nose, thumb and first finger, feels the tension building again. Charlie didn't know about the plan. Geena didn't trust her with it. 'You're making no sense at all. Where's the yellow rug? What happened with Daryl?'

Charlie clams up, nothing but fast breathing into the phone.

'Put Daryl on,' Geena says. 'What's he playing at? Are you still in the ute?'

A weird noise from Charlie, at the back of her throat. Geena listens out for some clue to where she is, some sound in the background, and thinks she hears a car.

'Where are you?' Geena says again. 'Put him on. Isn't he there with ya?'

'Shit, Geen, I'm outta coins. I'm gunna—'

And she's gone, disconnected the call. The number rings out when Geena calls it back and the kookaburras start up again in the yard as if they're having a go. Charlie's fifty cents would have got her ten minutes and they had all of two. She's seriously none the wiser about any of it, apart from the fact Charlie's not dead.

Charlie is not a bad kid. She hasn't had the greatest of runs at life, not with the way Mum died. Not with how close she'd been to Dad and how that turned out.

Sometimes Geena thinks Charlie's this close to being okay, within spitting distance of it, of sticking at something, of using her brain and controlling her temper, and then it all goes to shit again. She was going to surprise Charlie with the Gold Coast plan – it was always Charlie's fantasy more than Geena's, to move back to where Mum grew up. It was never something real until Geena took it and ran with it – and look where that's got them now.

The knock at the front door shocks her awake where she's dozed off in Mum's chair in the dark. It's real late, after midnight, her phone screen tells her when she blinks at it in her lap. The night is otherwise silent and she thinks she's imagined the sound, but it comes again.

It can't be the death knock. Charlie was fine three hours ago.

She creeps up the shadowy hallway with her shoes off, tiptoes into Charlie's room for a view of the empty street and front doorstep. All she gets is the back half of the man who is standing there – a dark suit and dark hair, cut off by a corner of wall.

Only one of him, and not in uniform. What does that mean?

He knocks a third time as she gets up to the inside of the front door, and she jumps – a lightning bolt discharging through her feet.

The hinges squeak as she opens the door and his eyes narrow, his hand still up and hovering. His left hand – the right arm is awkward at his side, his shoulders in the charcoal suit uneven. His arms and his torso look too long for his body, like someone distorted in a mirror. There's a metallic-edged body odour coming off him as well as the sage smell of some kind of cologne, and her gaze is sucked towards what's in his palm as he flips it open, the light from behind her catching it and her insides falling away from her. The police badge she's been expecting, but not like this.

His mouth opens and closes and twists, lifting dry lips into a sneer. 'Geena Kelly? I need to ask you some questions.'

The cop locks Geena in the back seat of a four-wheel-drive vehicle, a black Toyota he's got parked in a side street around the corner. He tells her to fasten her seatbelt and wait, that he'll be back to take her statement, and he disappears back around the corner towards the house.

She knows this is not normal procedure. It's after midnight and he should have a partner with him, a police-issue vehicle and radio. Why's he gone back to the house? What if he goes inside and smells the bleach, finds the blood the same way she did? She's not even certain she shut the front door properly; it all happened so quick, him taking her arm and marching her out of there.

He should have told her what he's investigating. He hasn't mentioned Charlie or Daryl or the stolen gold although that has to be what this is about; she's never broken the law before. But he should have a search warrant and she didn't ask to see one. That police ID could be fake. She's such a dipshit.

She's hankering bad for a ciggie and she doesn't have any gum. The cop wouldn't let her bring anything apart from her denim jacket, hung on a hook by the front door, and the sandals with wedge heels. She slipped her phone into the pocket of the jacket as she lifted it, and the shape presses flat and warm against her boob where she's moved it into the cup of her bra. The battery level is at thirty-three per cent, but who's she going to call? She told Lee they can't see each other, they mustn't contact each other. It's for the best; it's temporary. That's what she told him.

Charlie will be doing Daryl's head in by now. Does she think she can double cross him out of that gold? Is that what she meant on the phone, about Surfers Paradise? She doesn't know anything about it.

The cop is gone for thirty-five minutes and when he gets back in the car he smells of petrol. She doesn't remember that from before.

He winces as he threads his right arm through the seatbelt, catching Geena watching so that she drops her eyes. He wears a pair of charcoal leather driving gloves to match his suit, with cut-out holes across the backs of them where his knuckles are. She's never seen anyone drive in them before and they seriously creep her out. He's hardly Ryan Gosling but maybe he thinks he is. He zig-zags away through the quiet dark streets, jerking the car around each corner so she flies this way and that across the back seat, even with her belt done up. His eyes on her in the rearview mirror glitter like metal, relentlessly awake, but she's not going to say anything until she has to. She's aware of her rights.

They drive past three different cop shops on the way out of town. Each time she thinks he'll slow, indicate and park, that they'll go into one of those rooms for him to take her statement and read her her rights like he's supposed to, but he never gives the places a glance. The first time is a relief – she's still free, she's not a prisoner yet – but the next two times are anything but. Who is she kidding? She's already a prisoner.

He's not using the vehicle GPS and the screen is a blank black square that mirrors the dark outside the windows and reminds Geena of the inside of the empty safe. He's got a mobile phone on the passenger seat he flicks and jabs at intervals but she can't see what's on the screen. She wonders who he's in touch with, what he's saying to them and if any of it is about her.

Her alarm grows as they blast through the outskirts of the city and into the Swan Valley; she glimpses vineyards and post and rail fences, occasional fuel stops. The headlights and tail-lights of remaining city traffic thin out until the few vehicles passing them are big trucks, their lights high and blinding.

Once they get out onto Great Northern Highway – breaking the speed limit, from what she can tell from the back seat – it's mostly a single lane either way. She has a sense of the flat pastoral country ahead and around them, the night sky above and the city left behind, feels the extent of the clearing of mature trees and the emptiness beyond the lines of them at the sides of the road.

This is where the streetlights fall away into full dark and he starts with the questions.

'I want the names of your associates. How many of you are there?'

Geena meets his hard eyes in the mirror but can't keep it up. She looks at her arms wrapped around the top of her sundress instead, goose-pimples making tracks under the Toyota's air-conditioning. 'What associates? You haven't told me what this is about.' She's not giving up Lee and she can't shop Daryl without landing herself in it, possibly Charlie too. The last thing Charlie needs is a run-in with the cops.

'You know full well what this is about. Stolen property,' he says. 'Who is travelling with the girl?'

Does he mean Charlie? Surely he'd say if he did. 'I don't know anything about a girl. I think you might have made a mistake.'

'Has she been threatened or coerced in some way? Or is it money – she gets a percentage of the proceeds?'

Not Charlie, then. 'I don't know who you mean. You have to give me more than that. You have to give me her name.'

And if it's not a mistake? What's this girl got to do with anything? Shit, has Daryl taken off with some girl? Charlie doesn't have friends, not as far as Geena knows. Not apart from Saskia and she messed that up.

'What happened back there at the house?'

She flinches. 'I don't know.'

His eyes narrow. 'I'll tell you what this smells like – an opportunistic and highly unprofessional operation. Not co-operating will end badly for all concerned, particularly if the girl comes to harm.'

There's something real nasty about this cop and he's one hundred per cent right – Geena is way out of her depth here and no hero. But Charlie and Daryl are up ahead somewhere with the gold, at least she assumes they are, and possibly this girl too, so she sucks up the fear and gives as good as she gets.

'Am I under arrest? There are rules, even I know that.'

He says nothing, clicks the indicator and pulls out onto a darker stretch of road to overtake a truck. She feels the Toyota respond, the smooth surge of power that presses her back into her seat.

'What's the girl's name?' she says. 'Maybe I do know her. What school did she go to?' She leans forwards and gives it some cleavage and a tentative smile.

'I'll ask the questions.'

Her boobs might as well be invisible.

They pass the truck and keep driving, his dark-gloved hands on the wheel and the windows up and sealed against the night. Trees and power lines and stars like light globes dropping back into the dark.

Where are they going? How far out of the city? She doesn't care how he knows they took the gold, how he turned up on her doorstep, who he's communicating with via his phone. He knows and that's what matters. Maybe all she can hope for here is damage limitation.

'Listen,' she says. 'I don't know where it is, the stolen property, or the girl either. If I did, I'd tell you and you could recover it and we could all go home. That'd be real good, to be honest.' Still, it's painful to say it. The Gold Coast dream evaporating like desert rain.

'Is that right? I know precisely where they are,' he says. 'They're in Mount Magnet.'

TUESDAY

7

Charlie

Roadkill

I get the window open from the top bunk at Nao's aunty's – cooler out there than in here but it can't last. The sun over the fence next door makes me blink and the cash from the tin in the kitchen's in my pocket next to my phone. I found it last night, need it for fuel and shit, except how far's it gunna get me? Nao's buggered off someplace, gone from the bottom bunk. Lucky, 'cause I slept in and didn't mean to. Couldn't risk switching on my phone, could I?

Nao's got her aunty, the happy reunion. Orright, so it's not exactly been happy. She can work on it, but. It's not like she wants the gold, and not like Daryl's ute's got anything to do with her. I reckon I need both more than she does.

Can't believe Geen asked about Daryl last night on the phone, out on the main street where that payphone took my last fifty cents. She thinks I'm out here in the ute with him. As if! Once we get the money from the gold and a flash place in Surfers, she's not gunna mind so much that he's gone. She'll think he's done a runner. She doesn't even need to know he's dead.

I dangle the holdall out the window, far as it can go until my arm hurts. I listen a second, can't hear nothing, drop it. Screw my eyes shut but it hardly makes a noise when it hits the dirt. I turn around on the bunk to get my legs out the window and Nao steps into the bedroom.

Shit. We stare at each other. She frowns. 'What are you doing?'

'Thought you'd gone for brekky,' I say.

The ute key slides out my shorts pocket onto the bed, shiny metal. I snatch it up but she's seen it. Her eyes go big and then angry and she looks for the bag next to my pillow. 'Where's the gold?' she says.

I take the key and I drop out the window feet first. I grab up the holdall and run like fuck.

She catches me half-in-half-out the driver door. 'What the hell, Charlie?'

'Let go of me!' My heart sprinting, the bag squished between me and the door. Nao's two hands clamped round the top of my arm. I jab with my elbow and hit something soft, kick her shin.

'Ow!' She squeals and hangs on, hauls me out and slams the door. Digs her fingers into my hand and gets the key out of it. She's fucken strong.

'Oi, that hurt!' I stick my hand in my armpit and keep hold

of the bag. Both of us puffing and her hair all over the shop, bad as the other night.

'Where are you bloody going?' she says.

'Nowhere.'

'Rubbish. That gold's not yours.'

'Not yours, neither.'

'That key was in my bag!'

'Keep yer voice down, orright?' The street's dead quiet. The house behind her dark and the sun bright orange like a firework. 'How about you, sneaking round the place?'

'I wasn't sneaking.' Her face goes red, but.

'You're a shit liar. You can't wait to dump me. So what if I wanna dump you first?'

She squints her eyes. 'Look, if I wanted to take the gold, I'd have done it while you were asleep.'

I tuck the bag tight to my side. 'You reckon?'

'Yes. You sleep like a dead person.' She pulls a chunk of hair behind her ear, looks behind her at the house. 'I need to tell you something.'

'Don't change the subject.'

'I'm serious. It's—'

'You want me to keep quiet about ya lying to that cop? Not tell your aunty? Get me to an airport and let me keep the gold.'

She presses her lips down. 'You can't keep the gold. It's not yours to keep.'

'You don't even want it!'

'What gold?'

We spin towards the house and it's her aunty, come out the front door with the cowboy hat back on her head. She's got the tea tin in her hand with the lid off it. The tin I found the cash in. Least she hasn't got a shotgun. My hand goes to my pocket.

Nao glares at me. 'What have you taken? How much?'

'Nothing,' I say.

Her aunty says, 'Money.'

'Give it back.'

I put the bag down on the dirt drive and pull the notes out my pocket and Nao rips them out my hand. Looks down her nose at me like she's not even surprised. 'No need to chuck an epi,' I say. 'Now we've got fuck-all.'

She tells me to shut it and she stomps up to her aunty in her bare feet, puts the cash back in the tin and jams the lid down. They stick their heads together like they're having a whole conversation about what a deadbeat I am, and the aunty looks over Nao's shoulder at me with her hands around the tin and these little hot sparks in her eyes. They stick their heads together some more and I hear Nao say she's sorry. Her aunty pushes the tin at her and they have a whole convo about that too, like we're on an episode of *Home and Away*. And then the aunty takes her hat off and sticks it on Nao's head, so now she's got a hat *and* sunnies and I've got neither. Nao puts the tin in her suede bag and stomps back down the drive towards me.

'I'm driving. Get in.'

What choice have I got? I pick up the bag and squeeze between the front of the ute and the back of the aunty's car, and that's when I see the snake.

The one out the house, it's gotta be, dark and glittery in the light. I yelp and almost tread on it, jump back as it shimmies under the ute, my side.

'Get. In.' Nao rips her door open. 'Don't say a flaming word.'

'There's that—'

'Get in, I said!'

I get round my side, put the bag down. Hands and knees in the dirt, can't see the snake. Not under the ute, not under the aunty's car. We don't wanna drive over it.

'Now, Charlie!'

There's bushes along the fence, maybe it went in there except I still can't see it. I grab up the bag and get in the ute. 'That snake,' I say. 'The one from in the house. Did ya see it?'

'No. Don't talk. Put that gold on the floor. Do your seatbelt.' Her hand shakes but she gets the key in and starts the ute. She reverses out. No snake on the dirt drive. Her aunty stands there watching the both of us with her hand up against the sun.

'Dunno what happened to it,' I say.

Nao slams the ute in drive, looks sideways at her aunty, takes off down the street.

We're out on the highway before she says anything, upright in her seat with the hat on her head and the hot wind pulling at her hair. 'I was trying to tell you,' she says. 'It was on the news this morning. Your house burned down last night.'

'*Our* house? What the fuck? How d'ya know that?'

She turns her head. 'On the news.'

'How d'ya know it was ours?'

'I recognised the house. A firetruck out the front. The big townhouses either side.'

My hand goes to the phone in my pocket. Useless, no SIM in it. 'We gotta go back to your aunty, get to a phone.'

'We can't. She doesn't have one.'

'Get me to a phone!' The town back behind us and nothing

but flat scrub out the windows – the same bushes and red dirt. Geen's picture, hanging from the rearview, flapping in the wind. 'Why didn't ya tell me this before? Is Geen okay? Was anyone . . . ?' My brain in overdrive. My breathing too fast.

'I thought she didn't live with you, that she wasn't at the house.'

'She was last night!'

Her eyes go big. 'How do you—'

'Get me to a phone, Nao!'

Five minutes and she pulls off the highway at a roadhouse. A big place with a green corrugated roof, two massive trucks fuelling up and a payphone at the side. I get the door open before she parks. 'Lucky for your face this was here.' I'm halfway to the phone with the holdall before I remember I've only got ten cents. 'Fucksakes!' My chest's gunna explode, blood and guts everywhere. I spin around, straight into her.

'Here.' She's got that tin of her aunty's. Won't look at me but she gives me ten bucks. 'Aunty Mar's money,' she says, like she's making a point. 'Get change first, in the shop.' Not like her aunty's life savings, is it? Not even three hundred dollars.

I do it and I call Geen and she answers straight off. 'Charlie?'

'You're alive! Fuck, Geen—'

'Tell me where you—'

And that's my lot. A noise like she's dropped it and we get cut off. I feed in coins, over and over. Straight to voicemail, every time. I leave three messages.

'Geen. What the fuck? Don't go to the house. Call me back on this number. It's a payphone.'

I wait by the phone, the bag of gold on the gravel between my feet. Shadows standing out sharp and the day getting hotter and my neck burning. Nao puts fuel in and pays and comes back out with two big bottles of water. She cleans the windscreen off, gets in the ute and turns to look at me, her arm on the top of the open window.

Geen doesn't call back. I dunno if she sounded orright. I dunno what's gone wrong with her phone. Nao stares at me through her big sunnies like what do I reckon I'm doing waiting by the payphone? Course I'm gunna wait by the phone. I watch her mouth move and can't hear what she's saying. Little bastard flies trying to get up my nose and around the backs of my eyeballs so I gotta scrape them off my face.

Two more trucks pull in, fuel up and leave. The drivers chuck looks at Nao in the ute, both times. Stands out, doesn't it? Bright metallic green with the flash mag wheels Daryl put on it.

Fuck it. Geen's not dead. She's okay. Doesn't matter about the house. We'll get to Surfers with the gold and get our own house, not some shit rental. The gold's worth big-money thousands. A million, maybe. I pick up the holdall and head back to the ute. Just gotta get shot of Nao and everything'll be fine.

We pass a big cop LandCruiser, coming in the opposite direction, thirty minutes out from the roadhouse. Got my feet in my thongs on top of the holdall, gritty with dust. Hot wind blasting and the engine growling and both windows down. I see Nao tense up and check my seatbelt, then she's eyes front again, back straight with that hat on her head. The sun behind her shoulder makes the frayed edges of the hat stand out gold.

'That the same dude as yesterday?' I say.

'Don't remind me. I hope not.' She watches the rearview. The cop keeps going and doesn't turn around. Speed limit's a hundred and ten and she sticks on a hundred. Not convinced she's off her P plates like she told the cop yesterday but I'm not gunna ask her.

No other bugger on the road and the sun throwing the shadow of the ute out into the scrub. A few clouds, way up ahead of us, lined up on the horizon like they're in a hurry, like they've got someplace to go.

'So, your sister's okay.'

'Yep.' No point telling her nothing, told her too much as it is. Bet the house went up like a dead tree. We pass exactly that plus a flattened bit of roadkill, my side. Two crows hopping and fighting over it. A yellow sign with a kangaroo and a cow on it. 'What's that mean?'

'Livestock,' she says. 'Wildlife. Next stretch of highway.'

Makes me think of that cop again. No bull bar. Dunno how anything stays alive out here. I scratch the back of my hand, hot and prickly. Drink a bit of the water Nao bought and it's not even cold. 'Reckon you could drink your own piss if you had to?'

'I'd rather not find out.'

'Yeah, but if it would save your . . . look out!' Three big roos, outta nowhere. Red-gold in the sun in front of us, one after the other in slo-mo. I slam both hands on the dash.

Nao doesn't swerve, doesn't even slow down. Each one lands in the road once, sends up a puff of dust and takes off again. The third one's a near miss, her side, before they're across.

'Did you even see that? You almost hit that last one!' I turn in my seat, mouth open, but they're gone into the scrub.

'We missed them.' She grips the wheel, breathing a bit faster than she was two seconds ago.

'Yeah, but . . . fuck.' I turn back around. 'Tall as, aren't they? Giant. You weren't even looking.'

She cuts her eyes sideways at me. 'What, you've never seen one?'

'Course I have!'

She's got her tongue pushed into her cheek. 'Where, then?'

I tuck my fingers into my armpits but it's too hot and I pull them back out. 'Don't remember.'

'TV doesn't count.'

'I know that! Wildlife place or somewhere, I dunno.'

'You haven't.'

How would I? Only went to the zoo once, back in primary school. Only remember the penguins, 'cause they were Sass's favourites. I stare out the window. The same clouds there at the end of the highway. Another yellow sign: FLOODWAY. No more kangaroos.

Dunno why I'm so mad, like Nao's ruined it.

I scuff my thongs together, switch the radio on and get nothing except crackle. I try tuning it, but it does fuck-all.

'It doesn't work,' she says. 'I tried it the other night.'

Like she knows everything. Mum's playlist is on my phone but I'm not telling her that. I check the glovebox, zero music.

Nao shifts in her seat, glances over. 'Do you think someone did it on purpose?'

'Did what?'

'The fire at your house.'

'No way. How come?'

She checks the rearview. 'Think about it. That bloke outside your house, Sunday night. What if it was him?'

'Why would it be? Coulda been an accident. Nearly summer and dry as fuck.'

She chews the inside of her cheek. 'The houses on either side looked fine.'

'So?'

'So, he was looking for your bloke, Daryl, who stole that gold—'

'You don't know that.'

'We suspect that.'

Dunno why she's saying *we* all of a sudden. 'Why would he burn the place? You don't know nothing,' I say.

'He was right there. And do you know what else?' Her eyes meet mine and jump away. 'That fire destroyed evidence. Of you killing Daryl. What if he saw us with the body?'

Thirty minutes down the highway and Nao's still checking the rearview. Like she reckons that cop's gunna show up or the dude from outside the house. Like she's paranoid. The sun up higher and burning my arm, so I gotta keep my shirt on over my singlet. No sunblock in the glovebox, either.

'Charlie,' she says. 'I've got a plan.'

So have I. Just dunno yet how I'm gunna do it. How to keep hold of the gold and the ute, get that tin of money out her bag and get shot of her.

'You want an airport, right?' she says. 'You want to fly back to your sister?'

I nearly tell her about Surfers but I stop. 'Yeah. Where's the nearest one?'

'Newman. Five hours, maybe six.'

'Fucksakes.'

She pulls a crumpled map out her skirt pocket and pushes it at me. 'I got this back at the roadhouse. We're an hour and a bit out of Magnet. There's only one highway north.'

I can't tell which way up the map goes so I don't even unfold it, just stuff it down next to the gold. Can't get lost, can we? Not on the one road.

'This is what we do,' she says. 'We sell this—'

'The gold?' I look at the bag under my feet. 'Thought ya didn't want it?'

'Not the gold, the ute. We trade the ute, get you money for a flight home. There'll be flights to the city all the time – fly-in-fly-out, for the iron ore mines.'

'I know what FIFO means.' I squint sideways at her, up at Geen's picture, back down at the gold. 'What do you get out of it?'

'A smaller car, money for petrol. So I can keep traveling north.'

Dunno if I can trust her. For now, maybe. While I'm stuck with her. 'We got enough fuel to get to the airport?'

'There are places we can fill up. Check the map.'

'I need to stop at the next phone, call Geen again.' I drink a trickle of the warm water. 'I'm gunna get plastic poisoning.'

'I don't think that's a thing.'

'Course it's a thing. You should know, you watch the news enough.'

'What's that supposed to mean?'

We pass through two more Wild West towns – servos, pubs with verandas, parked-up trucks and utes. I try Geen both times, get fuck-all like she's switched off her phone, and leave messages. Nao fills up the ute at the second place, buys us rolls and me a choc milk, and we keep on going.

Another hour. A road train blasts past too quick and scares the crap outta me, blowing up dust and bits of gravel and shit, three trailers on the back of it. Never seen one of them, either, not until yesterday. Not telling Nao that, but.

What's out the windows doesn't change except the dirt and rocks get redder. Sometimes there's more of the grey hummocky bushes, sometimes less. Every now and then there's a thing on the horizon I reckon might be a hill but turns out to be nothing when we get up to it. No more towns or fuel stops, and the ute like an oven. An oven with a fan, 'cause of the open windows. At least it's got rid of the lemon air-freshener smell.

I point at the dash. 'There's aircon.'

'We need to save petrol.'

'Shit, do we?' I check the gauge, two thirds of a tank. 'How far is it now?'

'Are you going to keep asking that?'

Another road train and a Kombi van, going in the opposite direction. I bet even the Kombi van's got aircon. Nao says we've gotta go easy on the water – no shit. I put my face in the hot wind, rest my chin on my headphones. I think of turning on the phone in my pocket, playing something off Mum's playlist. The Divinyls, maybe. That'd work, except for Nao spitting the dummy when she sees me with my phone.

More roadkill, birds flapping up off it, shiny black wings. I think of them jabbing their beaks in, eating dead meat, and my brain goes to Daryl at the bottom of the lake. My guts go crook and I lick my lip, stare out the window some more. The highway's dead flat, dead straight, with one of those heat mirage things at the end of it. The clouds on the horizon are gone.

'Dunno how you can stand it out here. Creepy as fuck, like that movie, *Wolf Creek*.'

Nao twitches, turns her head at me. 'You didn't watch that, did you?'

'Didn't everyone?'

She presses her lips down. 'No.'

'Know what I'm talking about, but, dontcha?' Watched it with Geen, scared the crap outta each other.

Nao doesn't answer. She looks at the fuel gauge, down by half. The water's down by half, too. 'How much change do you have left, from what I gave you?'

'Eight bucks,' I say. 'Why? We're gunna make it, yeah?'

She swallows. 'Of course. Can I have a sip of that water?'

I give her some and she passes it back. Another thirty minutes go by.

It's fucken dangerous, out here. People die. I look across at Nao and wonder if she's thinking it. She's checking the rearview again, this little frown between her hat and her sunnies.

Winds me up, her doing that the whole time. It makes me think of sticking Daryl in the lake again. Her talking me into dumping him and not the other way around. She didn't have to do it, did she? Didn't have to chuck her phone in there, either. I don't notice I'm staring at the side of her face until she says something. 'What?'

'I know why you're out here,' I say. 'I've figured it out. Why you didn't stop at your aunty's. Why you wanna sell the ute and keep going.'

She shifts in her seat. 'You took Aunty's money. How could I stay, after that?'

'How thick d'ya reckon I am? You'd already decided you were going, first thing this morning.'

She frowns at the rearview.

'You watch that mirror more than the road,' I say.

'Of course I do. You killed a man. Someone burned down your house.'

111

Putting it all on me, when she's the one who's paranoid. 'Pig's arse. You're not worried about the cops 'cause of me. You're worried about them 'cause of you.'

'We moved a body in this ute, in case you don't remember. The police could already be tracking it.'

Makes me antsy, her saying that, and the back of my neck itches.

'Don't try to distract me,' I say. 'Why didn't ya let me call the cops when I wanted to, after Daryl? Why watch the news every chance you get? Give that cop a fake name? You're desperate to get to your aunty's and when we get there you act all weird—'

'I wasn't acting weird.'

'Yeah, you were. She picked up on it, too. You've been looking over your shoulder since I first saw ya, since way before Daryl. It's got fuck-all to do with me and fuck-all to do with him. You did something bad, back home. That's what this is about.'

She sits dead straight, the hot wind flapping her hair and nothing else moving.

'Bullshit me all ya want,' I say, 'but you did something. Killed someone, maybe. That'd make you as bad as me. Worse, depending on how come you did it.'

We pass a big bit of roadkill, my side. More yellow signs with kangaroos on. It gets hotter, the fan oven turned up to max. Nao shuts up. She doesn't admit whatever she's done but I know I'm right.

I don't like the way she keeps looking at the fuel, and when I lean across it's on less than a quarter. 'Shit, how much did ya put in it? How far?'

'We're almost there.'

Bullshit. Another hour goes by. Two road trains and a bus headed south with a sign saying PERTH in the front window. A flock of black cockatoos. Sticky little flies everywhere, sweat and red dust in every crack. The back of my hand still itching. Geen's photo keeps flapping like it's gunna take off and join the cockatoos so I pull it down off the mirror and stick it in my pocket next to my phone.

'How far now? I need to stop for a piss.'

Nao jumps and looks at me. Her mouth in a weird line. 'I don't think that's a good idea.'

I clock the yellow fuel light. 'How long's it been like that?'

She doesn't answer. My breathing gets scratchy. There's no point yelling at her; maybe it's gunna be fine.

The engine sounds funny for a bit and then it doesn't. What am I, a car mechanic? We go another twenty minutes and then the ute slows down, jerks, speeds up again. 'That you doing that?' I say.

Nao's leaning forward, pumping her leg on the pedal. I've got my hands on the dash, pushing at it, the inside of me panicking. And then the power goes out from under us and she crawls onto the gravel and stops.

'Are you serious?' I say.

'Crap. Crap. *Crap.*' She thumps the steering wheel with both hands and bangs her head down on top as the engine dies.

Back window – empty highway. Front window – empty highway. The sound of a crow, scraping at my brain. One half-full bottle of warm water and one melted Cherry Ripe. 'No fucken way. No *fucking*—'

'Shut up, all right?' She lifts her face off the wheel, screwed up and wet. Her sunglasses pushed up into her hair. 'Just *shut the fuck up.*'

Her eyes blink wide and we stare at each other. It's funny, except we're totally screwed and might die so it's not. 'Don't try to distract me,' I say. 'Like we're mates now or something. Because we're not.'

The sun's a metal spike to the head when I get out the car and the shadow from the open door is sharp black against the dirt. The knuckles of my right hand tingling and I wanna punch the shit out the back of the ute but I kick the back tyre instead. I get behind it where Nao can't see and I have a piss. It's either that or off the side of the highway and I can hear rustling out in the scrub as it is. Fuck knows what's gunna crawl up my leg if I go out there – something that only gets a drink every two years when some poor bastard runs outta fuel and has to stop here.

Hot piss splashes up off the gravel, splashes up everywhere, all over my feet and my thongs.

There's a sign up ahead and when I'm done I crunch up to it, squinting until the letters stop moving against the bright white and I can see what it says. A little spiky lizard's on the ground next to it giving me the eyeball.

The front part of the ute's splatted with dead bugs when I get back up to it – all over the windscreen and radiator grill. Daryl'd fucken hate that. I get back in and I can smell the piss on my thongs. Nao wrinkles her nose so maybe she can too. 'How long's five k?' I say. 'To walk, I mean.'

She looks at me. She's scrubbed the tears off her face but it's red and sweaty. 'You don't know how far five kilometres is?' I stare at her until she blinks. 'Sorry. Why?'

'Because that's how far the airport is.'

*

'There's at least gunna be a phone at the airport,' I say. 'You can walk it, easy. I can stay with the car.'

'Why do you get to stay?' She tucks a bit of hair under her hat, pushes her sunnies up her nose where they keep slipping down. 'I don't have shoes.'

'You can borrow my thongs.'

'They're two sizes too small.'

'You got a better idea?'

'Yes, I do. We stay with the vehicle, both of us. It's safer. We flag someone down.'

I cross my arms. 'No way. What are we gunna say to them? What if we're toast for a perv, someone like the dude in *Wolf Creek*? What if they take the gold off us?'

'Not everyone is a sex offender or serial killer, Charlie. We ask for help – someone with spare petrol. You can hide the gold, if you want to. I'm not walking five kilometres in the hottest part of the day. It's over forty degrees out there.'

'Out there? What about in here? We could die. We're gunna run out of water. We're gunna have to drink our own piss.'

'It won't come to that.'

'How d'ya know that? You don't. And whose fault is it—'

'If you say that one more time I'm going to scream.'

'Yeah? Well no one's gunna hear it.'

Forty minutes of hot wind and not one car – the air coming in at the windows smells like someone barbecuing dirt. I've got a hand in my pocket, clinking dollar coins against the gold, over and over. My body twisted around to keep the sun off my neck and the tops of my legs, except I can still feel them burning. Nao's flash silk top is wet with sweat. Half of her hair's come out the plait and stuck to her face. 'You could have walked it already,' I say. 'Shoulda gone myself. Coulda been there by now, got help, called Geen.'

My guts feel crook and I dunno if it's the water or the heat or all of the above. 'What if the next car's a cop? You gunna flag him down?'

'If you haven't got anything useful to say please stop talking.'

'Why should I trust you, anyhow?' I say. 'You killed a person.'

A noise comes out her mouth like it's an accident, like she can't help it. She pushes her sunnies up her nose, flops back against the seat.

'Not denying it, now?'

She turns and leans her head on her arms, out the open window.

'You'll get sunburnt,' I say.

After a bit I see her shoulders shaking. No sound, but.

Shit. I knew she'd done something bad.

A shadow goes over the ute, like a plane. I shiver and squint up there, out the window. It's a bird, a massive giant one.

Nao's watching it too, her head and the brim of her hat tipped up. She doesn't say nothing. It's so quiet out here there's a sound to it. Makes my ears feel funny. Never clocked that before now.

How screwed does it mean we are, whatever Nao's running from? Who did she kill? Are the cops looking for her?

'Sorry,' I say. 'Knew I was right, but.'

'It doesn't matter.'

'What happened?'

She turns back around, takes off her sunnies to wipe her eyes and puts them back on. 'I've messed up my life beyond all recognition and you're better off not knowing.' She's pressing on that cut on her hand again, twisting the Band-Aid. She needs to stop doing that.

'So, we're even,' I say. 'One dead dickhead each.'

She frowns. 'How do you know he was a dickhead?'

'Don't fucken worry, I can tell.'

She's hardly Hannibal Lecter, is she? She's not like me, either.

I always knew I'd go bad, 'cause I'm the exact same as Dad. I just didn't think it was gunna happen so soon.

I'm trying to figure out what we do now, if we need to change the plan, when Nao squeaks and bangs the door open. She's out the ute, into the road, arms flapping and I see the shadow of a car pull up. Then she stops like she's hit a brick wall and takes two steps back.

The car pulled in behind us is a blue and white police LandCruiser.

Fuck. I watch him in the wing mirror. Same hat and uniform and mirror aviator sunnies, but a different cop to yesterday.

He gets out and squats down, checking out the back end of the ute. He doesn't say nothing. I hear the crackly sound of a police radio from inside his LandCruiser.

Nao steps up to the front of the ute, her side. Looks a bit pale.

'He checking the rego?' I say.

She nods, shifting from one foot to the other on the hot ground. I look at the key hanging from the ignition, useless.

'Let's wait for another one, a family or something,' I say. 'Tell him we're okay.'

'But we're not okay.'

The cop leans in his car window like he's talking to someone. No one in there. He's on the radio. No, he's not. He's talking on a mobile phone.

I lean down and try to push the holdall back under the seat, except it won't go. My head swimming with the heat. 'What do I do with this?' I hiss at her.

'Act normal,' she says. 'He can help us. Keep calm.' She stands straight, sticks a smile on, rubs her hands down the sides of her skirt. She's not calm. Her hands are sweating and she's breathing funny.

I unfold the map and lie it over the top of the bag. 'Who's he talking to?' I say. 'What if he knows about—'

'Shh!'

'Afternoon, there.' He crunches up to Nao, looks at her bare scabbed feet and the Band-Aid on her hand and frowns. A tall dude with skinny shoulders and a big dimple in his chin. He squats down and looks in at me, tilts his head. I can't see his eyes behind the sunnies. 'Passing through? No country for unaccompanied young females, this. Remote. What seems to be the problem?'

Both my feet are on top of the map on top of the gold. My heart going hard like it's gunna die on me. 'Nothing,' I say.

Nao huffs and chucks me a look. 'We ran out of petrol,' she says. 'We've got a bit of cash, enough for half a tank, if you have any you can give us?'

Fucksakes.

He ducks down again, checks in the ute, front and back. That tilt to his head like a lizard. Twirls a finger at me. 'Step out of the vehicle please.'

'What? How come?' My eyes drop down to the map and the bag, back up again.

'Is there a problem?' he says.

'Yeah, she just told ya the problem.'

'Charlie,' Nao says.

He straightens up, checks the windscreen and squats down again. He's got this belt around his hips with things hanging off it. A black gun in a holster at the side. Probably got pepper spray and a Taser on there too. They pepper-sprayed Dad when they arrested him. They didn't have to do that. He was calm by then.

'No P plates?' the cop says.

'I'm not driving, she is,' I say. 'She's off her P plates.' He hasn't answered her question about the fuel. And why's he talking to me and not her? She's right in front of him.

He looks at Nao fidgeting her feet on the gravel, back at me. Not one car's gone past in either direction. I can't hear that bird no more.

He puts his hand on his gun in the holster, just rests it there. What's he doing that for? 'Step out of the vehicle,' he says. 'Keep your hands where I can see them.'

Dunno what this is, except not right. He herds us round the back of the ute, tries to get us to lean our hands on the back of it but it's too hot. 'Ow!' I say. 'That just burnt me.' I press my hands against my shirt, get the kick of my heartbeat through it. Nao leans on the ute, she's gotta be burning herself. 'What are you doing?' I say to her. 'Don't do that.'

'Face the vehicle,' he says. 'Arms out to the sides.' The rubbery stink of hot highway and the cop's sweat in my nostrils.

He pats us down like we're on *The Wire*, like we're drug dealers with guns and knives in our dacks. Then he starts at the back part of the ute, opens every door and searches it. What the fuck? I try to catch Nao's eye but she stares straight ahead. She's shit-scared of him and it pisses me off. Last up, he leans in the passenger door, lifts the map off the holdall and flaps it back on the seat. He pulls the bag out, sits it on the roof of the ute and unzips the top.

'Whatcha doing? That's not yours.' My head light like I might pass out.

He rakes in the bag like he's digging up rocks, zips it shut with a twist in his lips. He holds it out to one side and starts back towards his cop car behind us.

No way. He's taking it? No fucken way.

'That's not yours, mate. What about our fuel?'

'Stay right there, please.'

'Can he do that?' I say to Nao. She's facing the back of the ute like he told us to with her hands at her sides, not moving. I step towards him, my knuckles tight. 'Hey, mate, that's ours. You can't just—'

'Stay put, please!'

I see the snake when the cop's halfway back to his LandCruiser. It takes me a second 'cause it's looped and dangled in the shade under the bag. Like an extra handle, except the dude's got a hold of both handles.

The snake starts to move, uncoiling real slow. That was in the ute with us? How did it get there? I had my feet on that bag! I touch Nao's arm and she jumps like I've bitten her. 'Nao?' She hasn't seen it.

I take another step after the cop. 'You wanna put that down, mate.'

'Stay there, I said!'

'Seriously, mate!'

Another step forward and he swings around to face me, his back to the highway. 'I'm warning you,' he says. He unclips the top of his gun holster and I can't get my eyes off it, hot and panicky under my ribs. But the snake doesn't like him doing that. It flicks up and over the bag.

'That's a snake!' I yell. It wraps itself round his arm and he screams like a girl.

He drops the holdall and staggers back onto the bitumen, his arm jerking. The snake doesn't like that either. It thrashes and coils on the end of his arm, its head sat up like it wants to have a go at him. I step into the road and grab the bag where he's dropped it. I lift it and drag it back. He pulls his gun and shoots twice at the snake, can't see if he hits it.

The snake drops off his arm, sideswiping away but the cop's already falling. Backwards into the left hand lane with both arms windmilling the air.

It happens real fast. The gun flies up and spins against the sky. The snake skates away from the cop, across the hot road. Me and the cop watching it and neither of us sees the truck.

There's a massive blast of horn and a road train sucks past in a rattle of dirt and rocks and dust. My ears pop and it pulls like it's gunna take us under, and then it's gone.

Dead silence.

After a bit I hear Nao, her breath sucking in and out. The hiss of the truck's air brakes, further on down the highway.

I'm stood there with the holdall. I look for the cop. Can't see him.

'What just happened?' I say. 'Where is . . . ?'

'Don't look.' Nao's voice, wobbly. Her hands pushing at me. 'Take the bag. Get in the ute.'

'But . . . where's the . . .'

'I'll check his vehicle, see if he has petrol. Get in the ute.'

'But . . .'

'Do it, Charlie! Can you drive? Get in the driver's seat.'

She lurches towards the cop car. I see the gun, matt black in the road, and I stare at it. Can't see the snake. I pick up the gun and weigh it in my hand, heavier than what I'm expecting. Maybe the snake'll be back. More snakes, bigger ones. I stick the gun in the holdall and zip it back up.

I turn for the ute and I see the rest.

Bits of dark-coloured stuff, spread along the highway. The cop's blue hat and one boot. A chunk of his blue uniform. A blowfly buzzing. Looks like . . .

It feels like my tongue's floating in my mouth. Don't look. I do what Nao says: take the bag, get in the passenger door of the ute, crawl across to the driver's side so I don't have to walk on the bitumen. The key's still in the ignition.

Nao does something with the fuel – a jerrycan, the stink of petrol. She loads more cans onto the back seat and gets in. 'What are you waiting for?' she says. 'Drive.'

The ute starts third go. I get it in drive.

Down the highway we pass the road train, pulled over. The driver climbing down, waving his arms at us, his mouth cracked open angry.

I hear him roar as we pass.

I keep my foot down. Go straight. I'm not gunna freak. It wasn't our fault. If that snake hadn't've . . .

I watch the road. I do it better than Nao does it.

No road train in the rearview. No cop car. He's not coming back.

Nao turns her head at me. 'You okay to drive?'

'Was that the snake from back at your aunty's?'

'What snake?'

'It went under the ute, this morning. Couldn't see it. It musta got in the bag.'

'I don't remember any snake,' she says. 'Are you?'

I hold the wheel, breathing too fast. 'What?'

'Okay to drive?'

Course I'm not okay to drive. There's a cop that looks like prime mince roadkill a kilometre back down the highway. We've got his fuel in our tank and his gun on the back seat in the bag with the gold.

8

Geena

Alone With You

Geena and the cop are still on the road, in some back-of-beyond town, when she jerks awake. She has a moment of blissful calm before the events of the previous day rush back and the dread settles on her. Shit a brick – Charlie. Charlie and Daryl and the mystery girl and the gold.

They've been driving all night and she's busting for a pee, her tongue sticky in her mouth and an itchy hungry feeling at the back of her throat that's likely cigarette craving. Early morning sun glows through the tinted windows and Sunnyboys, 'Alone with You' plays on the car stereo as if Mum is indeed haunting her.

Where did he say they were headed? Mount Magnet. She's

missed the town sign so she can't be sure, but they're off the main highway and driving slow along a wide residential street, the occasional mature eucalypt in a front yard and the rest mostly dirt.

The cop punches a finger and shuts off the stereo. His hair is dark caramel in the daylight, a colour not unlike Lee's, with a side part to the left. He doesn't have good skin; acne when he was a kid, not that Geena can talk. He's got himself a pair of sunglasses on this morning, matt black rectangular frames with pale grey lenses she can see his eyes through. There's a two-litre bottle of water on the passenger seat, his suit jacket and his phone, and she can't see what else. He hasn't asked her anything more since last night. Does he think he's got all the answers? She doesn't even know if he's a real cop.

He's hardly a good one if he's not playing by the rules.

Her phone rings inside her bra – not on silent. Shit.

She scrambles the phone out and answers it, pressing herself away from him against the door. *Private number.* 'Charlie?'

The cop flings his arm at her, can't reach. He swerves into a driveway and brakes.

'You're alive!' Charlie says. 'Fuck, Geen—'

'Tell me where you—'

The cop swipes a second time and rips the phone off her. He ends the call, glowering and panting. In a bit of pain, it looks like. He turns Geena's phone off and slides it into the inside pocket of his suit jacket, passenger seat. 'That was stupid,' he says.

Bugger. Charlie's still alive, though. She's okay. He indicates and pulls back out, busy with the screen of his phone. They turn down a side street and left into another one. This is the kind of town Daryl grew up in, where the sheds are bigger than the houses they sit next to. The cop kerb-crawls past a tin-roofed fibro cottage with a flowering gum in the yard that's seen better days. He brakes and looks twice at the place like he might stop but changes his mind. Is this where Charlie is? Geena sits up straighter and he clocks her watching, jabs at his phone and takes off again.

She stretches the hem of her sundress down over her thighs, lifts her hair off her face and knots it. He has this way of staring at her in the rearview mirror, like he finds her disgusting to look at but he's willing to sink low enough to give it a shot. She's not used to men looking at her that way. She's given up on her boobs and pulled her jacket over the sundress – it's cold in the Toyota's air-conditioning.

They get back onto Great Northern Highway and pick up speed, heading north. Signs for the mining towns and remote north-west flash by and she wonders why they're leaving Mount Magnet, where they're going to next and what his plan is. She thinks of the riches in this country and remembers learning about the goldrushes at school, how men would find nuggets the size of their fists lying out on open ground.

'Who's Charlie?' he says.

'You need to tell me where we're going and why,' she says. 'Let me have some water and stop at a roadhouse for a pee.' He'll need fuel, won't he? She might find a way out of this yet. He asks her again who Charlie is and she doesn't tell him. He can't make her, not right now.

The petrol smell from last night has evaporated and she's not sure it was ever there. There's another smell, though, that makes her sick to her stomach. It's a layered-up medical smell of disinfectant and sticky fluids and blood, and it's getting stronger by the hour, overpowering his sage cologne. He's clearly not a well man. There's a dressing on the right side of his neck she only notices now. She can see it reflected in the driver's side window, poking up past the open collar of his shirt – white surgical dressing stained brown, with red shiny wet coming through the centre of it.

'Oh, shit,' she says. 'Excuse me? I think you're bleeding?'

He reckons it's a trick. He stares at Geena in the mirror and doesn't look down. The red fills the dressing and seeps into the white collar of his shirt. 'Seriously!' she says at him. She does not want this guy passing out in control of his vehicle. 'Your wound or whatever is bleeding, mate? Take a look.'

He glances down and his head twitches like there's a spider on his shoulder. He grunts and the vehicle swerves, gives a shimmy like it's testing him. He straightens it up, slaps his gloved left hand against the right side of his neck. When he pulls it away the fingertips glisten with blood and he quietly swears. 'You need to stop,' she says. 'Get that looked at. There a doctor in this town or what?'

But the town is back behind them and he seems dead-set on keeping it that way. He jiggles with the glove compartment and pulls out a first-aid kit. He's going to need more than that. 'You want me to get that for ya?' she sits forward.

'Thank you. No.'

He gets a pad of gauze against his neck. The blood comes through it and onto his gloves. The buzzing inside Geena is split between them crashing and her escaping. 'Jesus Christ, mate, do you want us to crash? We're gonna crash.'

He pulls over and phones a friend.

It sounds like he's calling in a favour, although he might as well be speaking in code. Her eyes drift over the console between the front seats, the child-lock light she spotted last night. Bloody hell, it's not switched on. He must have knocked it with his hand.

She almost rips the door open and tips herself out there and then, but in the middle of nowhere in a sundress and sandals? She won't get far before he catches her.

He asks his mate, Brunswick, to send a location to his phone, wraps gauze bandage around his neck until he looks like a guillotine survivor and sets off up the highway again. An hour along and he turns in at a driveway. There's nothing there but a road mailbox, a long gravel track lined with thirsty young blue gums and a post-and-rail fence. The blue gums look as out of place in the arid country as Geena feels. At the end of the drive there's a clearing, a sprawling veranda'd house and better-watered trees. Dogs tumble down the veranda steps at their approach.

Two kelpie-cross working dogs and a short-arsed terrier run yapping in circles as he turns and parks, making a good racket. She presses the window button her side and it works; her heart is in her mouth as the glass glides downwards, she's sure she'll be caught out by the electric burr. But his hand's up against his neck and the dogs are barking loud enough that he doesn't hear it.

A wiry old guy in a stockman hat steps off the veranda and calls the dogs back, looping around the car like it's the best game out. The cop tells Geena to sit and to stay like she's one of them as he exits the vehicle and locks it.

She's expecting a warning light to tell him, for him to notice and spin on his heel at the last second. But he limps away up the veranda steps with the old guy and the dogs, and the two men disappear into the house. The window at the side of her is wide open, the smells of coffee and sheep shit and eucalyptus floating in on a warm easterly breeze.

Geena searches the front of the car but there's nothing to find, not apart from the two-litre bottle of water the cop left on the seat. She takes it with her as she shimmies out of her window and ducks down behind the vehicle, doesn't know if the men might be watching from behind the dark windows of the house. He's parked the Toyota in the shade of a spreading fig tree, the paintwork dense black and sheened with dead insects and dust.

The chance at escape is stretched along her every nerve as she glugs down some of the water and checks out the track behind her, longer than it looked from the car. She might get lucky with a passing vehicle once she makes it to the road, and then again, she might not. She needs to get her phone back or find another one. She needs to get a hold of Charlie again.

There's no movement from the front of the house and the dogs are sleepy as all get out, panting up a storm in the shade; it's already that hot. She pees behind the Toyota and slips off her sandals, keeps hold of the water and her jacket, and tiptoes around the shady side of the house. There's a fenced paddock with two drooping horses under a tree, swishing their tails and stamping their feet at the flies. The dogs have a sniff at her but don't howl the place down. She's already in their territory; she's a mate – at least that's what she tells them. She's surprised how focused she is. It's one thing freaking out about what might happen. When it happens, you don't always react the way you thought you would.

Around the side are more steps up to the veranda, a window and a door, both open and flyscreened. She can hear muffled voices from behind closed doors in the hallway beyond. The coffee smell coming out is too civilised for this to be real and Geena's nicotine-craving itches. She goes to tiptoe further along the side of the house but one of the kelpies loops around and lifts her lip. 'Hey, bub, I'm not breaking in, okay? It's kinda the opposite.' She tries to sound soothing but the dog eyeballs her pretty hard so she backs up to the steps. The kelpie drops into the shade between Geena and the Toyota and she sees what she missed the first time: a chair in the hallway with a charcoal grey jacket on the back of it. The cop's jacket with her phone in the front pocket.

Okay, chill. Charlie and Daryl are up ahead somewhere with the gold, the cop on their tail because he's looking to recover it. Fair enough, and maybe they have to let him have it. But what's he going to do when he catches them? Shop the lot of them, most likely. What if there's a way to avoid that and keep the loot, too?

A door in the hallway opens, spilling light onto the jacket on the chair. She holds still while the old guy walks across, his boots echoing on the wood floor. He goes through another door and doesn't see her.

The cop's voice follows him. 'What are you looking for?'

'Local anaesthetic.'

'I don't want that,' he calls out. 'I don't want animal drugs.'

'Then you should have found a medic instead of a vet.'

He's getting medical attention from a vet? Okay, he is desperate.

The vet crosses back and disappears. Maybe he can fix Geena

up too if his dog bites her. She puts down the stuff in her arms real slow and the dog watches as she clicks the screen door open. Her heart is going like a bloody washer-dryer. She steps inside, waiting for the dog's teeth at the back of her knee but they don't come. She lets the door close without a sound and creeps forwards, her bare feet gritty on the boards.

The men's voices come through the half-open door to the right, louder now she's in the house. 'I need to re-suture it. That's a stab wound,' the vet says. Jeez, she thought the cop looked rough. More footsteps, a cabinet opening, the clink of metal against metal. 'You got antibiotics for it?' he says. 'Painkillers?'

'I got pills from the medic in the city. I don't need animal pills and I don't need anaesthetic. Get on with it.'

Hard man. She reaches the jacket, slides her hand into the silky inside pocket and retrieves her phone.

'What you need is a hospital.' There's the sound of a tap turning on and then off again. 'What about the young lady?'

'The young lady is fine. You're not squeaky-clean or Brunno wouldn't have sent me here.'

Brunno. Brunswick – the person he called from the car. It takes a couple of seconds for that to sink in. Okay, she already knew the cop was bad, but it doesn't help her nerves. She clicks her phone onto silent and turns for the door and stops.

It's not enough, is it, having her phone back? She's in the middle of bloody nowhere with a bad dude and no money. She doesn't know where Charlie is. She can't call the cops.

She slides back to the chair and searches the pockets, her fingers flying over the fabric and her breathing too loud. She pulls out his police badge and flips it open like he did last night – a blue and silver star shape that says WA Police. It looks real enough but there's no ID with it, nothing to tell her who he is, not even his rank. She slips the badge back and pats the other pockets: twin silver pens in the front one and a stamp card for coffees, three stamps out of ten and a logo on it of coffee beans strung up like fairy lights that nudges her memory but she can't place. Nothing else in the jacket: no wallet, no cash, no keys to the Toyota. Bugger. She heads for the door.

The men keep talking. 'That's some bruising to the chest,' the vet says. 'Broken ribs, possibly. Who did this to you?' A note of fear creeps into his voice. 'Not one of Brunno's thugs, was it?'

'Never you mind.'

'You had a chest x-ray?'

'No.'

'Painful?'

'What do you think?' the cop growls.

'Any shortness of breath? Dizziness?'

'Why? What does that mean?'

'Haemothorax. Pneumothorax.'

'Speak English, can't you?'

'Internal bleeding, damage to a lung,' the vet says. 'Rib fractures can do that. That'd need hospital, a chest drain.'

The dog outside pants her meaty breath, her head on her paws. Geena eases the screen door open.

'The quicker you do what I need, the quicker I'm gone,' says the cop.

She steps through the door and the dog leaps up, snarling and barking like Geena is outlaw Ned Kelly. 'Hey. Shh. Hey, bub.' She thumps down the steps. The dog snaps at the hem of her dress. Traitor. The door swings open and there's nowhere to run.

The cop stands in the doorway with an aggro face on and his

shirt off. She sees hard ropey muscles that look like they've been around the block a few times, and again the off-kilter perspective of arms and upper body that are too long for the rest of him. His torso is marbled with purple bruising and the angry wound at his neck is leaking blood. He holds a gun in one hand and his cop holster dangles from the other.

She didn't know he had a gun. Of course he had a gun, Geena. He's a cop. He must have had it down in the front of the car.

'I'll take that phone,' he says.

Back in the air-conditioned new-car-smelling Toyota, Geena is bloody furious at herself for letting that opportunity go, back there, when she might not get another one. For having had her phone in her hand and not called Charlie, not even found out where she is. The phone is in the glove compartment, where the cop put it after checking she'd not made that call. And as if that's not enough, he pulls into a deserted picnic area barely a kilometre along the highway – a line of gums shading a dry creek – and slides a police baton out of a black backpack in the front passenger footwell.

She experiences a flutter of disquiet and scans the picnic tables and under the trees but there's not a soul out there. He doesn't look at Geena while he telescopes the black metal out to its full length, three times that of the handle, and weighs it in his hand. She watches the flex of his fingers inside the glove as he does it. 'The power in this instrument,' he says, 'comes not from the effort one puts into each blow, but the speed at which one end travels relative to the other. The action is in the wrist, a little like playing squash.' His eyelid flickers and he still doesn't look at her. 'One of its advantages, with the requisite skill, is the ability to inflict pain and damage and not leave an external mark. But with you,' he says, 'I need not be concerned about that. Because you are disposable.'

She feels the inside of herself shrink, the air-conditioned car now excessively cold. There's something so controlled about the cop, so very different from Daryl, and she has no doubt he means what he says. He flexes the thing before collapsing it, zipping it away along with the gun. It takes him some effort to do so; she spots a subtle gritting of the teeth and a little more effort in his breathing, despite the clean white dressing over his freshly stitched wound. She remembers what the vet said: broken ribs, internal bleeding, the risk of infection. Bring it on, she thinks. It's her only consolation.

She thinks of the card in his jacket pocket and tries to imagine the ordinariness of him queueing for coffee but can't do it. She wonders how she can have been so exceptionally unlucky, and for a moment is afraid she might cry. But she sets her face and pulls her jacket straight. She's determined not to let her fear of him show, for herself and for Charlie. She watches skinny power-poles march past against a white-hot sky, marking the scrub with shadows, ticking down the time and distance, each one a little closer to where they're going, a little nearer in time to what will happen when they arrive.

It was one of Daryl's poker mates who told him the two-storey Mount Claremont home had a safe under the floorboards in the study with three-quarters of a million dollars-worth of gold in it. She thought it was a hoax until Daryl said he had it from a second 'reliable source' that it was true. Reliable being a relative term among these particular associates of Daryl's. Geena's always said she doesn't want to know what he's up to, but this one was in a different ballpark to his usual buying and selling-on of dubiously acquired goods. This one got under her skin.

She and Daryl even drove out to the house a handful of times and parked across the street, checking out the big square block and iron gates, the cream-painted exterior and the balconied second-storey windows, fantasising about how and when they'd do the job.

It was never real, though; it was never actually going to happen.

It's obvious now that the mate has played Daryl, wanted to drop him in it in retaliation for some previous screw-up or unpaid debt. Because she was right that it was too easy – a back door unlocked and the safe exactly where the mate said it would be, taking it and not getting caught. And who is the girl the cop was asking about? There's got to be more to the story.

The cop is still preoccupied with the screen of his phone, the same as he was last night – whoever is pulling the strings is feeding him information, Geena realises. He seems sure of where they're going and the countdown is like an alarm bell inside her head, growing louder by the second. She's going to need a different approach.

She takes a breath, smooths her eyebrows with a fingertip and licks her bottom lip. 'Making good time?' she says, like they're on a day trip to the Pinnacles.

He grunts. They pass a traffic sign: LOCAL POLICE ARE TARGETING SPEEDING. Not right now they're not, she thinks. He's likely got some kind of cop-immunity from traffic offences. He knows all the right people, like vets and medics who can fix him up when he doesn't want to go to the hospital, when he doesn't want anyone to know he's been stabbed and beaten. She can't help wondering what the other guy looked like and if he came off worse. She can well imagine he did.

'Um, you asked who the girl was driving with?' Geena says.

Eyes sharp in the rearview mirror.

'So, she's in the car with . . . the stuff you're looking for?'

A muscle twitches next to his eye. 'Now, why would you think that?'

'Look, I don't know who she is, I told you. But if she's with someone who has it, I *might* know who that is.'

A glance at his phone screen and back at Geena. 'Spit it out,' he growls.

'A man I know.'

'A man.'

'Daryl.'

'Daryl?' The muscle twitches again.

'Yeah. That's my . . . an old boyfriend.'

'I see. Not Charlie?'

The alarm bell jangles harder. 'It's got nothing to do with Charlie. She doesn't know anything about it. You can let her go.'

'Ah, Charlie's a female.' His eyes harden and Geena feels the vehicle pick up speed.

And she's either missed something, or screwed up big-time, or both.

Men think aggro is attractive, that hard man is attractive, but it's not. Why else did Geena fall out of the arms of Daryl and into the arms of his mate Lee? Because she learned that lesson, that's why.

The Toyota is still cruising, the soft reverb of the engine under the fake breeze of the air-conditioning and low classical music on the stereo. So civilised. Not. Geena has two fingers hooked over the coral necklace she got for her eighteenth, one of those rare truces between Mum and Dad the month before Mum died. Geena's pretending to sleep when the cop starts talking. 'I want a pair of eyes on Great Northern Highway.'

She flutters her eyelids open, white light stretched between them, and blinks them back closed. He's on the phone, not using a hands-free either. Another traffic infringement.

'South eastern Pilbara,' he says. 'You got a vehicle patrol in the vicinity, Brunno?' That name again. 'Tell him to expect my call.'

Empty silence, the hum of the Toyota. She keeps her eyes shut and her mouth open. He makes the next call.

'You on Great Northern? Yep, a metallic green Holden Rodeo twin cab,' he says. 'WA plates.'

Daryl's ute. Charlie inside it. The tension stretches – what Geena wants, what the cop wants. He reels off the rego of Daryl's ute. How does he know all that?

'I know where it is, mate. It's five clicks out from the airport and it's stationary.'

What does that mean? What have they stopped for?

'Yep, could be,' he says. 'Get them to stay where they are. Make it a routine stop. I'm thirty-five, forty minutes out.'

Geena blinks wider and sees why he's not on a hands-free. The mobile phone he's talking on is not the same one he's been looking at the whole time.

He's got two phones. He's got a burner.

'Some stolen property. A private matter. Do not search the vehicle,' he says. 'I don't want the passengers alerted. Let me know when you've got eyes on them. That's all I want.'

The Toyota slows. The ticking of the indicator. She thinks of them, Charlie and Daryl and the girl, stopped up ahead on the highway. She's torn between getting to them – giving the cop the gold and getting it over with, getting Charlie back safe – and what? Something worse.

Daryl can be violent, Geena freely admits that. He can be a rough, stupid bastard and over the last day and a half she's been genuinely worried he might have hurt Charlie. But she'd pick a fight with Daryl over this cop any day of the week. He's armed and bloody dangerous. He's not a normal cop. He's got a burner phone and bad friends.

She doesn't want him anywhere near Charlie.

The gravel shoulder crunches under the tyres as he brings the Toyota to a stop. He unclicks his seatbelt and she feels sick as a dog, like someone's tripped a switch. She cowers away when he opens her door. 'Time for a change of scene, Geena Kelly,' he says.

'I'm not getting in there,' she says. 'There's no need for that.'

They're standing at the side of the highway behind the open boot of the Toyota. He's pulled a couple of jerrycans of fuel and more bottles of water out and stacked them by the back tyre. He's got his shoulder-holster contraption back on over his shirt, with big sweat patches looping under the arms. He wants her to get in the boot. She's not getting in the boot.

'I won't try anything. I'm all out of ideas,' she says. 'I'll be real quiet.'

The emptiness of the country either side of them is truly dizzying now she's out of the car. A landscape she's known about theoretically but never ventured into, now unfolded around them like a map. She thinks of a line from that movie she loves so much, her second favourite line in it: *We're not in the middle of nowhere, but we can see it from here.* It's mulga scrub, Geena knows. Low bushes more than trees and a lot of arid ground in between. A heat haze shimmers over the furthest reaches and she wonders the cop doesn't feel the effect of it, like a kind of gravity, all that flat country between them and the horizon.

Closer to them are the shredded remains of a giant truck tyre, ripped and spread in pieces along the edge of the bitumen. Beyond that a single tree, top-heavy and bent at the crown, the shadow of it outlined against the dirt. She can taste the dust on her teeth.

There's a hot easterly wind mixing with the heat coming up at them from the exhaust, somewhere a bird crying, thin and high-up near the sun, and her skin is burning. It's early afternoon, she reckons, the hottest part of the day scouring the backs of their necks. The cop has produced a cap for himself in addition to his reactor sunglasses; the lenses darker now, out in the sunlight. There's almost a day's growth of stubble on his face, caramel coloured with salty flecks of grey.

'You'll do as I say,' he says.

The boot is spacious-looking and could be cooler than it looks. But Charlie's so close, and bad shit always happens to the girl who gets put in the boot. Everyone knows that.

He slides the gun out of the holster.

He wouldn't have brought her this far if he was going to shoot her. Still, she should be smarter. She should know better. She's overconfident because he's pulled the gun on her instead of that police baton thing and she misses her cue – that moment of electric stillness when a man is about to crack the shits with you. 'Listen,' she says. 'I promise to—'

He hits her across the face with the gun. It takes a second to register it, her hand flying to her cheek as the pain flames and he grips her upper arms and bundles her in. He bangs and scrapes her shins over the searing back of the car as he does it, shoves her hard in the back and slams down the lid.

Her legs burning and blood in her mouth and she swears he's broken her face.

Pitch dark. The engine and the road vibrate through Geena's aching face. It's a hatchback boot but something's fastened across the top of it so she can't get upright, can't see out of the back window. She doesn't know why he's put her in here or what he's going to do when he gets to Daryl and Charlie. They need to hand over the gold. This is clear to her now, and she should've come clean and promised him, out there, before he hit her.

She's on her left side with her denim jacket balled up under her head. The skin is puffy and tight under her right eye and there's a cut inside her cheek – blood mixing with the dust in her mouth – but she doesn't think it's broken. A tooth at the top right is loose and she can't stop probing it with her tongue. Her shins are scraped and bruised and painful, and that Sunnyboys tune is stuck in her brain. But she's not giving up, not with Charlie still out there.

The guilt is unwinding in Geena's gut, the same slipperiness as she imagines her organs having. It didn't take much for her to spark Daryl's vanity about stealing that safe, give him the extra little push he needed. It was his need to impress as much as anything, to equal his more decently criminal mates and prove he could.

She'd never have done it if she'd known it would come to this.

There's no gap between the seats, no place for a chink of light to make it through from the front. She digs with her fingers across the fake carpet underneath and in front of her, broken nails snagging, until she finds a dent where the carpet lifts and she gets a nail and then a finger under and pulls it up. There's a handle in the hard floor and she hooks that up too, a space beneath. She has to roll backwards in order to do it and something presses into her from behind when she does, a metal bar angled across the deeper recesses of the boot.

She can't get the compartment fully open, not lying the way she is, but she finds the rim of the spare wheel and what feels like a jack, and deeper in, something else – cool smooth metal with a crossbar.

A wheel brace. She shifts herself, every muscle tensing with the effort. She works the thing loose and gets it out from the space. It'll do the job, whatever that is. Bashing his brains out or the gun out of his hand or bashing her way out of his crummy vehicle.

Could she bash his brains out? She doesn't know. She lies quiet and he's on the phone again, still driving. She can't hear the words but they're short and angry and he ends the call. A big truck rattles past, the only bit of traffic she's heard in a while. The Toyota grinds over a cattle grid. They keep rolling, another half hour or so, until she feels the car slow and the tyres bump onto the gravel shoulder. Her breath coming harder. They stop and the weight in the vehicle shifts. His door slams shut.

Her hands ache from gripping the wheel brace. She waits for it, but he doesn't open the boot. She listens out and hears nothing. They've gotta be out there.

She lifts the wheel brace and starts belting the shit out of whatever metal bit she can find. The inside of the back makes the best sound, and she clangs it for all it's worth. 'Charlie, in here! I'm bloody in here. Charlie! Someone? Help me.'

The back springs open on the cop's angry face. The gun held low in his left hand. 'In here!' she yells out.

He wrenches the wheel brace out of her grip and tosses it over his shoulder onto the surface of the highway. It skids and bounces and she watches the white light reflect off it, yelling Charlie's name until she's hoarse.

Charlie doesn't come and her yells get quieter. Charlie was right there. She was out there, she had to be. The cop stands and waits. 'Where is she?' Geena says, her heartrate slowing. 'What have you done with her?'

'Be quiet. There's no one out here to hear it.' He glares down at her, his lopsided shoulders blocking the sun. A little almost-grunt with every breath. The angle of him is all pain.

'Let me out,' she says. 'Please.'

'You think you're more use to me alive? Barely. The only reason I'll pull you out will be to shoot you in the head.'

The wheel brace is miles away, dead on the bitumen. She listens out but there's nothing, not apart from that same cry of a bird. She thought they'd stopped on the road, that Charlie would be here. 'I need water,' she says. 'I'm real thirsty.'

His eye twitches, that little aggro tell he has. 'Not now.'

He goes to slam the lid and she hears the sound – the crackle and squawk of a radio nearby. He blinks. She yells out, 'Help! In here!'

He cracks the lid shut. Pitch black. Footsteps on the gravel, walking away.

That was a police radio, that was another car. A real cop car, parked in front where she couldn't see it. She kicks the door with her bare foot, a dull thud.

The cop gets back in and they drive two minutes and stop. The weight shifts again and his door slams. She hears him call out, 'What's happened here, exactly? You seen two young women in a green Holden Rodeo?'

Who's he talking to? Real cops? Charlie? Geena yells but her voice is all out. She bashes on the inside of the lid with the heels of her hands and the metal bar behind her shifts. It's not a part of the vehicle. It's only when she gets an arm up behind her and explores the full length of it that she realises what it is.

She thought he'd slipped up back there and was admitting it: that he does need her alive, that she is more useful to him that way. But the thing at her back is a shovel, brand new, with no dirt on it. The kind of thing you'd use to dig a shallow grave if you were that way inclined and had need of one. The cool of the blade seeps into her fingers.

She hears one gunshot, and a second one. The sounds punch through her.

He gets back in the front and drives.

9

Nao

Backpackers

The open windows blast hot air, and it's only as we come into Tom Price I see that the weather has changed – heavy-bottomed clouds gathering over iron roofs as the sun dips low in the sky. Neither of us has looked anywhere but the road, but I wonder if Charlie saw it, the roadhouse barely a kilometre past the stopped truck, the name of it marking a line on the map: Tropic of Capricorn. The clouds have tracked us through the gorges and the spinifex country and I'm reminded we're traveling north into the wet season.

Charlie passes the speed limit sign and doesn't slow. Her eyes have been wide-open and bright the whole way, the tip of her tongue clamped in the gap between her teeth. I glance over at her. 'Charlie?'

She twitches. 'What?' But she slows the ute, and yawns, which is the most normal thing she's done all day.

'There'll be a motel here,' I say. 'We can stop.'

'Orright.'

We're low on petrol again. There are two more jerrycans in the back from the police cruiser. We shouldn't have taken them, but there was no way we could have stayed where we were. *Don't think about it.* But it's impossible not to. What was left back there on the highway. The buzz of flies in the silence. The truck driver's face as we passed him.

A new crime to add to the list. *Cop-killers.*

We cruise through town – wide streets, sprinklers on lawns, bore water staining the kerbs. A flock of feral corellas takes off in a screaming crowd. Suburbia, except I don't imagine suburbia being normal ever again.

Charlie pulls into the first motel we see and parks around the back. I notice the stares we get as she does it: an old bloke watering his lawn, his head tracking left to right as we pass. A kid on a bike, slowing and wobbling. The place isn't used to strangers.

There's a sign for reception. VACANCIES, lit up pinky-red. 'Wait here,' I say. 'I can give them my card number. They won't want paying until the morning.'

Charlie looks like a possum in headlights and hasn't let go of the wheel. But we'll be fine here. No one knows us. We can take a breather, eat, sleep, make a plan. Find a place to sell the ute, get Charlie money for her flight home.

The air is like warm water as I walk away towards motel reception, the heat and stillness closing down on the small town. I realise I'm kidding myself about pretty much everything when

I see what the kid and the old man were staring at: the spray of blood along the driver's side door.

Cop-killers.

The woman in reception is drinking a neon pink slushie in air-conditioned chill and watching an old episode of *CSI* on a TV at one end of the counter. A gecko grips the wall above her head. She sucks loudly on the straw as I fill out the form she slides across at me. Name and address: not real ones, obviously. She's got a crop of pimples on her chin to match the slushie and she sees me staring.

She's not happy with the form when I slide it back. 'Rego number.' She stabs so hard at the box her pen punches through the paper. 'Both names if there's more than one of youse.'

I say I'll check the registration and be back, fumbling the words.

I think of the police officer, taking down the ute's number, talking on his phone. Why was he doing that? Why didn't he use his radio? Then searching the ute and taking the gold he knew was there. Who was he talking to?

I heard the radio in his vehicle, squeaking and crackling against the silence. It wasn't as if it was out of order. Charlie heard it too.

A memory looms as I slip out of the door: Warren, cold and controlled, marching me up the stairs to his study. I shudder and blink it away. There is no way these things are connected. We've been unlucky, that's all it is.

When I get back to the ute Charlie's staring at the side of it, holding the bag of gold tight against her. The blood spatter is near-black in the dimming light, the metallic green of the paintwork glowing.

'Didn't know that was on there,' she says. 'Didn't see it . . .'
Her voice is scratchy, barely there.

'Don't look at it. I'll wash it off. There'll be a tap somewhere.'

'Don't see how it got on there.'

'The truck was going so fast, I guess it was . . .' I swallow.
'Charlie, let's not either of us look at it. We've driven over a big
kangaroo, that's all. That's what it looks like.'

'No it fucken doesn't.'

'Yes, it does. Go inside and take the bag. Unit Fourteen. I'll
move the ute into the back corner of the car park.'

I give the woman in reception a fake rego number and a
made-up name for Charlie. It's not as if she's going to check.

Everything in the motel room is brown, except the fridge in
the corner and the tiny TV up on the wall. I bring in the empty
water bottles and my uni bag with Aunty's tin of money. The air-
conditioning doesn't work when I switch it on, and the ceiling
fan stirs the heat around like soup.

Charlie is hunched next to the gold on the bed furthest from
the door. 'There a payphone in that office?'

'Inside the door, on the right.'

'Can I trust ya not to do a runner with this if I go and
call Geen?'

It's like a cartoon anvil in the bag, it's that heavy. 'How far
do you think I'm going to get with it?' For now she can think I
want nothing to do with it.

She sniffs.

'And don't tell your sister about . . . you know.'

'What?'

'Anything.'

She bangs the door behind her on her way out. I keep the curtains closed and watch her through the gap – her bright blonde head, those headphones around her neck, the charcoal cloud massing over the motel roof – around the corner to reception.

I click the lamp on next to my bed and take off Aunty's hat, pull out her tin and count the cash we've got left. There were questions in her eyes this morning, but softer ones. She told me for the third time I have Dad's face, our family's face. 'You look after it, Nomi.' She said Charlie and I would need water, lots of water, and repellent. I'd like to think that telling me these things and giving me her hat and the money means something, that I might be more welcome in her house next time, if there is ever such a thing.

There's nothing else in my bag except three one-dollar coins and the cards I can't risk using, a set of study notes from before the exam and my almost-empty tube of foundation, SPF fifteen. Charlie bangs the door again on the way in and thumps back on the bed.

'What happened?' I say. 'That was quick.'

'Went to voicemail.' She slumps against the headboard, flicking the end of her headphone cord.

It makes me queasy, her wearing those pointless headphones. 'What do you think that—'

'Dunno, do I? Doesn't even ring.'

'So, she's out of battery,' I say. 'Or she's got no signal, or she was on another call. You can try again. Is there someone else you can—'

'No there's not.' She eyes the tin on my bed. 'Can we get some proper food? Did ya get cash from that . . . cop car?'

'No, I did not.'

'Shit. We need cash.'

'We'll get money when we sell the ute. We should be okay in a small place like this but we'll have to do it quickly, before ...'

'Before what?'

'Before there's a description of it out there.' Aunty's money is eighty dollars and change. I take out forty. 'I'm going to see if there's a chemist open, get some stuff to dye our hair. We should stay in, keep a low profile. I don't want the people here finding out my card doesn't work. I've only given them the number.'

She glares over tight-folded arms. 'How come ya keep saying *we* without asking me what I reckon? You're not doing nothing to my hair, neither.'

'He might give a description of us too, the driver of that ... road train.' I close Aunty's tin and put the forty dollars in my purse. Charlie watches me the whole time. 'You know we couldn't stop at that airport, don't you? Not after—'

She shrugs.

'An airport's a bad idea, anyway. Too much security, all that CCTV. You'd be better off getting a bus back to the city.'

She scratches the back of her hand and the back of her neck, looks at the bag of gold on her bed. 'Not going back,' she says.

'But your sister—'

'Gunna go Surfers Paradise,' she says. 'Gold Coast. Got no house, now, have we? Got fuck-all, according to you. Have to figure it out, but. Geen can fly out when I get her the cash.'

I don't know if this makes things worse or better. At some point she needs to know she can't keep the gold and can't sell it. She can't. That police officer knew about it. How many others do? It leads right back to Warren. The thought churns in my stomach.

'And how are you going to do all that?' I say.

'Dunno, yet, do I? Give us a shot, I'm thinking on the go here.' But I see the way she watches the bag. She hasn't let it out of her sight, not apart from the phone call just now.

'We killed a police officer, Charlie.'

'Did not! That wasn't our fault!'

'No, I know that.'

'Was your fault if it was anyone's. You pulled the dick-head over.'

'I didn't pull him over. He was police. He'd have stopped either way.'

She picks at a thread on the brown bedspread. 'That snake was the one in your aunty's house. Musta got in the car. I had my feet on that bag the whole way, coulda killed me.'

'He did us a favour, then, taking it out of the car. If you'd kept calm, not started yelling, it might not have—'

'Bullshit! How come you did exactly what he said? He was taking the gold. He was no good. Told ya we should walk to the airport, get fuel ourselves. But no – you know better, always do, and he was no fucken good.' She pulls harder on the thread, lifting and tenting the fabric on her bed and I want to tell her to stop. 'How did he know, but?' she says. 'Who was he on his phone to?'

A twinge in my gut like it's me she's pulling at, not a thread in the bedspread. The sound of the fan is too loud, the hot air grinding around like the blood in my head. I'm back in Warren's study two days ago, staring at the space where his safe should have been.

'I don't think we should talk about it,' I say. 'I'm going to wash the ute before someone sees it.'

I cart water in the empty bottles. The sun is setting bougainvillea pink, the humidity pressing down like it's going to storm. No one sees me clean the blood off the ute and fill the tank from the jerrycans. There's only one other car in the car park.

The last of the water goes on the back of my neck and the sick feeling settles. I don't see why I have to explain myself to Charlie. I shouldn't have let slip to her about Warren, either, back there on the highway. I won't do it again. We need to focus on what's in front and not behind, stick to the plan: trade in the ute for a smaller car and some money, dump the gold and go our separate ways.

I fill the two bottles of water and lock them in the ute before I move it. I ask the woman in reception if there's a chemist open, and she points me further down the main street. The gecko on the wall hasn't moved but her TV show has changed to a true crime documentary. I keep my eyes fixed on the counter. 'Is there ... somewhere in town I can trade in a vehicle? I mean, and buy another one?'

She puts down her slushie and looks me up and down, lingering on the blood-stained Band-Aid and my scratched feet. I resist the urge to cover one foot with the other as the heat creeps into my face. Charlie's right: I need shoes. I've kept my sunglasses on but I wish I'd had a shower before coming back in here. I wish I'd done something about my clothes.

'No car dealers in town,' she says. 'You'll have to go to Hedland, or online. There's websites for that.'

'Do you have internet, a computer?' I swallow. 'For guests, I mean?'

'What, got no mobile phone?' She leans forwards across the desk, her gaze raking my outfit, my face and my hair like she's memorising the lot. 'Where are youse down from again?'

I take a step back and try not to run for the door. 'We're on our way south.'

She narrows her eyes. 'There's a caff,' she says. 'Past the chemist. Open tomorrow, seven a.m. Got a laptop they let folks use.'

I trip out of the reception door, my feet scraping the footpath like they belong to someone else. I feel her eyes through the window until I turn the corner onto the street.

The door of Unit Fourteen is locked when I get back from the chemist. I rattle the handle and scan the footpath. I cup my hands around my face at the window, the narrow strip of room and two beds between the curtains, the ceiling fan lazily spinning. I don't see the bag of gold. A bubble of panic. Where the hell is she?

The change in the weather behind me is like someone has opened a door, and a gust of wind flattens my hair against the glass. I turn my head as Charlie rounds the corner from the street with a plastic carrier bag dangling from one hand.

'Where have you been?' I say. 'What's that?'

She pushes past me, turns the key in the lock and trips inside.

Hot food smells from the bag. 'Where did you get the food?' I say. 'I said we should stay in.'

She eyes the bag I've brought back from the chemist. 'What, like you did?' She unpacks plastic containers onto her bed, a bag of prawn crackers, paper napkins and plastic forks. 'Was the only place open. Noodles and fried rice, special offer.' She points at a door in the opposite wall. 'Seen that? Opens into next door – number thirteen. Empty, thank fuck. I locked it, our side.'

The smells waft across the room with the heat. I see she's stashed the gold under her bed. I sit on mine and notice Aunty's tin, the handful of one and two-dollar coins in the bottom of it all that's left. I open my mouth to have a go and close it again. Seriously, what is the point?

'Any vegetables?' I say.

'What?'

'I'm vegan.'

'Shit, that figures. Yeah, in with the meat, but.' She hands me the fried rice and a plastic fork. 'Got ya Diet Coke. Didn't know if . . . ' She goes red as she hands it over, slippery and cold. She's got full fat Coke for herself.

'That's fine. Thank you.' What I need is a large glass of Chardonnay but I swig the Coke and pick pieces of baby corn and broccoli out of the rice. 'How many people in the Chinese place?'

She shrugs. 'Couple. In those orange mine uniforms.'

'Anyone ask you anything?'

'Like what?'

'About what you're doing here? How you got here?'

Her eyes meet mine and flip away. 'Nup.'

I put the container down and go to the window. The street is dark now except for the lights from the two houses opposite and one streetlight. I can see the top of a palm tree, tossing. 'Wind's picking up.' I turn back to the room. 'There's a café with internet, apparently. Open tomorrow morning. But . . . I think maybe we should keep going. To Port Hedland, that's the next big town.'

Charlie chews with her mouth open, hunched over the plastic container like a bird. 'Fuck that. We only just got here.'

'It's a bit close, that's all. To what happened . . .'

She glares over a fork full of noodles. 'Thought we weren't gunna talk about that.'

'We're not. But the woman in reception—'

'What?'

'She was looking at me. I don't know.'

She rolls her eyes. 'Yeah, 'cause you look like shit.'

'She said Port Hedland would be better, to sell the ute. And it's further away. You could get a bus north from there, keep going through the Top End to Queensland. That'd be safer than flying, less money.' Charlie keeps shovelling food. I tip the boxes of hair dye out onto my bed, the comb and the pack of adhesive dressings. The pair of scissors that make me feel sick when I pick them up. 'We can do our hair and go after that, while it's dark. Did you try your sister again?'

She twitches a shoulder. 'Still not ringin'.'

'I'm sure there's an explanation.'

'Bloody better be.' She rummages in the carrier bag. 'Forgot – I got ya these. Was a dude lighting up outside the Chinese place.' She pulls out two battered cigarettes and a book of matches – red with a golden dragon. She catches my eye as she holds them out. 'Geen smokes when she's stressed out.'

My throat full like I might cry. I stand and take them. 'That's . . . thanks, Charlie.'

She makes a face and looks away. 'Still shit for ya. You seen the warnings on them packs? You should give up.'

'I don't smoke very often. Thank you. Really.' I take the cigarettes and the matches and go to the door.

'Asked the smoker dude what the price of gold is. Know what he said?' she says. 'Almost eighty bucks a gram. Know what that adds up to?'

I turn around. 'That's more than—'

'Three-quarters of a million bucks, yeah. Eight thousand for one bar. And I'm shit at maths.'

It's a life-changing amount of money, and not only for her. All the more reason to get rid of it.

I get the cigarette alight on the third match, my back turned to the wind outside the room. It's harsh and grates on my lungs and goes fast to my head, the smoke stinging my eyes along with my whipping hair. But Charlie's right about the stress and it helps.

I prop myself against the wall with one leg up behind me the same way Ertan does when he's early to class and waiting for the rest of us outside the law building. My ex-classmates. My ex-class. There is no point thinking about these things now.

There's a dark four-wheel-drive parked diagonally across the street, the cab light a yellow rectangle. The light clicks off as I watch it, and though I smoke half the cigarette and grind it out against the rough brick wall, no one gets out before I step back inside.

I hack at my hair in the bathroom until my hand aches from the too-small scissors and I try to ignore the weight of it all being gone. I apply the bleach, stuffing my braid and scraped up handfuls of hair into the plastic bag from the chemist. We can dump them somewhere north along the road.

I scrub everything in the shower, my silk top and bra and undies too, and I put them back on wet along with my skirt. I can't seem to get my nails clean, no matter how much I work at them; the edges of polish flaking. I clean the cut on my hand and stick one of the adhesive dressings over it. There's a small scab and a bruise on my head but the most visible thing is the black eye, that and the swelling in my cheek where I fell against the wall. I cover what I can with the end of the tube of makeup. The rest will be hidden under the hat and sunglasses and I can hold onto both for now.

When I put my head around the door Charlie's asleep on her bed surrounded by empty takeaway containers, her lips moving in a dream. She's not going to give me crap about the hair, at least not yet. It's come out ochre yellow in short thick tufts. I tell myself it's the colour of the sun on the country up here but it's really not. It's horrible. It should make me want to cry or yell or spit, or at least feel something near to normal, but there's no such thing as normal now.

The room is a box of hot air despite the wind bashing a branch against the outside front wall. My top is drying on my skin as I turn on the TV from my bed and mute it, pull the photo of Dad and Aunty out of my skirt pocket. The colours wash out in the brown light of the room, the rocks and water behind them merging together, but the words on the sign are clear – SALT-WATER GOLD CORPORATION. In the Kimberley, Aunty said. Someone in Broome will know where the place is and give me directions.

There's a part of me now that is doing more than running. I want to find out how Warren got hold of the gold, how it ended up in his safe. Not legitimately, judging by his reaction when it was taken.

It's an insane thing to consider, to go there and ask questions.

It's the opposite of what I need to be doing. But it's the cause of everything, isn't it? Why shouldn't I want to know? It's like the photo has taken the lid off something. I hope Aunty understands about me taking it. I know she didn't want me to go there.

There's something more, too – what she said about me not remembering Dad's accident. Something at the back of everything else, washed out and faded like the background of the photo. Aunty didn't mention Warren once, despite all her talk of Mum, the entire time we were there. She's afraid of him, I realise. It's why she didn't want me in her house.

My eyes shift to Charlie, one arm over the bag of gold like she's spooning a puppy. I need to explain to her why she can't keep it. It'll be worse, now she knows how much it's worth.

I push the photo back into my pocket and surf channels for the evening news.

There's nothing on either Warren or Daryl turning up dead in Perth, and it's been almost two days. This is not right; I know it isn't. Who cancelled my credit card if it wasn't the police? The feeling is like someone staring so hard between my shoulder blades it's as if they're poking me with a stick.

I've been expecting an appeal from Mum, I realise. One of those press conferences. *'You're not in trouble, darling. You've only gone and killed your (cold, controlling, police officer) stepfather. Please, come home.'* She must be back at the house by now. Someone will have found him.

But what if they haven't?

'What's that?' Charlie, sitting up and blinking.

'I didn't say anything.' My heart skipping too fast. I see I'm squeezing the cut again, a line of blood speckling the clean dressing.

'Whatcha doing?'

'Watching the news.'

She jerks upwards, scattering plastic containers. 'Yeah?'

The story changes. A state government investigation into police corruption. 'Don't worry,' I say. I stare at the mess she's made of her side of the room. 'There's nothing. Nothing from Perth, either.' I click the TV off and drop the remote.

'Put it back on.' Her face is white, staring at the screen. She hasn't said a thing about my hair.

'What?'

'Put the TV back on!'

The images glow in the darkened room. The triple-trailer road train against the red dirt behind. And then the words, scrolling at the bottom, that make my stomach turn over and over. *Breaking News.*

'That's not . . .' I say.

'Yeah, it is.'

Remote Great Northern Highway double fatality.

Double?

I swallow down the nausea. The words keep scrolling. *Tragic accident or double homicide? WA Police sergeant dead of multiple injuries. Truck driver second victim.*

'Turn the volume up,' Charlie says.

I fumble the remote.

'. . .*confirmed the driver of the three-trailer vehicle was the victim of a shooting. Local police will speculate no further at present, and neither victim has been named. But one thing remains clear: this was a brutal act that has left two men dead, sparking fears an armed gunman is on the loose in the remote East Pilbara region of Western Australia.*'

The story ends and the next starts. The weather – a cyclone. Images and words washing out into the room. The wind bangs what sounds like a whole tree against the outside wall.

Armed gunman.

Charlie stares at the TV and then at the bag, her chest rising and falling in the light from the screen. 'Someone shot that truckie?' she says. 'What the fuck?'

The wind has picked up even more, the rain spraying in gravel bursts against the window. I press against the thin wooden headboard of the bed, staring at the gap between the curtains. The four-wheel-drive is still across the street, outside the halo of the streetlight. Dark grey or black. Two sets of headlights have raked along its side since Charlie clicked off the TV.

She comes out of the bathroom, her hair in a pixie crop, *Natural Dark Brown*, out of the packet I gave her.

'Want me to cut yours for ya?' she says.

She's miles away, speaking underwater. I swivel my head. 'What?'

'Your hair. I can fix it if ya want.' She comes around between the beds with a towel and the scissors. 'It wasn't us, yeah?' she says. 'That truckie. We didn't do it.' She's speaking too slowly, like there's something wrong with my brain.

I blink at her. Her singlet is the colour of strong tea now, my silk top too – drying on me for the second time tonight. It was Charlie's idea to use the hair dye, to cut the sleeves off my top and shorten the hem of my skirt, after the news about the truck driver.

'Someone did it,' I say. 'Someone behind us on the road.'

'You reckon they saw us?'

'I don't know.' I check the window again, the dark shape. *Just a parked car.* But the light went off as I was watching, didn't it?

There's someone sitting out there, waiting.

'Charlie? I think we should go.'

'What?'

'Leave now. Go out the back way. Get back in the ute.'

She plants a fist on each hip, the scissors in one hand. 'That a joke?'

'Do you see that four-wheel-drive, across the street? The interior light was on, earlier, when I smoked the cigarette you gave me, and now it's not.'

'So?' She moves to the window. 'What, you reckon there's—'

'Don't touch the curtains! Don't let him see you.'

'Calm down, fucksakes.' She peers into the gap. 'What, that LandCruiser? Someone visiting a mate.'

'The light in the cab went off and no one got out. There's someone sitting in there.'

'Is not,' she says. 'Can't see nothing. You're being paranoid.' A ragged shape spins through the splash of light from the streetlight: rubbish, a palm frond. There's a rush of wind at the window and she steps back. 'Not going out in that, neither.'

'I need to tell you what happened, the thing in Perth. Then you'll get it, you'll see why we have to go.'

She stands between me and the window so I can't see out. A frown flickers between her eyes as she weighs it up. 'Orright, tell me if ya want. Let me do your hair, but.' She moves closer, hovers a hand and touches my shoulder. I flinch, but she slips the towel between me and the headboard and wraps it closed. She starts cutting, the tufts of yellow hair falling against the towel. 'Learned this off Geen,' she says. 'Not real good at it.'

But she is. I'm surprised by her steady fingers, not what I expected; the way she moves my head, the tug of the scissors and comb. It's grounding, when everything else feels like it's coming apart and dissolving. 'It was my stepfather,' I say. 'The thing that happened.'

I tell her the lot. Warren waking me up and pushing me ahead of him up the stairs. My wrist hurting from the way he held it and knowing, from the charged silence once we got into his study, that whatever this was, it was bad. Worse than the usual stuff about what I was wearing or doing or eating. Worse than his obsession with me getting 'ideas' now I was at uni and how he didn't like me to have an opinion on anything. The rug was folded back to show the space under the floorboards and my mind raced as he spoke. *You fail to arm the alarm. You fail to secure the back door. My safe is removed from the room directly over your head and you expect me to believe you know nothing of it?*

'I didn't see how I could have slept through all that either,' I say to Charlie. 'I thought it was a joke. But I'd been up so late, the whole week; studying, an assignment and then the last exam. I'd had a few drinks the night before, celebrating with friends. I'd slept late and fallen asleep again in the afternoon. Warren had been out all day and didn't know what time the safe was taken. And he doesn't do jokes, not really.'

Charlie's hands in my hair stop moving.

'Keep going,' I say. 'Please?' She starts again – the rhythm of pulling at a chunk of hair, snipping, smoothing, pulling again. I check the space between the curtains. No change.

He stood in front of his desk, gripping the edge and leaning on it at the same time. The square space in the floorboards between him and the wall. He asked if they'd threatened me, made me stay in my room. I told him no, I didn't know they were there. Had I been scared, and stayed in there of my own accord? Had I called the police? No, I told him, I hadn't heard anything.

She stops cutting again as I tell her this, her fingers frozen and the scissors glinting in the light from the bedside lamp. I bite the bullet and tell her about Mum's 'accidents', three in the last year. The stories she'd have ready and how each time I believed her. She'd broken a bone in her hand because a pot plant fell on it, bruised her cheekbone when she walked into the bathroom cabinet in the dark. I press on the cut on my hand. I have to get this out, the whole way.

'He was holding onto the desk like he wanted to snap it. But not like he was about to lose it, like he knew exactly what he was doing. I could see every tendon in his hands.' I glance up at Charlie: the tightness around her eyes, her mouth a little way open. 'He asked if I'd spoken to Mum, if I'd called her in Bali that day. Did I think she knew about the safe going missing? He turned his head and met my eye and I knew – that he'd done those things to her. And he could see that I knew.

'I ran, Charlie. I shouldn't have done that. He caught me at the top of the stairs. He caught me by my hair.'

I race through the last part, wanting to get it over. My face, slammed against the wall. The adrenaline flooding. His hand in my hair at the back, twisted so I was held there, suspended above the stairs. 'It felt like it was happening to someone else, not to me,' I say. 'The stairs are very steep. Mum fell down them and she . . . ' I swallow. 'That was her third accident. There's a table up there, on the landing. I threw out my hand and grabbed the first thing.'

It's suddenly cold and I pull the towel tighter. I can't look at Charlie. 'I stabbed him with the pair of scissors I picked off the table. He fell the whole flight with them sticking out of his neck.'

The wind makes a sound and we both jump. 'There was a lot of blood,' I say, 'and he wasn't moving. I panicked and ran.' I drag my fingers down over my face. 'The worst part is, I'm starting to think he might not be dead.'

Her blue eyes are pale in the darkened room, her mouth still open. 'Didn't ya check? Call an ambulance?'

'He wasn't breathing. His neck was at this weird angle.'

'You did with Daryl. You checked his pulse.'

'Yes, because you asked me to.'

'You stabbed a dude and pushed him down the stairs and—'

'I didn't push him! He fell down the stairs.'

'Same difference. You didn't check.'

'I told you; I panicked. I knew I'd stabbed him, and he wasn't moving ...'

'Breathing, you said!'

'Both. He was ... there was a lot of blood, more than I'd ever seen. It wasn't very real ... have you finished cutting my hair?'

She nods and backs off, eyeing me. Scissors and comb in one hand. 'Same as Daryl. You didn't let me call the cops.'

My fingers are twisted in the towel at my throat. 'That was different. You saw the body – there was no point. And you didn't want your sister to find out.'

She doesn't get it. What my chances are. Someone like me, having killed someone like Warren: a senior police officer. I'm not so different to her, am I? One parent down and the other absent. I was hardly going to call Mum. She knew what he was capable of and she'd left me with him. She'd still gone away.

I put a hand up to my hair and feel around – my ear, the back of my neck. Shorter than Charlie's, almost smooth. 'You've done a good job on this.'

Her eyes narrow. 'How come you wanted him dead? Did you nick it, like he said? The safe?'

'No, I did not.' *Your bloke Daryl did. The gold was inside.* I will explain it to her, that Warren said he knew where the safe was and had her address on his phone. But there's mistrust in her face as it is; now is not the time. I drop the towel on the bedspread and brush itchy shards of hair from my damp top. 'I didn't want him dead. I thought he was going to push me. It was a split second, like you.'

She sniffs. 'Like me. And now ya reckon he's not. That a good thing?'

He won't have picked himself up in a hurry. At the very least he'll have needed blood and a hospital. I go to the window, the vehicle still out there and dark. 'You don't know him.'

'What, he's been behind us the whole way? Nah. Got one like that, has he? A LandCruiser?'

'That doesn't mean anything. He knows people. He will have sent someone.'

She drops the scissors on the bed. 'He's probably dead, like you reckoned.'

The window frame rattles, the branch out front banging. 'Do you think we could drive in this?'

'Don't be a dick. The weather's epileptic. Cyclone, the news said. Cyclone Bertrand.'

'That was north, though. This is the edge of it, maybe.' There's a lull in the wind and rain and the sound of snoring comes through the wall from next door, deep and regular. 'I don't think that room's empty.'

She swears, steps up to the dividing door and checks the handle, then drags over the wooden chair from across the room to wedge it underneath. She pulls back the cover on her bed and makes a face. Tugs it back across, gives the pillow two thumps and lies on top in her singlet and shorts.

Rain batters the roof and the window and a metal bin lid clatters away. 'There's more. About my stepfather. I think he sent that police officer, the one on the highway. I think that's why he searched the ute, how he knew the gold was there.'

'What? How come?'

'Because … my stepfather's a detective.'

She bolts upright. 'Like a PI, ya mean?'

'No. Like, a police detective.'

'That another joke?'

'No.'

'Ya didn't think it might be good to tell me that? A bit earlier on?'

'I am telling you. I'm telling you now.'

'And you tried to kill him? Fuck.'

I'm about to turn away from the window when red and blue lights strobe through the rain. The police cruiser tracks right to left, headlights scraping the wet road. It turns towards reception and disappears.

Who called them? Was it him – backup, for the four-wheel-drive?

'Charlie?' I scan the room, my heart banging. I take in the

plastic takeaway containers and Coke cans, the tufts of my hair all over the bed. 'Is there a way out the back?'

'Bathroom window,' she says. 'No way you'd get through it – not being funny.' She catches my look and her eyes widen. 'What?'

'Police,' I say. 'Outside reception.'

She leaps up. 'Fuck. Fuck. Shit.' She snatches up her shirt and gets the gold out from under the bed, pushing her feet into her thongs. 'Don't stand there, get your bag!'

I don't know if I can. I don't know if I can keep running.

There's a knock at the door, muffled against the rain. 'Police officers. Open up.'

'Nao!' Charlie shoves my jacket and bag at me. The gold is clutched to her side. She rips the chair away from under the door handle and unlocks Unit Thirteen.

'Police! Open up in there.'

'Charlie. Maybe we need to face them.' But before I can finish, she's got the door open and she drags me through it. 'What about the . . .' We fall into the room and pull the door behind us. ' . . . bloke,' I say.

He's sat up in bed, blinking, his mouth working like he's been chewing in his sleep. 'You're dreaming, mate,' Charlie says. 'We're not in it, orright?'

She pulls me across the room. It has the same layout – one bathroom, one window, one door. I'm dragging my feet and she doesn't notice. I hear more knocking from next door. 'Police officers!'

'It's no good, Charlie. The front door's the same as ours.'

The bloke in his bed puts on a pair of glasses, lifts a mobile phone to take the shot.

'Don't make me, Dickhead.' Charlie swings the bag and knocks the phone out of his hand. It hits the wall with a crack. 'Move and I'll deck ya.' She's breathing like an angry rabbit. He freezes, but there's no way out of this. More knocking, muffled voices. She grips my arm. 'Here.'

It's a corner room, the door on the side wall instead of the front. She's thinking better than me.

She twists the handle and gets it open. Sheet water pours off the veranda. The wind buffeting. 'Fuck, it's pissing elephants,' she says.

Reception is around the corner to the left; the laneway and car park to the right.

'Police officers!' Another voice. 'Knew there was something about 'em. Not your usual backpackers.'

'The woman from reception,' I say, turning towards the sound.

'Not shit-hot at this, are ya?' Charlie drags me the other way, up the laneway and into the car park. She stops dead and circles, raindrops like golf balls bouncing up off the wet surface. 'Where's the ute?' she yells over the wind.

'The what?'

'The ute, Nao!'

'I moved it.'

We exit the car park; running, stumbling, panting. Right, left and then right again, at least I think it was. 'Whatcha move it so far for?' Charlie clutches the bag, her voice snatched by the wind. Rain sluicing her face and hair.

'I was worried.'

'How much further?'

'Another block.' We cross a driveway – curtained rooms,

warm and dry – through a pool of too-bright light. I look over my shoulder.

'See anything?'

'No.'

'Where are they?'

I expect them, too – a blast of siren, a blur of lights – but the street is dark. 'There.' The ute, halfway along.

'Gimme the key.' I hand it over and we pile in. Our clothes are plastered. Charlie slicks the wet off her face, stashes the gold behind her seat. I check the mirrors, empty. Rain lashes the roof, the windscreen, the windows. The wind is beating at the ute before she's even got it going.

'They behind us?' she says.

'I don't think so.'

She starts it, clicks the wipers on full. 'Not sticking the lights on,' she says.

'What?'

'No bugger out, is there?' She eases out from the kerb. 'Can't see nothing, but.'

'Put the fan on. Here.' I press the button.

We snake through black streets, windows up, hot and humid in the cab. The rain muffles everything and makes it unreal. The beat and whine of the wipers is like the blood in my ears.

I keep my head up, scanning the mirrors and back window. Mailboxes, house lights, cars on driveways. 'Dunno which way,' Charlie says. Her wet fingers are tight on the wheel.

She takes a left and a right. I see a wash of red and blue and my gut tenses. 'That's them,' I say. 'Police cruiser, other end of the street.'

She swears.

The cruiser enters the street as we leave it and the ute planes sideways. 'Careful!' Charlie turns left, over a bridge lined with streetlights. Too visible. The wind tugs like it's got a hold of us but lets us go again. 'We could be driving into it,' I say. 'The weather.'

'No shit. Know where we're going?'

'North. We need to get out of town. No.'

'How about that map you had?'

'No good for up here.'

'Fucksakes. Why aren't they following? Are they?'

I check behind. 'I can't see them.'

We come to an intersection, a sign too dark to read. 'Which way?' she says.

'I don't know. I can't read that.'

'Can't do this by myself, Nao! Which way?'

'Right. It's a big road. Right should be north.'

Something wet and heavy splats the windscreen. She wrenches the wheel into the turn and it slides off. 'What was that?'

'Rubbish,' I say. 'Something dead.'

Sideswipes of wind, the hiss of wet tyres. We take a long hill and the lights of the town disappear.

She glances at me and clicks on the headlights. 'Can't see.' The flare is a shock, the two of us lit up on the dark road. She hunches closer to the windscreen. 'Can't sell the ute now, can we? After that truckie got shot?'

'I don't know.'

'How we gunna get money if we can't sell it? How do I get to Surfers?'

'I don't know, Charlie.'

We head north, towards the turnoff to the national parks. The wind is tugging less hard but the windows stay fogged and Charlie keeps ten kilometres per hour below the speed limit. A sign flashes in the headlights as we leave the town limits, the usual warnings on entering a remote area: NO FUEL OR WATER AVAILABLE. NO MEDICAL ASSISTANCE. UNFENCED ROAD.

We rattle across a cattle grid, the first of many. Charlie doesn't blink. I watch the mirrors but we're the only thing out here, and I start to breathe a little easier. No one in their right mind would take this road, not in weather like this.

We're an hour out of town when I register the headlights behind.

WEDNESDAY

10

Charlie

Double-Take

'Charlie? Jesus, you're not asleep are you? Charlie!'

The ute pulls left. Into a pothole and out. I blink my eyes open and yank it back. 'Course not.'

Fuck, I reckon I mighta been. There's streaks of light in the sky where a second ago it was dark. What's she expect, driving all night with the ute sliding all over the road? I yawn and click the wipers off. 'Storm's over.' Warm air in at the windows. My shorts and shirt dried out from last night.

'Can you go a bit faster?' Her eyes are fixed on the rearview. 'Actually, no. Pull over, that next tree.'

'Make up yer mind.'

I do it. Pull over. She gets me to turn the headlights off and kill the engine, and she gets out but I stay sat there. I check she's not looking, bend and unzip the holdall in the back, quick as. The dead cop's gun still at the bottom, under four layers of gold bars. Shoulda moved it but where to? I only picked it up 'cause of that snake.

Reflex. A dumb one, Geen would say.

Wonder where she is. I hope she's not freaking about the house and she hasn't reported Dickhead Daryl missing.

I zip the bag shut and climb out, rub my face and arms and stamp my feet. It's still mostly dark. Spooky fucken quiet. Steam coming up off the dirt, that smell of wet euc you get after rain. There's a few trees now, little scrappy ones either side of the dirt road. The wet dirt sticks to my thongs in lumps.

Thought Nao had gone for a piss except she hasn't. She's just stood there, squinting back down the road. Her feet are chunked in dirt too. 'This road's shit,' I say. 'Can't handle a bit of wet.'

She goes up on tiptoe.

'Whatcha doing?' I check where she's looking. Lumpy scrub and sky and bugger-all else – still makes me crook to look at it. Plus something rustling out to the side that scares the crap outta me until I see it's a kangaroo. 'Flat out here, or what?'

'That's why it floods.'

'Does it?' I rub the back of my neck. 'How come you know? About the road?'

She frowns. 'I don't know. We did road trips when I was small. I don't really remember them, though.' She walks around and opens up the back of the ute and climbs up. Takes her a few goes to get up there and she stands on tiptoe again.

'What's this?' I say. 'Stargazing? Geen's into that.'

She chucks me a look. 'Has your … has Daryl got a set of binoculars? Check the glovebox.'

'I already looked in there.'

'Not for binoculars, you didn't.'

There's nothing when I check except an empty pack of condoms. Gross, and who was he screwing in the ute? Not Geen, that's for sure. 'Nup, nothin',' I yell up at her.

'Come up here,' she says. 'Look at this.'

'Why?'

'Just come up here.'

I climb up next to her. The sky's a bit lighter and there's dots of stars. The road and scrub are solid dark, but, so you can see the two cones of light, way off and coming our way. 'Fuck. Police?'

'I don't think so. I noticed the headlights last night. I thought they'd gone.'

'Reckon it's following us?'

'There's no one else out here. The road's terrible, you said so yourself.' She's pressing on that bandage on her hand again. 'He's been behind us since we left Tom Price. I think it's that four-wheel-drive, the one across from the motel.'

Fingers of sun come up over the scrub and the headlights wink off as we watch. 'Shit, can't see nothing now.' I jump down. 'We need to get going. Port Hedland, that's the next town, yeah?'

'Up on the coast.'

'Okay, we dump the ute. Get another car, quick as. Could be the cops, from last night.'

She's still up there, her mouth in a wobbly line. 'I don't think it is. I'm scared it's Warren. That he's sent someone after us.'

'The dead cop stepdad?'

'It's not a joke. It won't be, not if he catches up to us.'

'I know it's not. Get down. You can drive. I'll keep a look out.'

We get going. The ute slides on the wet dirt road, the engine loud through the windows. The sun rising all gold and splintery over the scrub and a load of tiny parrots making a racket out to our left, skimming the tops of bushes, between trees. Nothing in the rearview.

My neck and the backs of my hands are prickling, mainly 'cause of how weird Nao's being. 'How's he followed us?' I say. 'With the rego number of the ute?'

She keeps the headlights off and leans forwards, pulling against her seatbelt. 'Not without surveillance cameras, not out here. He followed our lights.'

'Not the whole way from the city. Didn't see him at your aunty's, did we? How'd he track us to the motel?'

She turns her head at me, big round eyes. 'Holy crap, you're right. What if there's a tracker, GPS or something, on the ute?'

'On Daryl's ute? Nah. How'd it get on there?'

She checks the mirrors. Presses harder on the gas, the ute revving and slipping. 'Jesus. Get the bag. Have a look in it.'

No way. 'Why?'

'I need to explain some things. How I turned up at your address, for a start.' She skims a hand up to her hair, drops it back on the wheel. 'Open the bag. Look for a tracker. If there is one, it's in there with the gold.'

The leather holdall's on my lap, zipped open, angled away from Nao so she can't see in it. I've checked the lot, each drawstring bag with a bit of gold inside. She keeps turning her head to look. 'No tracker in 'ere,' I say. 'How come it's—'

'Check the lining.'

'I already did. Not here.' I dig the whole way around the bag a second time, under the gun, inside and out.

'You're not doing it right. Let me do it.' She takes a hand off the wheel and I slap it away. The ute slides sideways.

'You're driving! Watch the road.'

The sun up now and getting hotter, cooking my arm through the open window. The scrub either side of us flat dirt again like the trees all died. Ripped up bits of cloud and blue sky. 'It'll be small,' she says. 'You've missed it.'

'Might not even be one.'

'There is one.'

We hit a pothole full of water, splash in and out. 'How d'ya know?'

She looks at me and back at the road. Her face covered by the big sunnies again so I can't see the bruise round her eye. 'The thing that happened, with Warren. He had your address, on his phone. The location. He told me that's where we had to go to get his safe back.'

'Why? He's a cop. Coulda called it in.'

'Because he's obviously not a good cop, Charlie!' She glares at me, breathing hard. I don't get why she's so mad. 'He can't be, can he? You're right; he didn't call it in. He took it out on me instead. But how did he have your address? It was because of Daryl. He stole the safe.'

'Daryl? What's it got to do with—?'

No way. I stare at the holdall, the weight of it on my knees.

'*This* was in your stepdad's safe? That's who Daryl nicked it off?'

'Warren didn't say what was in the safe,' she says. 'But I recognised the bag. And how else would he have had your address? There has to be a tracker. Daryl was at your house on Sunday evening. The gold was sitting out there in the lane, in the ute.'

'That's how come you showed up? And you didn't even tell me? After—'

'Tell you what? That I'd just stabbed someone and I thought you'd stolen his safe?'

We eyeball each other. The scrub flashing past behind her shoulder. 'He coulda been after us the whole time and you didn't tell me.'

'I didn't know that. Not until now.'

'Watch the road,' I say, and she looks away. What else is she not telling me? She lifts a shaky hand off the wheel and puts it back on.

'Sorry,' she says. 'It proves it, though. It proves Warren's alive. He cancelled my credit card. I should have guessed when there was no dead body on the news.'

'Just ... give us a second, orright? Shut up for a second. It's a fucken lot to take in.' My head's weird and I can't sort it. I wish Geen was here, wish I'd told her what happened with Daryl first up. Wish we'd stayed in the city and none of this shit had happened.

We pass one of them yellow FLOODWAY signs. Sheet water on the road and the ute sprays it up either side.

'What colour's that LandCruiser?' I say.

'Dark grey or black. Dark tinted windows.'

I check out the back. No LandCruiser. No dust either 'cause the road's too wet. Flooded potholes reflecting sky. 'We need to not bullshit each other, orright, Nao? This is serious.'

She chews her cheek. 'I know.'

'What else?'

'I think Warren's alive back in the city. He told the cop on the highway to take the gold and when that went wrong, the bloke in the four-wheel-drive shot the truck driver. It's Warren who sent him after us.' She glances over, pushes her sunnies up her nose. 'After *me*. It's the bloke we saw outside your house. I don't know why he went back and burned it after we lost him that night, but he found us again.'

She still might be guessing half of it. Either way it's bad. 'Orright. Keep going. Fast as you can get it to go.'

'The road, Charlie.'

'Yeah, I get it.'

We go for an hour, her arms out straight and her lips pressed together. The fuel creeping lower and both of us watching the rearview. Another racket of tiny green parrots I reckon might be budgies. More of the FLOODWAY signs. Each time we pass one there's more wet on the road – one time it's like a creek and Nao has to slow right down. I remember her saying about it flooding. Flat sheets of water out in the scrub, from the rain last night. The smell of it through the open windows.

Shit, my phone – the rain. I slide it out one-handed, try to switch it on. Nothing happens. I keep pressing but it stays blank. I shove it back before Nao clocks me, then pull out the receipt with Geen's number on it.

'Fucksakes! Geen's number,' I say. 'Washed out in the rain. How am I gunna call her now?'

'Let me see.'

The back of my throat's got a lump like wet sand. I push the receipt at her. If the phone's wrecked the number's gone forever.

She hands it back. 'There's nothing on it. You can't remember it?'

'No, I fucken can't.' I wrap my hand around Geen's keys in my pocket, the Surfers keyring, press until the hard square feels like it's a part of my hand. The scrub changes again – hummocks of grass, a few trees. Fuel on a quarter of a tank. 'I need internet. Get a message to her. How far's Port Hedland?'

'A couple of hours, if the road holds up.'

Not gunna make it, are we? Too far. I don't say it, but. 'What's the dude gunna do when he catches up to us?'

'He's after me,' she says. 'It's me Warren's sending a message to.'

I roll my neck, wipe my hands on my shirt. 'What's the message?'

'That he's alive. That he wants his gold back. That he's not going to give up.'

'What's that up ahead?' I say. A glint of sun off something shiny. Nao presses the brake and slows. It's two vehicles stopped in the road. 'Wrong colour, yeah? Not him?'

One's a white LandCruiser and the other a yellow Kombi van, side by side: the LandCruiser new and shiny, black tyres caked in red dirt. The Kombi van rusted with surfboards piled on top. No way to get around 'em.

Nao sticks her hat on, she's out her seatbelt and out the door. 'Wait here.' She leaves the engine running.

The sun hot on my shoulder and arm. I stick my head out and crane a look: a tree and a sign for the national park. The road dips down and it's like another creek across the middle of it, a big one. I check the rearview, still nothing.

I lean down, unzip the holdall and pull the gun out. It's heavy like it was when I first picked it up. I ram it down the front of my shorts and pull my flanno shirt over the top.

'What are you doing?'

I jump. Nao's stood at her open window.

'Nothing. Stashing this so no one gets a look.' I zip the bag shut, shove it under my seat from the back. 'Can we get through?'

'I doubt it. It looks deep. There's a boy in there, doing a walk-through. We don't have a snorkel.'

'A *what*? How deep's it gunna get?'

The end of her mouth twitches. 'Are you serious?'

'I'm not swimming,' I say. 'Could be anything in there. Piranhas. Leeches. And what about the ute?'

She smiles, first time I've seen one on her. Blink and you'd miss it. 'Jesus, piranhas? The snorkel is for the ute, to get it across the flooded part.' She points at the two vehicles in front. 'See the tubes sticking up on the driver's side? We don't have one.'

'Can we nick one?'

Her mouth opens and shuts. A dude in wrap-around shades comes up behind her. 'Likin' the green utility. Si-ick,' he says. Blond dreads, dirty boardies and a sunburnt nose. Wobbly head like it's on a string. I don't like the way he's sticking his peeling nose in to check out the back seat. 'Where a you chicks travelin' to?'

'Anyplace except for here,' I say. 'Long way from the surf, aren't ya?'

The dude steps past Nao, lands two hands on the top of the open window. Leans in close and he stinks of weed. Thanks, bro. 'Road-tripping,' he says. 'Like you two gals.'

Not the only kind of tripping he's doing.

'You gals out here alone? What happens if you blow a head gasket?' He lifts his shades up, red eyes, drops them back down. 'We're headed into the campsite, after. You chicks wanna join? Wanna be careful, out here in the boonies. No knowin' the characters you might run into.'

'Like you, ya mean?' I say.

Nao steps up, chucks me a pointy one. 'She means thanks. Thanks for the offer but we're okay as we are.'

He has a perv at Nao's legs in her cut-off skirt, frowns at her trashed feet and double-takes her face. He checks out the ute again, the outside of it this time. 'Green utility . . . far out. You gals watch *Crime Stoppers*?'

My gut scrunches. 'No, mate.'

'Yesterday,' the dude says. 'Shooting, was it? Great Northern Highway. Coupla gals wanted as witnesses.'

The gun's heavy and cold against my skin. 'Coincidence, mate. There's utes this colour all over the state.'

'Fugitives from the law,' he breathes. 'You can still join, no biggie. Got any food?'

A yell from up ahead. 'Jez! She's real deep, mate. Come and look.'

The dude backpedals, one hand up in a wave as he shambles off. 'Not you two chicks, anyhow. Different hair.'

He drifts between the Kombi van and the LandCruiser, towards the water. 'He for real?' I say to Nao.

She's hovering, her mouth in a flat line. 'Descriptions of us and the ute.'

I try to smile. 'Different hair.'

'They'll be looking for the owner of it. Daryl.'

'Doesn't mean they'll find him.' I check the gun in my

waistband and climb out. 'Can you see that LandCruiser following us?'

She goes up on tiptoe and gives me a shake of her head.

'Don't you reckon he shoulda caught up by now?'

Holding her hat on, squinting back along the road. 'Maybe.'

'Wait here. Get the gold and your bag and get ready to run.'

'Where are you going?' she says. 'We need to get across that water. It's deep, he said.'

'I know we do. I'm gunna get us a snorkel.' Might be a vehicle attached to it, but.

Nao's not into the plan and then she is, thank fuck.

We leave the ute and come up between the LandCruiser and the yellow Kombi, parked on the slope a few metres back from the water. The gun still in my shorts with my shirt pulled down so Nao can't see it. Not like I'm gunna use it. She's doing this weird half-crouch with her bum out like an emu. What is she, Army Reserve? There's a blonde chick checking her phone in the passenger seat of the flash white LandCruiser. Rules that one out, worse luck.

The crossing's wider than I reckoned, twenty metres maybe, more like a river than a creek except the water's not moving. A dead tree marks the other side of it. Jez and his mate are halfway across, up to their waists in brown water, the mate with a stick like he's checking out the bottom.

Nao's got the holdall. I give her an elbow. 'Don't let those pricks see it.'

We keep low, one of us either side of the Kombi van. The surfboards cast lumpy shadows Nao's side and we check the wheel arches and inside it for the keys. The back of my neck and my arms buzzing.

Nao nods at Jez. 'What if they're in his pocket?'

'Just look!'

Jez and the dude stop what they're doing and glance our way. I duck.

And I clock the huntsman spider.

Big as my hand, on the windscreen of the white LandCruiser. The girl hasn't seen it. I wave at Nao. 'Get round here. Change of plan.'

I flick at the spider with the tail of my shirt so it runs across the windscreen towards the girl, go around and knock on her window. 'Open up!' The girl drops her phone, picks it up. Hasn't seen the spider. The inside of the Landie's flash, with a load of new gear in the back. Most likely full of fuel, too.

The girl slides the window down. Tight ponytail, nose stud bling. I see the key in the ignition and get a blast of cold from the aircon. 'Yes?'

Rubberneck Jez looks over, frowns.

'There's a giant huntsman spider on your windscreen.' I point at it – little hairy feet stuck to the glass. 'You wanna get out here and get that off.'

She checks it out. A wrinkle between her blonde eyebrows. 'And why?'

'It'll find its way in. They're buggers for that. Get out here and I can help you.'

Blank face, cool as Kylie. 'Leaf him,' she says, some European accent. 'I'm not scared of spiders.'

Fuck.

Nao mouths something from the other side of the car. I shake my head and step back where she can't see me. The dudes in the water are climbing out the opposite side, pushing each other and pissing about. Fuck it. We need it more than they do. I lift my shirt, show the girl the gun and her face goes white. 'Just get out the car and leave everything in it,' I say.

She clutches her phone, can't get her eyes off the gun.

'Not next week! Do it now or I'll take that phone.'

She drops out the door and I yank her out the way.

Nao and me pile in. The smell of leather seats and Juicy Fruit chewing gum. She looks confused. 'How did you—'

'Just gimme the bag.' She does and I stash it.

The girl turns a circle on the road, flapping her arms and yelling. 'Marcus? Marcus!' Dunno where Marcus is.

Jez and his mate start back from the other side, shouting. The water halfway up their legs already.

'Lock the doors,' I yell at Nao. 'Go!'

She fumbles the key. 'Do your seatbelt . . . I'm not sure about this, Charlie.'

'Just drive!'

She starts it and crawls forward, bottom of the slope. The front end dips in the water and I get one arm in my seatbelt. 'Watch the water,' I say. 'Not too fast.'

'Do you think I don't know that?'

The tyres spin and grip. I hang onto the door. The slope levels out but water comes up fast both sides, the engine straining.

'Head for the dead tree. Got it in four-wheel-drive?'

'Yes. Don't talk, Charlie.'

The girl's still back on the road, yelling. A tall Black dude in a baseball cap pops out from the scrub behind us and starts to run. That'll be Marcus.

Jez wades closer, his mouth open. He stumbles, changes tack.

I can't see where his mate is. Brown water up over the tyres, the smell of it everywhere.

'Faster,' I say.

Nao mutters. The engine changes up and water laps the hood. We tilt sideways. It starts to come in around the bottom of the door.

'Slow down!' I say. 'It's too deep, it's coming in the doors!' Her side, too. 'What if we can't—'

'Shut up, Charlie. I can't concentrate.' Her foot on the gas, the Landie grinding forwards. Water frothing at the bottom of the windscreen like we're in a car wash. Jez coming at us from the side with his mate behind him.

We're halfway to the dead tree when there's a massive clunk and she stalls it.

Jez grabs the bull bar, his tongue in the corner of his mouth. 'Start it, can't ya?' I hear the panic in me. Think of the dude in the LandCruiser back behind us, what he's gunna do if we don't make it across.

Nao tries the engine. Nothing.

Jez gets two hands on the bull bar. His mate stumbles, recovers, heads across in front. I see Marcus in the wing mirror, waist-deep and closing behind. Nao's still fumbling.

I feel the gun under my hand and I don't wanna have to shoot someone.

Marcus gets a hand on the back door, bangs the window with the flat of it and grapples with the handle. My feet are wet and water's still coming in. 'Nao?'

The engine starts.

She revs it and backs up, yanking Jez's arms but he's cling-ing onto the bull bar like that spider. He holds on and so does

Marcus. I grip the gun. I can shoot one of them in the leg or the hand or something. I'm probably gunna miss.

Nao pulls right. Marcus drops back and we rip Jez off his feet, legs kicking. Brown water up in his face but he doesn't let go.

Jez's mate's halfway between us and the other side, arms out wide. 'Don't kill him,' I say. 'Don't run him down.'

'I'm not going to kill him.'

But she goes straight for him, she floors it. Water streaming past both sides, the level dropping as we start to climb out. Jez yells at his mate and lets go. His mate dives out the way and they both go under.

'Shit, did you hit one?'

I turn in my seat and see two heads pop up.

And then we're out, Jez hauling his mate onto his feet, shaking water out his hair. Marcus and the girl, phones out, taking pictures. Nao accelerating onto the flat dirt road.

I stick my head between the seats and watch them disappear behind, Jez's beat-up Kombi and Daryl's green ute too. Nao's breathing funny in the driver's seat. She stops on the road and we open the doors, wait while all the water rushes out.

'You orright?' I'm not gunna think about the girl's face when she looked at the gun. Not like I woulda shot her, is it? 'Check out the back. There's a whole fridge back there.'

'They'll call the police, Charlie.'

'That Jez was stoned as. He's not gunna call them.'

'The other two, then. Or they'll come after us. This is a good vehicle.' I see the worry on her, remember her giving Beer Gut Dude his water bottle back, except we're way past that. 'It'll be on the news,' she says.

'We're already on the news. We're on *Crime Stoppers*. Just

keep going north so I can get on a bus out the state and you can get away from the dude coming after ya. It's gunna be fine.'

The sun's low and orange and swimming in heat as we come into Port Hedland. It's all palm trees and wide streets, with dirt and corrugated iron the whole way to the horizon. Every truck and car's covered in dust now the road's dried out, but the carpet in the Landie is wet and stinking, even with the aircon blasting. The radio playing some country song and Nao humming like she knows it.

No bugger following us, far as I can see.

'Thought it was a big town. Reckon there's a bus station?' I've checked out the stuff in the back, the girl's blingy studded handbag, her wallet and cash. I got the gun back underneath the gold without Nao seeing it.

'There'll be a bus station.' She pulls into a servo on the way into town and fills up the LandCruiser. I give her some of the girl's cash and she doesn't ask. We keep on going into town and she parks in a big car park out front of Woolies with palm trees lining the watered grass verge. The car park's half full: shoppers and trolleys and kids, dogs panting in the trays of utes with their tongues hanging in the heat. Every vehicle light coloured or silver, and red with dust.

Nao turns the engine off, wipes the sweat off her face and does a three-sixty scan of the car park.

'How come he's not caught up to us?' I say. 'Reckon he got across?'

'Maybe he went around, took another road. We still need to find the tracker, remember?'

She won't let that go. Probably never was one.

'There's seven hundred bucks left of this cash,' I say. 'If it's enough to get me to Surfers you can keep the rest: the flash LandCruiser, the food and spare fuel and camping stuff. That's a top deal, there's heaps of good stuff back there.'

She gulps water and wipes her mouth. 'Only because you don't want any of it.'

I shrug, pull the holdall of gold onto my lap. I imagine getting off the bus in Surfers with it, imagine calling Geen and telling her I've got it. 'What we gunna do about this? I don't get the idea you wanna give it back to him. Don't reckon you wanna keep it, neither.'

She checks the rearview, back down at the gold. 'He won't give up, Charlie.'

'Be better off without it, then, wontcha? Can't come after ya if you don't have it.'

She keeps staring at the bag, puts a hand up to her yellow hair and I can see her brain working. She frowns and looks up. 'Do you still have the one in your pocket?'

What the fuck? She's changed her mind about it, somewhere back down the road. 'What, you wanna keep it now? Thought you wanted to dump it?'

She presses her lips down and I know I'm right. She's still bullshitting me, after everything. After I got us outta there last night, pulled the gun on that girl today and got us to here.

The back of my throat's weird. I would've asked her, I almost did. Did she wanna come to Surfers with Geen and me? To get away from him, to get out the state. Well, now I'm not.

'Go ya halves, then. Four hundred grand each.' I try a smile except it doesn't come out right. 'My final offer.'

She pushes her sunnies up her nose. 'It's not as simple as that.

I think I know where it came from – a place in the Kimberley. I think Warren stole it.'

'So?'

'So, he's not the only one who wants it back.'

'What, you want to return it? There a reward out for it or something?'

'No. I don't know. We still need to find the tracker in it.'

'Nah, I don't reckon there's a … fuck.' I clock a black LandCruiser, three rows in front, cruising right to left. My chest gets tight when I see it. 'Is that him?'

She jerks her head up, the colour washing out of her. 'Oh God,' she says. 'Can you see who's driving?'

'Tinted windows, can't see shit.' It turns at the end and I lose track of it. One car behind it a dark blue Commodore pulls into a parking spot, a shitload of antennas on the front end of the roof.

Something about it, like I've seen it someplace before.

The LandCruiser turns again, one row closer. 'How'd he get here? Wasn't even behind us.'

Nao's eyes are too big, staring. 'He went another way.' She rips the holdall off my lap and gets her door open. 'I'm going to find the tracker.'

I grab a handle, try and yank it back. 'It's not in there, I'm telling ya. I unpacked the lot.'

'You missed it. I'll take it into the shopping centre, use the women's toilets. I'll lock myself in until I find it.'

'No way! Ya can't.' I undo my seatbelt and pull on the handle but she won't let go. 'I'll do it. You look for him, see who's driving. He'll come round again.'

'You won't do it right!' She's out her door, stretching the bag between us like liquorice. 'Drive around. Keep moving. Meet me back at the main doors.'

The handle breaks and I'm left with fuck-all. I grab for her shirt and miss. 'Nao!'

She slams the door and she's gone into Woolies with the lot. Not forgetting the gun at the bottom of the holdall. She'll go apeshit when she finds it.

The double doors slide shut behind her and slide open again for a dude with half a carton. She's left her jacket and hat, the messenger bag with her purse in it, the credit card that didn't work. My breathing does that thing – in and out like a chook with no head. She's still bullshitting me and now she's gone. What if she doesn't come back?

The black LandCruiser drives by, real slow, down the row in front, headed for the shopping centre. Only one empty car space between us. The driver wearing sunnies and a black cap pulled down low. Can't see more through the tinted window.

I catch sight of the back passenger as he cruises by, only see her 'cause she's pressed up against the glass. It's like the whole thing happens in slo-mo: her tanned shoulder and cheek, the yin and yang fish tattoo. Dark blonde hair off her neck in a knot.

My heart doing tumbleturns. I know that hair, that shoulder tat. She looks right at me and her mouth opens.

'Geen!' He's got her in the back.

11

Nao

Deadly

I go to the end cubicle and lock it, pulling the bag of gold onto my lap as I sit on the closed lid of the toilet. The air-conditioning chills the sweat on my face, my heartrate up from running but slowing, slowing, slowing down. I lean my head into the wall; there's a mechanical hum and the distant sound of Christmas music. And it's not even December yet.

My head is full of Warren. I can't get him out of there. Thoughts and fears scramble over one another, competing for attention. The thought of him three days ago at the top of the stairs, and the thought of him now.

I flinch, and the bag of gold waterfalls off my lap onto the floor.

Warren was closest to being like a real dad in primary school, in those first years after Dad died when I didn't do well. His rules were there but I didn't notice them because I was trying so hard to be good. He'd help me with homework when Mum was busy or away for work, he'd listen to me reading. It was only when I started to do better he backed off. Didn't he want me to do well and to go to uni? Apparently not.

The undermining got worse in high school – criticising an outfit, my intelligence, the way I wore my hair. Not allowing friends to the house. He'd tell me I was selfish if I questioned him, remind me of everything he'd done for us and say Mum's anxiety was down to me.

When you live with these things you tell yourself they're normal, until you realise they are far from normal and you haven't been paying attention. He'd been so much worse the last few months, almost as if he knew what was going to happen to his precious safe in advance. And until Sunday night I didn't know the half of it.

But Warren's abuses are bigger, even than that. They've leaked out into the world, or that's where they started. He has mobilised people: the officer yesterday, the man in the four-wheel-drive. A truck driver has been shot.

Warren is a corrupt police officer. Did Mum already know this? He reminded us of his seniority often enough. Did she know about the gold in the safe too? I can't shake the feeling of him, returned from the dead. I want to go back to Aunty and ask her what to do, tell her I've made a mistake and I can't keep running.

But I'm not at Aunty's place, I'm here, and falling apart is no good.

I wipe my eyes and the sweat off my forehead, and I bend and unzip the bag – a ripping sound in the quiet. The zip sticks halfway and I tug it past. Someone bangs into the toilets and I stop.

A sharp body-odour smell. I hold still, one hand on the zip, the back of the other pressed against my teeth. The door next to mine creaks open, creaks shut. A wide gap between the wall and the floor: two man-sized feet in Blundstone boots, red dust deep in the seams.

I shrink against the opposite wall. He's followed me in here from the car park – the man in the black four-wheel-drive. I've wasted minutes, I should have been quicker. The bag is too close to the gap where the boots are. The broken handle is trailing underneath.

There's a rustle of fabric. The feet shuffle. The sound of peeing, like rain into a bucket.

The fear lets go in one breath and I'm weak with relief. I grab the handle and slide the bag towards my feet. The person flushes, the door bangs and the tap goes on and off and she leaves.

The jingly music and air-conditioning descend back.

Okay. Get a grip. Charlie's waiting. I hope she's okay, that she's not panicking or doing something too Charlie. That she keeps her head.

The leather holdall is a dead weight as I lift it back up. It's only ten kilos, the size of a small dog, but it slips and slides on my knees like a bag of hammers. I pull out one of the pieces of gold – so heavy for such a small, flat thing – and there's the embossed logo: *SGC*. Jagged waves below the letters, like teeth.

The GPS tracker is not among the bars of gold or anywhere inside the bag, but stitched into the place where the handle attaches, between the leather and the lining where the handle has now pulled away. It doesn't take much to work it free. A black plastic teardrop shape barely bigger than a SIM card. I drop the bag to the floor, click off the back and there's the SIM.

Transmitting.

And just like that the road ahead opens up. The thought is like a rush of blood – there's no way he can find us without this. If I time it right, I can get it onto a vehicle. A truck, something commercial, on its way south. I remember the sign for the bus station, out through the shopping centre.

Charlie and I can keep going and he can't follow.

I push the tracker into my skirt pocket, heft the bag out of the cubicle and balance it next to the sink to wash my hands. My nail polish is chipped beyond repair, a crescent of red dust underneath each nail, even after scrubbing them. My dyed silk top has darkened with sweat and lost a button low down. I tuck it deeper into my too-short skirt, lift the sunglasses and check the bruise around my eye. I've used the last of the makeup but it's starting to fade now, and Charlie has improved the cut of my yellow hair. I expect a kind of visceral horror at all these things but it doesn't come. I don't look like me, anyway, which is the whole idea.

The new plan forms under the grey washroom light. Dump the tracker. Get to Broome and ask for directions. Find the mine site.

I need to go there. I have to know why Warren has sent people halfway across the state for the gold, why he's had a man killed. Once I know, I can decide what to do with it.

The Christmas music is louder again, exiting the toilets. I turn left towards the bus station.

When we get to Broome I'll put Charlie on her bus to the

Top End and say goodbye. That will be a little harder now – I can't quite imagine it – but it has to be done. It's not as if we're friends. We ended up this way out of necessity, that's all.

No half-million-dollar apartment on the Gold Coast for her and her sister.

They've got each other. She'll get over it.

It's busier at the other end of the mall – evening shoppers, lots of orange and yellow high-vis uniforms – a shift has finished at one of the mine sites. I've got the tracker in my hand and the bag tucked under my arm, the unbroken strap looped over my shoulder. The bus station is opposite the exit: a bus waits in a bay and passengers line up, the driver checking tickets. I'm almost at the doors, passing Harvey Norman, when I see it: the wall of TV screens, like something out of the nineteen fifties.

The grainy CCTV images plastering each make me trip over my feet and stop: a photograph of the green ute; Charlie and I at the roadhouse outside Magnet, me with long hair and Aunty's hat, our eyes down like criminals; an inset image of Daryl.

God, it's so unfair. Neither of us deserves this. But there's no mention of Daryl's dead body on the screen. Not yet.

I tug the hem of my skirt down and start walking again, my heart skipping and my eyes sliding sideways. The news story cuts to the road train – *Truck Driver Shooting* – and footage of us driving away from Millstream in the stolen vehicle. How have the police connected all of this together?

The ute, that's how. They'll have the registration of the stolen four-wheel-drive, out in the car park with Charlie, and she doesn't know. The story changes, the Corruption and Crime Commission investigation: new evidence linking WA Police with organised crime. I duck my head and pick up speed. The mall is a sea of mostly-white faces and the pony-tailed security guard at the doors of Harvey Norman swivels his head.

But I look nothing like I did in those images from the road-house, and his eyes skim down to my feet and then away. I can't work out if my lack of shoes makes me more visible here, or less; it feels different, the further we are from the city.

The air outside is a wash of tropical night, the reflections of sunset fading out of the sky. The bus driver checks the last ticket and the final passenger climbs aboard. The sign in the front window of the bus says PERTH, safely in the opposite direction from where we're going, and the luggage compartment yawns open. I dart across the street and a cyclist swerves and swears. I trip up the kerb and run the last few steps, throw the tracker into the luggage space where it skitters past rucksacks and cases.

'Whatcha want in there?'

I spin around, one hand to my throat.

The driver, his gut straining the buttons of his shirt, grips the compartment door with one hand. 'You lost something?' He frowns at the luggage stacked inside.

'No, thank you.' I shift the bag of gold on my shoulder.

'You got a ticket? You need one?' He's chewing gum, his mouth working. He takes in my feet, my stained clothes and the broken bag.

I shake my head.

His gravelled voice softens. 'Listen, you want to travel – you get a ticket.' As if he thinks I'm trying to hide in the hot dark space under the bus. The shame flames in my cheeks as he slams the compartment and walks away.

He's on the bus with the doors suctioned shut before he swaps around the sign in the window. He reverses loudly from the bay and pulls out, the headlights blinding me, raking the street and the trunks of palm trees, and then gone. Not on its way safely to Perth with the tracker on board, but north to Broome. Exactly where we want to go next.

It's dark by the time I get back to the entrance where I said I'd meet Charlie, and of course she's not there. I've taken too long, but where is she? She can't be gone, not without the gold.

I wait, because that's what you do. I stand in the shadows by an air-conditioning vent, the night filled with food smells and exhaust, the handle of the bag cutting into my shoulder. The car park starts to empty, too dark to make out anything more than headlights and taillights. The doors slide open and closed beside me, knots of shoppers heading to their cars, glancing at me, the girl alone, and quickly away.

The shame in my face settles and stagnates like a bruise. *This top was once a really good top*, I wanted to say to that bus driver. It's worse that he was kind. *You should see the shoes at the bottom of my wardrobe.* Say what you like about Mum, she picks out a good pair of shoes.

Mum even supported the idea of me studying law, at least at first. I wonder now if that support went deeper than I realised. But it wasn't effective, and in the end I bought into the story that Warren's deteriorating behaviour was down to me doing what I wanted. I'm not running to Mum now.

Charlie doesn't come. I don't have money for water. I don't have my bag or my jacket. I don't want to go back into the shopping centre or anywhere near the bus station. I try to squash the fear that Charlie's gone wherever the four-wheel-drive has gone, because there's nothing good about that. She'd never leave the gold behind, not willingly.

I wait far too long, until the place is deserted, and when she still doesn't come I start to walk, my feet scraping with tired and half-healed-up cuts and the rest of me wired up with worry. The stink of diesel and the tang of salt is in my nose once I get out onto the road, curving south before it joins the highway north. Hurrying vehicles, red and white lights. I don't know what the time is but it's late. I try not to think about the *Wolf Creek* movie, Charlie freaking herself out about that. No one stops for the Black girl, walking.

No one walks out here.

Three times I stop and change the bag of gold from one shoulder to the other. A shape at the bottom of it keeps digging into my side. I get thirsty, and the dark presses down. I see a pair of eyes out in the scrub and my breath freezes until the shape turns away. A dingo, maybe, or a big feral cat. Tall highway lights line up with an orange glow, a cloud of huge whirring moths around one of them, until I hear the cries and look again and I see they're not moths at all, but seagulls. And then the road changes and the lines of lights fall away, and there's nothing but the gravel hurting my feet and the occasional vehicle as it passes me by. And stars. The stars up here are like nothing I've ever seen.

The last song on the radio as we drove into Port Hedland starts to play in my head – Kasey Chambers, 'Runaway Train' – and my eyes get hot and I can't see where I'm putting my feet. But I keep walking, and the song fades out, and only then, when I am small and invisible against the dark country, do I run through the worst-case scenarios lined up in my mind.

The police have tracked Charlie down and she's in custody.

She's being questioned about the stolen vehicle, the truck driver, the officer on the highway, what happened back in Perth or all of the above.

She's seen or heard the news and done a runner. But she wouldn't have, not without the gold. She thinks *I've* done a runner. This is worse. I missed her in the dark and she's waiting back there in the empty car park.

Worst of all is the last: that the man sent by Warren has her, and this is my fault. That now the tracker is gone he has no way to trace me or the gold, and she'll end up in the scrub with a bullet in her back.

The red ute passes. I only notice as it stops ahead of me on the shoulder. The red and white lights as it reverses back.

I snap my head up and spin into the scrub. The bag a dead weight, rocks and twigs piercing my feet.

Run. But out here? Which way?

The crunch of tyres. A car door slams like a shot and I trip, twist an ankle and drop the bag. The strap drags on my arm, pulling me around in a circle.

'Can I give you a ride?' A man's voice.

I grab up the bag again, my heart thumping. I put my foot down and it flares with pain.

'Sister? Sorry if I . . .'

I stop and turn back, puffing. A tall Black boy, in the glow of his stoplights. Footballer's shoulders in a West Coast shirt. He's on the balls of his feet, a beanie hat in his hands like he's about to pass the ball. 'I'm real sorry if I scared you. It's . . . But . . .' He glances over his shoulder and back again. 'It's not for walking, out here. There's nothing until Broome, not unless you count Eighty Mile Beach.' A shy smile. 'And I wouldn't.'

I rub a hand over my face. There's a low throb in my ankle and my feet are pricking. A fire's been through here, days or weeks back. I take in the ash and scattered pieces of charcoal, the blackened skeletons of bushes. 'I know.'

He takes a step towards me and stops. A truck passes and the slipstream rifles his thick hair. He's got most of it tied back in a ponytail.

'You did scare me,' I say.

'Yeah, shit. Sorry 'bout that.'

He talks fast, still on the balls of his feet. He's nervous. Has he recognised me from the news? But he'll have water in the ute. I can sit down. 'That's where I'm going,' I say. 'Broome.' The words are out before I can stop them.

He lifts his eyebrows. 'Reckon it'd take the best part of a week to walk it. Don't know that I'd recommend that.'

I hold the bag in front of me like a shield. Pointless. It's not like it'll be any use if he tries something. 'I wasn't going to walk the whole way.' I test out my painful ankle.

'Nah, course you weren't. If you want a lift, but?' I see him catch my expression and he takes a step back. 'I mean, I don't want to ... you could sit in the tray if you want?' He turns to the tray of his ute and makes a face. 'Second thoughts, it's a bit far and she's feral with dust.' He nods at me. 'That all the stuff you got?'

I pull the lumpy bag against me. 'Yes.'

'That'll fit in the cab. I'll stick the dogs in between, in case you ...' He frowns and blinks. 'I hope you like dogs, eh?'

'Dogs?'

'I got two.' A single high-pitched bark from the cab, and a whine. He shrugs and grins.

I step closer, out of the scrub and back onto the edge of the highway. He seems jumpy, his eyes wide. Maybe he has recognised me. It's hard to tell. I can't decide if I'll be better off on the road with him or out here taking my chances alone.

'Broome,' he says again. 'That's where we're going, straight through. Six hours or so. Who needs sleep, eh?'

I take another step towards the ute. What's the worst that can happen that hasn't already happened? He calls the police? Crashes the ute? I'm savaged by his dogs and left for dead?

'That'd be good,' I say. 'Thank you.'

The dogs' names are Gecko and Gus – Gecko is a brown terrier and Gus is a kelpie cross with a scarred muzzle and ripped ear – and the boy's name is Sam. The cab of his run-down red ute smells of dog breath and Minties, and after a lot of sniffing and several attempts by Gecko to get his tongue up my nose – 'Gecko! Leave it. Sorry 'bout that' – the dogs curl around each other on the bench seat between us. Gus keeps one blue eye open, watching me, while I press against the door, stretch my skirt down over my thighs and try not to fidget my throbbing ankle. I've tucked the bag of gold under my feet, the same way Charlie does when she's not driving.

Hip-hop thumps out loud as Sam starts the engine. 'Shit, sorry!' He turns the volume accidentally up instead of down. 'Shit!'

'It's fine,' I say. 'The music's fine.'

He nods and drums the wheel as he pulls onto the highway. 'Briggs. Deadly.' Another quick smile. 'You know Briggs?'

'It's fine,' I say again. The thump of the music is calming, pushing other things out of my head. I watch the unspooling highway and scrub in the headlights as we get up to speed, the occasional flash of a rabbit's eye out in the dark.

Sam's a student teacher going home to Broome for the Christmas holidays. He's wearing the blue beanie although the wind blasting in at the windows is warm. He's still on edge, blinking fast as he hands me a bottle of water – 'It's a fresh one, yeah' – but he doesn't say anything to make me think he's seen me on the news. He offers me the Mintie packet (I take two and try to put one back and almost make him drop the lot) and talks non-stop-fast over the noise of the engine and music and wind, and that's good because I don't have to say anything back. I'm scared if I open my mouth a whole lot of stuff will fall out of it.

The locations of a string of dead blokes, back as far as Perth.

Police, good and bad. Warren. Mum. Aunty.

Charlie.

I don't want that final thought to drop into place but it does, because I'm watching the white lines take us further and further from where I last saw her. I have absolutely no way of finding Charlie. I don't even know her last name. She's somewhere out there in the dark and I don't know a thing about her except how bad she wanted the gold; how bad she needed the money.

A lump in my throat takes me by surprise.

Sam says, 'Who's your mob in the Kimberley? You going back home for Christmas too?'

I shake my head, can't talk. He misinterprets and says, 'Family, eh? Complicated. Flaming nosy. Can't shut me up.' He's quiet for a second, throwing me glances. 'I'm gunna drive right through.'

I swallow past the lump in my throat. 'That's fine.'

'How long since you've been back to country?'

'Sorry?'

'That's where you're going, yeah?'

I stare at him. 'How would you know where I'm going?'

He frowns and looks back at the road. 'I don't, except you said Broome . . . and your face. You've got connections up there, yeah? Family.'

I run fingertips over my cropped hair and down across my cheek. He can tell all that from my face? I can't even tell that. 'I don't know where I'm going,' I say. That sounds insane, and it is. Because what am I doing up here, really? What do I think I'm going to find?

'No worries if you don't want to talk about 'em. I get it.' He nods with the music. 'I'm not normally a motormouth.'

'You're okay. I'm grateful for the ride.'

He looks back at me, his eyes wide. 'I'm a bit . . . I took something. To study for my last exam. Messed up my sleep so it's back to front. I'm a bit wired up.'

My hand tightens on the strap of my seatbelt. 'Are you serious? What, like speed or something?'

'A mate sold it to me. Stupid. Shoulda studied more, not left it last minute.' He smiles but cuts it short when he sees my expression. 'I'm right to drive, honest! Only took it for the exam. Just gotta get there before the crash.'

'The crash?'

'Hell, no! I mean sleep.'

I glance down at the dogs. They don't seem worried. 'Do you do this a lot?'

'Nah. First time. Honest.' He tries a smile again. 'Don't tell my dad, but!'

'I'm not all that likely to meet your dad.'

'Nah, course not. Yeah.' He rubs his face and pushes the Mintie packet at me. 'We can stop at Sandfire, for fuel and a leg stretch and that. She's about halfway.'

I take a Mintie. 'You're not going to, are you?' I say. 'Fall asleep? I can drive if you—'

'Nah. She'll be right.'

He goes quiet and I stare out of my window. It's after eleven p.m. by the clock on the dash and I'm worried now if I don't keep him talking he won't stay awake. The scrub is sparser here, the highway running closer to the coast. The headlights flash up red dirt, more blackened areas from the fire that's been through, and the occasional sign. I ask Sam about his uni course, where he's studying, and then of course he asks me the same. I tell him about Ertan wanting to practice entertainment law, Mel and her native title ideas. It's easier to talk about them than me, and when he asks I say it's early days and I haven't decided. It's half true but I wish I'd made something up, because I'm ashamed Sam sees more in my face than I do, and I don't want to tell him about Dad. That pretty well the only thing I know about Dad is he was planning to go back to school and study law, and I only know because Mum let it slip. And then Warren's in my head saying what did I expect, that it stands to reason I was never going to make anything of it.

I squirm the crumpled photo from Aunty out of my skirt pocket.

'It's here,' I say. 'Where I'm going. This place.' And I reach across and hold out the photo – the Saltwater Gold sign, Aunty and Dad. Sam clicks on the light in the cab and blinks.

'The old mine site? Shit, man!'

'You know it?'

He tilts his head and squints at the photo, long eyelashes against his cheek. 'That your brother and sister?'

Gus has both ears pricked watching me so I ease the photo back and put it in my lap. 'My dad and my aunty.'

Sam glances down at the dog. 'Gus! Pull it back in, mate,' and the dog closes one eye and settles. 'Don't mind him,' Sam says. 'Thinks he's security. Bardi Jawi country, up on the peninsula – that's the old Saltwater mine site in your picture, eh? You got people up there?'

'I don't know,' I say. I think of all the things I could have asked Aunty but didn't. And it's like the wind has gone out of my plan without Charlie, even though it has nothing to do with her. 'I haven't . . . I'm not sure how to get up there.'

'You pretty much head out of town past the pearl farms. She's a shit road but there are signs. Keep going until the road dies on you, 'bout two hours.' If he thinks it's strange I don't know where I'm going he doesn't show it. 'That's a nice waterhole in your picture, outside the old site. You want to be careful, but. Big saltwater crocs up there. No swimming!' He's talking very fast again. 'I could take you . . .' He fidgets and looks at me, glances down at Gus. 'I mean, if you don't have a vehicle.'

'You keep saying, "old". You mean the mine's not still there?'

'Not since the robbery. Corporation shut it down after, went broke. They reckon there's still gold up there, but. In the ground.'

The bag shifts under my feet. A pull like I felt back at Aunty's place. 'Robbery?'

'Yeah, the big gold robbery. A lot of bad feeling. Still unsolved, that is.' He looks at me again. 'A hundred kilos of gold taken and three blokes shot and killed, one of them a detective from the goldfields. They reckoned it was an inside job. You don't know about that?'

A rushing in my ears. I put a hand to the dashboard to steady myself. A detective from the goldfields. That was Warren's department back when he met Mum, when they first got married – the gold detection unit in Kalgoorlie.

That's how he got hold of it, and he shot and killed a colleague to do it. But a hundred kilograms? That's ten times what's in the bag at my feet.

I imagine the weight of it, impossible to carry. The questions line up in my mind as a truck roars past us in the opposite direction, its headlights turning everything to light and then dark before it's gone.

12

Geena

Wide Open Road

The Toyota is still speeding, out on the open highway, when the sun drops low enough to the horizon for Geena to see it through her window. Out to the left and a little behind the car, so they're still headed north.

It's been a brutal drive, hours and bloody hours with one stop for fuel, she doesn't remember where, after he almost bogged the vehicle and gave up on the dirt road they were on early this morning. The cop let her out of the boot last night during the storm, parked across the street from that motel, with the proviso she didn't talk or try to escape or basically do anything at all. Where was she going to run to in weather like that? He probably figured she'd make no more trouble, anyhow, that she'd be scared enough not to, after she listened to him shoot whoever he shot back there on the side of the highway.

And he'd be right about that.

Two shots. Two people in Daryl's ute, according to Lee. Two shots for two separate people, or to make good and sure for one person?

She's spent the day mashed into the back seat not drinking the water or eating the curling sandwich the cop bought her. She's headachy and nauseated and maybe it's cigarette craving or maybe she's getting the flu, but what does it even matter? She's thinking about the shovel in the boot, wondering if she's next for a bullet and why he hasn't done it already. Wondering if she might as well ask to be next because Charlie could be dead and if she is it's Geena's fault.

So no, she hasn't asked him who he killed back there and maybe she doesn't want to know.

They're way past anyplace she's been to before in WA. The Pinnacles on a school trip was probably it. She feels real sad about it, how shitty it is that she and Charlie never made it out of the state, never made it across to Surfers and the Gold Coast after all.

The country has changed and she only notices it now: spinifex grasslands, the hummocks of grass rushing past on either side, dry again after the rain. The landscape is dead flat, like someone has taken a giant set of shears and chopped it back for the sky to sit easier on top of it. The course of the road is perfectly straight and not deviating even for a second, like the cop has drawn it himself with a sharp pencil and a ruler on a map, which is exactly the way she imagines he'd draw something. It seems like every five minutes there's a dead thing at the side of the road or even in the centre of it – sad-looking bits of roadkill – and not a whole lot else. The only traffic they've passed today has been road trains carrying iron ore, but she's likely missed a fair bit.

The sun sinks lower. The ghost of a line of ridges is visible out to the west of them, little more than corrugations on the horizon. They cross a cattle grid and she shifts away from the window, the vibration hurting her face. She twists her necklace in her fingers and watches the back of the cop, his tight shoulders and uneven breath. He's not bled to death yet, worse luck. She reckons he's on his own now – he made one call to his Brunno contact last night that didn't sound like it went too well – and she knows this is probably bad news; the cop's options narrowing down alongside hers.

He hasn't said one word to her the whole day. What kind of an arsehole does that, shoots someone and keeps going like nothing has even happened?

She clocks a big heap of roadkill, dead-centre of the highway, while they're still a fair way out from it. They gain on it fast but the cop doesn't slow. He must have seen it. It's big enough it's going to take some getting around.

It's only when they get close that the heap breaks apart like a heat mirage and she sees it's a crowd of birds, feeding on whatever is dead in the road. The bird bodies and wings float up and flap and pull apart, real slow like it's a Sunday and everyone is out for a drive and lunch and no one's got a worry in the world.

Too slow, and the cop clips one of them – she thinks it's a wedge-tailed eagle, it's that big. He hits it hard with the front top part of the car and the thud shakes her. He keeps his foot down.

Geena flips around in her seat to see it tumble in the slipstream, over and over like it's out of its element, caught underwater and dumped by a wave. It flaps one wing but the other is wrong and busted-up, and the bird gets taken out by a truck going in the opposite direction.

She blinks three times but every trace of it is gone. Dust in the wake of the truck. The cop doesn't bat an eye.

And maybe it's because he doesn't give a shit or maybe it's because she might as well be that bird for all the power she has in the back seat of the Toyota, but it makes her mad. And mad is better. Mad is real good, actually.

'Did you not see that?' she says. 'Couldn't you have slowed down?'

He doesn't answer.

Fuck him and his OCD pens lined up in his jacket pocket, his neat backpack and wiping the top of his water bottle each time he has a drink out of it.

'Why am I even here?' she says. 'You can at least tell me why I'm not dead like the others, can't you? Why shoot them and not me?'

His eyes don't move from where he's watching the road, slowing down now because there's more traffic around them. There are power poles and palm trees, and they're coming into a town as the sun is setting; she hasn't seen the sign so she doesn't know which one.

'I don't see why you can't tell me,' she says. 'You know where that gold is, you're tracking it with your phone or you've got someone doing it for you. That's bloody obvious, mate. Why not shoot me too, after you shot the others?'

His eyelid twitches in the mirror.

Why shoot them at all? she thinks. What's gone wrong? 'Talk to me, can't you! Who died back there?' Her voice breaks on the last part and she can't finish. She bites her lip and stares out of the window. *Was it Charlie?*

He's silent for that long, making the turns, watching his phone and the traffic, that she doesn't think he's going to say. He gives her the stare in the mirror, the you-are-a-piece-of-shit stare like he'd be real happy to stick her back in the boot, and says, 'No one you know.' He turns into a shopping mall car park, full of people with supermarket trolleys and kids and normal lives, and he scans the rows as they drive past parked cars and utes and LandCruisers.

She doesn't know whether to believe him or not about what he's just said. But it can't have been Charlie, she realises – not if he's tracking the gold and he hasn't got it yet. It stands to reason that Charlie, Daryl and the girl are still out on the road.

It stands to reason, too, that the only reason any of them are still alive is because he needs them that way, Geena included. Her hunch yesterday was not as far wrong as she thought; she's his bargaining chip, at least for now. This scares the shit out of her as much as it reassures her, but it's better than nothing.

The cop passes a bunch of empty parking spots, up one row and then the next, checking out the vehicles. He's not parking; he's searching. He's looking for Daryl's ute and they've caught up to them.

Geena scans the vehicles too but can't see the green ute. She doesn't want to see it; she wants them to be gone. The Arsehole is bent over his phone and she watches out of the side windows and the wing mirror – cars and spaces and people.

She doesn't know what makes her look – the flare of

orange-gold light on the windscreen, maybe. But she clocks the girl in the passenger seat of a parked white LandCruiser, one empty parking spot between that and the Toyota as they pass. A pissed-off-looking girl with a heart-shaped face and a gap between her two front teeth. Their eyes meet and the girl blinks and Geena sees the word form on her mouth: *Geen!*

Jesus Christ, it's Charlie, with different hair.

Geena faces front with her heart banging off the insides of her ribs. Not a doubt that it's Charlie. Alive. No one else in the cab with her. Has she stolen that LandCruiser?

The Toyota gets to the end of the row near the shopping mall and turns left past the entrance. Geena watches the white LandCruiser shoot backwards out of its parking spot. A squeal of tyres and it follows them, closing the gap. The cop is still focused on his phone and he hasn't seen Charlie, but why would he recognise her? He doesn't know her. And she's changed her hair since Sunday, cut it short and dyed it brown. She's full-on disguised herself.

Why in hell has she done that? Geena doesn't want to think what else might have happened between back home and here, how anything could be worse than it already is.

The cop turns down the side of the building and Charlie follows, seriously up the Toyota's backside. Geena forces herself not to look. She sits tight and faces front, catching glimpses of the LandCruiser in the wing mirror. There's red dirt halfway up its sides but the top half looks brand new. Where's Daryl's green ute?

The cop circles the building, back to where he started. He snaps on the Toyota's headlights, daylight fading outside the windows. Charlie sticks behind them and flashes the LandCruiser's lights, two, three times. Geena wants to scream at her to back the hell off.

Charlie can't have the gold or the cop would be following her, not the other way around. She needs to stay safe. She needs to back off and turn around. There is literally nothing Geena can do to tell her this, nothing that won't draw his attention to the vehicle behind. The cop turns down the side of the building a second time and heads for the exit. He's sitting straighter, his gloved hands tight on the wheel, and Geena feels the energy crackling off him, his excitement at getting closer to what he wants.

The LandCruiser's horn blasts twice and he snaps his head up: 'Bloody clown.' Geena sits on her hands as he takes the exit onto the street.

They come up to the bus station as the streetlights on both sides of the road flicker on. The cop slows as a bus pulls out in front, a sign for Broome in its front window. Geena checks the wing mirror – Charlie's one car back, a silver sedan in between them.

They drive out of town like this, the cop behind the bus and Charlie behind the sedan, a steady stream of oncoming traffic as the sky grows darker. It's like a back-to-front car chase – the cop straining forwards and Geena wanting to be two cars back next to Charlie, her damn useless phone in the glove compartment. Charlie doesn't try anything, doesn't lean on the horn again. She'll give up, won't she? Or she'll run out of gas?

Geena knows she won't bloody give up.

The Toyota follows the bus onto the highway, traveling north. There's less traffic now, only a few big trucks heading back into town. They pass an airport, arcs of white and orange lights, and over a railway crossing. The sedan behind turns off. The cop keeps steady behind the Broome bus while the LandCruiser's headlights stay a safe distance behind.

Geena holds the left side of her face in her hand – the side that's not hurting – and watches the wing mirror. The LandCruiser pulls closer. *No, Charlie.* She sits forwards. 'You could overtake that bus,' she says to the cop. 'He's not even doing a hundred.'

He grunts and grips the wheel, his hands at ten and two o'clock like a driving instructor. A truck passes in the opposite direction. The cop is sweating, she can see the beads of it on his forehead in the mirror. She checks his dressing for fresh blood but there's none.

The LandCruiser edges closer, the indicator flashing to overtake. 'Clown,' he growls. 'What's he playing at?'

'You should seriously overtake that bus,' Geena says.

'Sit back and be quiet.'

'But you—'

'Sit back!'

The LandCruiser pulls out to overtake. Hell, Charlie's only on her P plates, she's never even been on the freeway. Geena watches out of the side window, her bottom lip caught under her teeth. She can't see Charlie in the cab in the dark. She'll never get between the Toyota and that bus.

A pair of high-beams, oncoming, a kick of fear in Geena's chest. That's a truck, can't Charlie see that? She's going to prang it head on.

She comes level, too close. The truck headlights get brighter. She's not going to judge it right.

'Can't you pull over or slow down?' Geena says. 'Give her space?'

'Be quiet.' They hit something with a soft thud and he swears. A rabbit.

He pushes forwards, the truck headlights filling the windscreen. 'Slow down!' Geena yells.

'Quiet!'

Charlie swerves and drops back, losing speed. Geena spins around and watches her – the headlights receding and sliding over into the left lane as the truck blasts past.

Jeez, Charlie Bear, that was close. Geena watches the indicator blinking orange on the LandCruiser and then the hazard lights. It pulls off the highway and stays there, and she doesn't know what that means except for now Charlie's in one piece.

She turns and sinks back into her seat. The cop doesn't get it, her panic gone over his head. 'The clown grew a brain,' he says. 'Or blew a head gasket. Same difference.'

The Arsehole, that's what she's calling him from now on, stays behind the Broome bus the whole trip and they get into town in the early hours of the morning, close to three a.m. by the clock on the dash. They stopped for fuel somewhere in the dark and pressed on, the cop giving no sign of needing to rest. Geena has slept in snatches and drunk the water and her head's clearer. Maybe not the flu, maybe the nicotine withdrawal letting go of her bit by bit.

Hell of a way to quit smoking. Charlie will be rapt when Geena tells her. She hopes she gets that chance.

They follow the bus the whole way to the bus station, The Arsehole leaning forwards again, his breath quick and shallow, rolling his neck after the long drive. He threads the Toyota along streets lined with palms and boab trees, low corrugated roofs and red hanging lanterns and a sign that says CHINATOWN. The place is up-cycled country town flash with its galleries and outdoor cinema and you can see the money there under the verandas and behind the windows. There's no one on the street, not even one drunk girl or boy weaving back from a big night out. The sky above is pearled with stars.

A set of headlights behind them takes each corner the same as the Toyota. Geena sits up straighter. Charlie. Has she caught up? When did that happen?

The cop parks a half a block back from the bus and watches every passenger off it while sitting rigid in his seat. There are exactly three of them – a skater girl, an old Indigenous guy and a crusty-looking backpacker – and he's not happy. The tension in his jaw is more than just his busted-up ribs. He was expecting someone to get off that bus with a holdall full of gold.

The skater girl gets a ride with a mate in a van, and the backpacker and the Indigenous guy wander off up the street. Geena expects the car behind the Toyota to pull up and give one of them a ride, but it doesn't. The car just sits there, two car spaces behind them with the headlights winked off. It's not a white LandCruiser – the paintwork's dark and it's not the right shape. She watches it in the wing mirror but the interior stays dark and no one gets out of it. The Arsehole hasn't spotted it; he's agitated, checking the screen of his phone. The bus driver disappears into an office and the cop exits the Toyota before realising his mistake and coming back for Geena's phone out of the glove compartment. He leaves a second time and locks her in.

She doesn't give a shit, not now. He can do what he wants,

because Charlie's safe. Charlie's back there on the road and she'll flag someone down and whoever they are, they can't be worse than him.

She watches the cop knock on the window of the bus driver's office and the two of them reappear and open up the luggage compartment of the bus. The driver has a good look in there and obviously doesn't find what the cop's hoping for, because there's a bit of a tense exchange of words. Then the cop shows him what he's got inside the backpack and she can imagine how that part of the conversation goes because the driver gets back in the compartment on his hands and knees and searches it again.

He doesn't find it, and when the cop climbs back into the Toyota, something has changed. He sits a moment before he starts the engine, scratching at the dressing at the side of his neck, and it's the first thing she's seen him do that has no purpose.

He's lost the gold, that's what's changed.

She expects he'll take it out on her but that might come later. For now he's deflated, the burning drive diminished. As he steers the Toyota back through the streets of Chinatown, the headlights behind them wink on and follow. He doesn't even notice.

The cop is going to make a mistake. Like last night on his stakeout across from the motel. He didn't do a good job of that, did he? Geena reckons she noticed more than he did. One car in the car park, no green ute. No sign of anyone at all until the Indigenous girl stepped outside the room for that smoke. She was only in the light for two seconds as she opened the door, talking to someone inside the room. After that she was out there in the shadows for the duration of her cigarette, its red tip floating in circles. But The Arsehole didn't see her, digging around at his feet where he'd dropped his pain meds after the aggro phone call with his mate Brunno.

Geena sat there wishing she was out there with a ciggie too, and hoping it was Charlie inside the room instead of back down the highway with a bullet in her head. She thought the Indigenous girl looked familiar, her stance as she propped herself against the external wall, and she realises now where she's seen her before.

She was doing the exact same thing outside the house in Mount Claremont, the last time Geena and Daryl scoped it out. She's the mystery girl the cop was asking about; it's her house they stole the safe from. And not only that. Geena pictures the café across the street, the tiny car park where Daryl would park the ute, hidden in among peppermint trees and the morning rush.

The sign with coffee beans strung across it like fairy lights, the same image as on the stamp card she found in the cop's jacket.

That's when Geena understands: the cop is connected with the girl. It's his house across the street from that café. It's his safe they stole and his gold he's been chasing the whole time.

It's personal for him. And surely she can use that.

She doesn't know how Charlie and the girl have got mixed up together, but why else was the cop watching the room? Why else give up and move on after the police raided it and no one got dragged out? There's always a chink of light, Geena thinks. He'll let his guard down. He'll get tired or sick or he'll get slack and she'll escape. She'll find her way back to Charlie.

The car behind the Toyota passes under a streetlight. Geena catches a glimmer of midnight blue and a forest of antennas on the roof. It's only a glimpse but her heart gives a squeeze. Seriously?

She keeps quiet, facing forwards. That car is either a plain-clothes cop or it's Lee. The fake antennas on his Commodore he reckons mean he won't get pulled over by the cops.

Has Lee followed them the whole way from the city?

That brings her back to the thing she's been trying hard to avoid all day, which was easy enough with the rollercoaster of hope and fear about Charlie, the stress and guilt and cigarette-withdrawal. If there were two of them in the ute when it drove away from the house on Sunday night, and one of them was the mystery girl, then where the bloody hell is Daryl?

THURSDAY

13

Nao

White Creek

It's after midnight and Sam and I have lapsed into silence but his music keeps up its thumping beat and as far as I can tell he's still wide awake. I need to ask him more about the mine robbery but I don't know where to start. It scares me – three dead men and a hundred kilos of gold, the gold squad connection to Warren. I know in my gut he killed those men. What I don't know is what he did with the other ninety kilos.

My head swivels as the parked four-wheel-drive looms out of the dark and flashes past. 'Did you see that?'

I feel Sam hesitate, the ute slowing. 'Someone changing a tyre.' He frowns into his mirror, slows some more and indicates. I ask him to stop and reverse the whole way back.

The lump is there in my throat but it can't be her. We're an hour outside Port Hedland and I don't know why she'd have come this way. But I can't get my door open quick enough as Sam parks on the gravel shoulder. I trip and land on my crap ankle and I don't even feel it.

I see the cropped hair and pale face and I practically run up to her. 'Jesus, you're alive. And you're not with the police. I was so worried.' I want to hug her but then I'm not sure. It's awkward and the moment's gone, plus she looks quite angry.

'So fucken worried you fucked right off.' She's on the ground by the back tyre with what looks like the entire contents of the four-wheel-drive spread around her, a wheel brace in one hand and grease streaked up her face.

'I got held up. You were gone. I waited over two hours.'

'Yeah? Well shit happened. We gotta get back on the road.' She fits the wheel brace on and screws up her face. 'I can't get the nuts off. Who's he?'

Sam hovers behind me with his beanie in his hands. The two dogs are shadows beside him, the warm wind rippling their coats. 'Um, Sam, this is—'

'Where's the bag, Nao?' She glares past me.

'Oh. Crap. Hold on.' I hobble back and lift it out of the ute, the dogs sniffing around me.

'Fucksakes.' She stashes it by her side when I bring it back. 'I don't believe you.'

'Sam picked me up, Charlie. He really saved my life back there and I'm amazed we passed you, because—'

'There's only the one road.' She swipes sweat and grease across her forehead. 'I need to talk to ya. We gotta get going, orright? Like, right now.'

There's a tension in her voice that scares me. 'What's happened?' I think of the black four-wheel-drive and check both directions along the highway but it's empty. Charlie says nothing and looks pointedly at the bag and then Sam until I get the hint.

Sam doesn't want to leave but I tell him we're fine now, which is not in the least true, and I walk him back to his red ute. 'I'm not too happy with this,' he says. 'I can get that tyre changed, quick as. We can head off together. Safer, eh? At least until Broome.'

'Thanks, but we're really okay.'

'Nao!' Charlie says. 'Don't piss about.'

Sam frowns as he hustles the dogs into the cab and leans in the window to his glovebox. 'Here.' He writes something on a scrap of paper against the roof of the ute and hands it over along with the rest of the Minties. 'My number. In case you ...' He shoves his hands in his pockets and shuffles his feet. 'No signal up on the peninsula. It's good in town, but.'

I haven't asked him any more about the mine but I say thanks and put the paper in my skirt pocket next to the photo, and he frowns again and tugs his beanie back on. I limp back to Charlie as he drives away.

'Just help me.' She puts the wheel brace on and stamps on it. It doesn't budge and her foot slips off and she swears.

'Give it to me.' I pick it up and kneel and fit it back on. 'We could have asked him to help. He's okay. He's—'

'The dude in the black LandCruiser's got Geen.'

I drop the wheel brace and stare at her.

'That's how come I ended up here,' she says. 'I followed them out the car park.'

'Oh, God, are you sure?' I look along the highway again.

'Course I'm sure. She saw me from the back seat. Dude with a black baseball cap and black gloves in the front, driving. She looked shit-scared, too.'

My stomach turns over. 'Black gloves?'

'Yeah, as if he needs them. What for?'

I lean against the car and try to swallow the nausea. 'Like, leather driving gloves?'

'Dunno, maybe. Couldn't see too well. You orright?'

Breathe. 'I'm fine. Just give me a minute.' I wipe the sweat off my face.

'You don't look orright.'

'I'm fine, I told you.' *Don't think.* I straighten up and fit the wheel brace, lean hard on one end until it hurts my hand and I feel the nut loosen. I do the next one. 'Where's the jack? We need to get this tyre changed.'

'I know we do.'

'Start putting some of that stuff back in the car.'

The only person I've ever seen wear a pair of leather driving gloves is Warren. He has them custom made so he can still use the touch screen of his GPS. Warren is the man in the black four-wheel-drive. He's back from the dead like I thought and he's taken Charlie's sister.

I can't tell her this.

It gets light a little before five a.m. – there's a soft line out ahead of us, a purpling of the scrub. I check the rearview mirror: black empty space. I've got the air-conditioning turned off and my window open to catch the wind and keep me awake. My teeth ache from the night's hard driving, the space behind my eyes too, hours and hours with one stop for petrol at the place Sam mentioned last night.

There's a sense here of having crossed a border into a different kind of country. There are small trees and thick tufts of grass, everything greener and the dirt growing deeper red as the sky lightens. Pindan. I don't know where the word comes from but I know it's right.

The section of highway I drove with Sam could almost have been a dream, except for the note with his phone number in my pocket and the Mintie wrappers scattered in Charlie's lap. I glance over at her, curled in the passenger seat, asleep, as the light changes on her face. Her feet are on top of the bag where they've spent so much of the last few days. She looks like she did on Sunday night, driving back from the lake, apart from how dirty her clothes are – everything rouged with dust – plus the colour in her arms from the sun, the extra freckles on her nose. Her knuckles have healed, they're not cut and swollen anymore. She looks peaceful and I don't want to wake her.

I haven't told her about Warren. All night I've wanted to turn the vehicle around, head south or inland, anywhere but follow him, but my feet and my hands have kept us pointing north. There's no choice now, we have to get Charlie's sister back. And I don't want her to see how afraid of him I am.

We pass a dirt track on the left and grind across a cattle grid. Her eyes spring open. 'Geen?'

'Not yet,' I say. 'We'll find her.'

Charlie blinks and checks the mirrors. There's a snail trail of drool at the side of her mouth and she rubs at it with the back of her hand. 'Where are we? We caught up to him?'

'The top end of Eighty Mile Beach.'

The exhaustion hits like a slow crash into a brick wall and I realise I've been fighting it for at least the last hour. I slow and turn off at the next track, the tyres sliding and then gripping as we come off the sealed road onto the dirt.

She sits up. 'This where he went?'

'No. There's been no sign of him.' I focus my eyes on the track. 'We're not going to catch him up, Charlie. We're still an hour outside Broome and we need to sleep.'

She goes for her seatbelt. 'I'll drive, you sleep. We gotta keep going.'

'No, listen.' I yawn and put a hand on her arm, her skin hot. 'Let's both sleep, just for a couple of hours. I won't be able to think straight until I've slept, and we need to make a plan. Work out where to meet them so we don't run into the police.'

She sinks back into her seat.

'He's going to follow the bus and end up in Broome,' I say. 'That's where it stops.'

'What if he gets aggro when the gold's not on the bus? What if he does something to her?' She scratches the back of her hand. 'Can't you call your stepdad? Tell him we've got it?'

Her words drop my stomach like a dip in the road. 'His number was in my phone,' I say. 'I don't have it.'

'Your mum, then. You know her number, yeah? Get her to call him.'

'What, and tell Mum the whole story? She'll call the police.' And what if Mum already knows the story? The gold in the safe, the things Warren has done and where his money has come from. Money for school and clothes and holidays Mum's job could never have stretched to. Why have I never questioned these things?

The track ahead narrows, the thick scrub pressing in from either side. 'He's got no reason to hurt her,' I say. 'He just wants the gold back.' I don't know if I believe this.

We emerge onto a rocky shore as the sun rises – a creek mouth and tangle of mangroves to the right, red-winged parrots skimming the tops of the trees. The smell of ozone and mud, and a silvery channel of water snaking away across white sand.

Charlie sniffs. 'I hate the beach.'

I blink at her. 'And you want to go and live on the Gold Coast?'

'That's different,' she says. 'It's got money. It's not a shithole.'

I park the vehicle on a platform of rock screened by mangroves, room for one car and a view back up the track.

Charlie turns in her seat. 'We're gunna give it back to him, yeah? Swap the gold for Geen?'

'Of course.'

'No bullshitting, remember? We can't fuck it up.' She blinks in the early light. 'You're not gunna change your mind, try and get that reward money?'

Her eyes are wide and desperate and I so nearly tell her about Warren. I'm this close to telling her. But what is the point in scaring her? How is it going to help?

'There's no reward money,' I say. 'It was never about that. We arrange to meet the bloke and we give him what he wants.'

I jolt awake to the sound of surf and the cry of a bird. Another dream about dark water and a hovering fear that solidifies as I remember where I am: Eighty Mile Beach. Warren and Charlie's sister. The sun is baking the canvas of the swag and my watch says four p.m. Shit – ten hours sleep – we've way overslept. But he'll have to sleep, too, won't he? I unzip the swag, screw my eyes tight against the light and the flies, and grope for my sunglasses.

Charlie's flaked out on the back seat when I get to the vehicle, the little bush flies walking up and down her bare arms and legs. I go to wake her but stop. A few more minutes to get my head straight. She murmurs and I hear her move in her sleep, the creak of her skin against the leather seat. She's got one of the rucksacks down off the roof-rack, a lime-green one, with the top of it open and pieces of clothing strewn across the front seats.

There's a sarong at the top of the rucksack and I wrap it around my face against the flies. I wear Aunty's hat, push my feet into Charlie's thongs and brave the burning sand to the water. My ankle is a dull ache in the deep sand but better than it was. The beach is dead straight as far as I can see in both directions, the tideline littered with shells. The light off the water is piercing and I can feel my skin burning. Another rule broken; Warren impressing on me, as far back as I remember, to cover up and keep out of the sun.

They were confusing, Warren's rules. Different ones for me than for Mum. That particular rule – to keep out of the sun and keep my skin pale, as futile as that was – was yet another way not to acknowledge Dad. I tried to do it, too; I tried to fit in.

I step out of Charlie's thongs and let the water wash across my feet. I shiver when it does, cold against the breathless heat of everything, but my feet are better than they were and I like the feel of them in the sand. Saltwater country. I look north, towards Broome and beyond. I'd like to think there's something there for me, that in some way at least I'm getting nearer to Dad, but all I can sense is Warren there, waiting. I peel the dressing from my hand and clean the cut in the salt water. There are no box jellyfish in the shallows, or are there? I watch for them but all I see is my own shadow.

The light here pushes everything out to the periphery – thinking, remembering, even the feel of Warren's fingers twisted in my hair. I don't have to feel anything like that again. Warren gets the gold he stole and Charlie gets her sister back. A simple trade and the only option we have.

But when I try to imagine what's on the other side of it, of giving Warren back the gold, there's nothing except a blank empty space that feels worse than running. I'm afraid that swapping the gold for Geena won't be enough for him. That she and Charlie will be punished, because of me.

'Nao?' Charlie's voice is thin across the sand. I don't turn right away but she calls again, louder the second time.

She's perched on the edge of the back seat with the door open when I get back to her, her bare legs dangling and a pair of too-big designer sunglasses on her face. 'How come ya didn't wake me?'

'I overslept. Sorry.'

'Thought you'd nicked my thongs.'

I slide my feet out and hand them up to her. 'Where did you get the sunglasses?'

She nods at the rucksack, takes the thongs and whacks at the flies. I notice how bony she is, her sharp elbows and collarbones. And I can't tell now whether the marks on her neck are bruises or dirt.

'Know what I reckon?' she says. 'Let's wait for it to get dark.'

I look at her, surprised.

'Be cops in town, won't there, plus we're probably still on the news. No good for Geen if we get caught, is it? It's only a couple more hours.'

'Okay,' I say. 'Let's eat something and drive in after sunset. It'll be harder for anyone to ID the vehicle. You can find an internet place and get your Facebook message to her.'

We sit on the bonnet and eat cheese and bread from the car fridge as the sun tracks lower and the waves turn to gold. Charlie smears herself with insect repellent out of the rucksack while I smoke the other half of the cigarette she gave me; I'm scared she'll see my nerves if I don't keep myself calm. I go down to the water to wash my hands and when I get back, she's got that keyring out of her pocket, the one of her sister's. A sun-gold photograph in a plastic square. She starts to talk, still perched on the bonnet behind those sunglasses that are too big for her face.

'Know what's different about the east coast? Sun comes up over the ocean instead of going down.'

The image in her hand is the Surfers Paradise sign with the sun behind it. 'Yes. I know.'

She stares past my shoulder at the water. 'Geen and me need to get someplace new, someplace decent where the bullshit won't follow. That's how come Surfers. 'Cause my mum lived there when she was a kid, used to tell us stories about it. Plus ... my dad's in Casuarina Prison.'

'Oh. Okay.'

She swipes at a fly. 'Ya don't have to say nothing. Probably better if ya don't.'

'Okay.'

She sniffs. 'Mum and Dad was always fighting when Geen and me were little kids. We never had no money after Dad lost his job and anyhow he mostly gambled it down the TAB. No big deal except Mum ended up dead four years back and Dad's in jail for it.'

For a second, I hover between moving towards her and not doing it, worried it'll mess things up with her, and then the moment is gone. 'I'm sorry. I didn't know that.'

'Course ya didn't, how would ya? He cracked Mum's head on the brown bathroom tiles. I don't even reckon he meant to. And I was scared Geen'd go the same way, 'cause of Daryl. That's why Geen and me are ...' She swallows and swipes at her face, knocking the sunglasses sideways so I see the fiery sun in her eyes before she straightens them up. 'The landlord's gunna chuck us out so he can bulldoze our shitbox house and build a better one. So who cares if some fucker burned it down? Anyhow, now ya know.'

It makes sense of her, this, like an image coming into focus. The image is of Charlie curled around the bag of gold, asleep on her bed in the motel room. I've been such a snob, haven't I? Because we're not as different as I thought. And we're not out of this yet.

It's not like I can stop Charlie from coming to meet him; she'll never agree to that. I'll have to think of something else.

The sun sets and the mosquitos descend as we pile the food and camping gear back into the four-wheel-drive. I smear the registration plates with mud and wash my hands in the creek, and Charlie reverses the vehicle, turns it five points of a star and nudges it onto the track.

It's dark with no traffic in either direction when Charlie turns onto the highway towards Broome. The wheels thrum on the sealed surface, a smooth sound that's already less familiar than the dirt.

The gold in the bag feels different under me – the same pull through my feet as at Aunty's place – and I don't know what that means. I wish we had the rest of it to bargain with, the other ninety kilos, but he'll have offloaded it years ago. It's probably all over Australia by now.

'Charlie?' I watch her pale profile as she drives. 'I need to tell you something. It's not going to change the plan, okay?'

She frowns. 'Good, 'cause we gotta stick to it.'

'I know we do. It's . . . I know where Warren stole the gold from. Sam told me the story, last night. Plus, there's a load more of it.'

'What?'

'There's more gold. A hundred kilos was taken. We've only got ten.'

She grips the wheel. 'That a joke?'

'No.' I tell her what Sam told me, the dead men and the con-nection with Warren, the crime unsolved. She glances at me and nods, a startled animal look, but she doesn't ask me anything else so I don't have to lie.

'When you message your sister, tell her we'll meet them out of town, on the road to the pearl farms. We can meet at the turnoff to one of them, make it the second one. There'll be signs but I can give you directions.'

'How come there?'

'It's remote. No police.'

'Everywhere's fucken remote. What if the dude says no?'

'I don't think he will. He'll want to get it done.'

She turns her head from the windscreen, her eyes wide in the dark. 'What we gunna do if it goes wrong?'

'What do you mean?'

'Are we gunna have to kill the dude?'

'God, no. Of course not. Why would you say that?' She doesn't know what she's saying.

She looks back at the road. ''Cause I'm like Dad, aren't I? I'm gunna end up like him.'

'No, you're not. Don't think like that.'

'Yeah, I am. Daryl, that cop on the highway, all the shit that's happened? My fault, 'cause I got aggro, you said it yourself. I'm the exact same as Dad and there's fuck-all I can do about it.' She sniffs. 'If it kicks off and goes wrong with Geen I'll probably kill the dude. I'm just saying.'

'No, Charlie. We only need to keep our heads. It'll be fine.'

And maybe it will be. Maybe I'm imagining the worst. But I look away, out at the rushing landscape, and I feel that yawning hole again, on the other side of everything. There must be a way to keep her out of it.

She says, 'Anyhow, you're not a whole lot better. You stabbed your own stepdad.' And then she swerves and brakes and my head snaps forwards, frozen for a second before we're fishtailing across the highway.

'Go with it!' I say. 'Turn into the skid.'

'Can't, I'm gunna hit it!'

'Hit what? There's nothing there—'

We meet the gravel on the other side, bouncing and grating and the headlights drawing a circle – half a white-painted truck tyre, a sign on a gate, the pale trunk of a gum – before she gets some traction under her wheels and we slide to a stop. Dust rises in the flare of the headlights, and beyond it the bright white of the tree. We're both catching our breath as Charlie stares at the empty road. 'Didn't ya see it?' she says. 'Giant cow, middle of the highway.'

Something brushes my memory. 'I didn't see anything. Give me a minute, will you?' I clunk the heavy door open and climb out, my ankle throbbing dully after the skid. The air is warm – the smell of melted bitumen, the heat of the day coming up into my feet – but my back between my shoulder blades is cold. It's that sense of being watched I associate with Warren, but there's no one here apart from Charlie and me, the whirring of insect wings out in the dark, and the stars in a milky-way spread overhead.

There's nothing on the highway in either direction. I don't know what it was Charlie saw.

I detour to the tree on my way back to her – an old spreading snappy gum set back between the highway and a metal five-bar gate. The bark is pitted like bad skin, I see in the headlights as I get close. I glance back at Charlie, the cab dark above the lights and the engine idling.

The tree has a scar at about the level of my shin, a wide bite from the white trunk like someone's taken an axe to it and given up. The word *scar tree* comes to mind, but I know it's not that. I bend and put a hand to the wood above the scar – warm and vibrating. I see the paint and bend closer. Flakes of sky blue. That same feeling returns between my shoulder blades. I twist my neck but there's nothing there. I let go of the tree but my fingertips prickle where they touched it.

Charlie rolls a window down. 'Gunna be much longer?'

'No. Just wait.'

It's nothing. A collision. Someone ran into this tree.

But I'm remembering Aunty, her eyes digging into mine – *Accident, is that what you call it?* – and at the same time Mum, explaining to me at six years old that Dad has died. I don't know why I feel so sick. I already know all this.

There's a scratching sound above my head and I look up to see a black cockatoo, only its beak and its eye visible against the dark. It looks back at me, not moving, like it's waiting for something.

There's that brushing of memory again, softer than a feather. Thoughts, landing. The feeling of safety, just out of reach. Saltwater country. Pindan. How I knew about the roads through Millstream flooding. These things come from Dad, although I don't have the memories that go with them.

Listen to your liyan, Nomi. Pay attention to it. I still don't know what Aunty meant by that.

Charlie revs the engine. The tyres crunch the dirt. There's more, itching at the back of my mind, and I'm annoyed she's hurrying me. Until she switches the lights onto high beam and they pick out the sign on the gate: WHITE CREEK STATION.

And I remember it: our crumpled blue bonnet against the tree. The airbags and the taste of dust, specks of it floating in the air like gold. Mum in the driver's seat, asking if I'm okay, angry at the other car we've swerved to avoid. I see the steer in the middle of the highway, its wet black nose in the seconds before impact. The dark-coloured station wagon on the wrong side of the road.

I turn and throw up into the dirt, sour milky vomit from the meal we had at the beach. My blood pushes too hard like there's not enough space for it, like it's looking for a way out. I tilt my head up. I can't see the black cockatoo. Why can't I see it? It's not there.

I walk back to Charlie, wipe my mouth and get in the car.

'You orright?' she says.

'I'm fine. Just go.'

I'm not fine.

Dad wasn't in the car with us. He didn't die in the accident.

14

Geena

Lucky Star

Geena wakes up on her hard single bed in the motel in Broome and clocks right away that The Arsehole is not in the room. She sits up and slips off the bed, light showing around the edges of the curtains. She tried so hard to stay awake. She doesn't know how long she's slept for.

The air-conditioning unit is making a racket with the same barbecued chicken smell as last night coming out of it. The bathroom door is open and all his stuff has gone from the other side of the room – the backpack, the suit jacket, the cop holster. Holy hell, is it over?

She crosses to the door on tiptoe, her mouth dry, and presses the handle.

And it doesn't open. She rattles it, pulls on it, thumps the door with the heels of her hands. 'Hey, can anyone hear me out there?' There'll be housekeeping, someone in the next room. 'Hey, I'm locked in here! Let me out. Someone? Please. I'm in here against my—'

A key scrapes in the lock. She steps back as it swings open, and it's him.

'Be quiet.' He opens his jacket to show her the gun in the holster and there's a waft of his cop BO. His hair is dark with grease and dirt and he's sweating, his face greyer even than yesterday and the salted-caramel stubble creeping down his neck.

She wobbles backwards until the backs of her knees hit the end of the bed, crawls back over it as far as she can go and stays there, small against the wall and the faded red bedspread.

He locks the door and pockets the key, an old-fashioned one with a black plastic tag. His chest looks the wrong shape, the right shoulder tensed up on the side where the wound dressing is. There's blood on the dressing but it's old and brown. His breath is fast and shallow. Is it worse? 'No need to look like that.' He grimaces as he unzips his backpack and drops a sad looking sandwich and a bottle of water onto the end of her bed.

He's playing nice but she doesn't trust it. She's been expecting repercussions since they checked in here. Ever since he lost his gold she's been waiting for aggravation, for the crack of his gun in her face again. All he did last night was alternately pace or sit upright on a wooden chair in his half of the room, with the gun in his left hand and his injured right arm at his side, but she knows what else is in that backpack.

The motel is on a Chinatown back street and has seen better

days. Either The Arsehole is strapped for cash or he's keeping a low profile, and she thinks it's the latter. She didn't miss the look he threw at the cop shop on their drive into town last night, or the way he detoured to avoid it.

She sucks down some of the water but doesn't touch the sandwich. She needs a cigarette.

He takes his jacket off, the muscles in his jaw gripped as he hides the pain, and folds it over the back of the upright chair. The gun and the cop holster stay strapped on over the top of his shirt and he comes back across to the foot of her bed. There's a phone in his left hand and it takes Geena a second to see it's hers. She notices the missed calls on the screen and her heart gives a kick. Charlie. Where is she now? She glances at the curtained window.

He leans down and places the phone on the end of her bed next to the uneaten sandwich. Is he giving it to her? Is he letting her go? She stares at it like it's a trap.

'I need you to contact your sister,' he says.

Shit. Did she tell him Charlie was her sister? No, but he's figured it out, or got one of his cop mates to find it out for him.

Still, what harm can it do? Charlie's back there on the side of the highway. She's out of the picture. She's dumped her phone or she's lost it along the road, otherwise why's she been calling Geena since Monday from random private numbers?

She reaches and grabs up the phone and scoots back to her spot against the wall.

He gets her to listen to the voicemails on speaker. Charlie's not left any since Tuesday and there's nothing useful in them, just different payphone numbers she asks Geena to call back. She sounds upset, sure, it's not an easy listen, but she's safe, that's what Geena tells herself. She's dumped her phone someplace, like Geena thought.

He makes a note of the payphone numbers and Geena calls them but each one of them rings out. 'Dial her number,' he says.

'She never picks up. Not even when—'

'Make the call.' That tic in his eyelid.

Her eyes dart to the backpack. 'Sorry.' It comes out hoarse. He's worse like this, quiet. She knows how fast he can change.

She dials Charlie's number and listens. 'Straight to voicemail. You want to hear it?' She tries to smile but her face won't do it. The phone shakes in her hand as she holds it out.

He gets Geena to leave Charlie a message, word for word, and she does it. She can't flirt, she's well past that, and she doesn't know what else she's got. She repeats what he says: he wants his property returned to him. Time is running out. Charlie needs to call back because lives are at stake, presently and predominantly, Geena's. He enjoys watching her say this last part, she thinks – the ghost of a lop-sided smile.

He retreats to his side of the room with Geena's phone after that and sits upright on the chair. The day glows gold through the closed curtains and she watches him from her bed. He surfs channels on the TV, the small flat screen angled away so she can't see it, charges up all three of the mobile phones including hers, but Charlie doesn't call back.

She's not going to call back. She's back there on the road. She won't get the message. She's hundreds of kilometres away from *him* and Geena needs to keep it that way.

A tap drips in the bathroom and three times the cop goes in there to try and sort it but he can't. She watches his growing aggravation at the constant *drip, drip*, how he flinches and blinks at the bathroom light when he first switches it on, and the next two times leaves the room dark.

He's in pain and sleep deprived, isn't he? He's been awake the whole time.

Watching his patience tick down is like watching a piece of rope, stretched and fraying. Sure, he's pale and sweaty and his breathing's not right and he hasn't slept, but he might not die of any of these things. She knows what will happen first; his patience is going to snap. What happens when Charlie doesn't call back?

Geena watches the gun in the holster, how it shifts with each shallow breath. How every few hours he punches two tablets out of a blister pack and dry swallows them. She thinks of the shovel in the boot. He won't shoot her in a motel room. He's not the type to make a mess. He'll wait, he'll take her out bush.

The key is still in his suit jacket, folded over the chair. Geena's phone is on the desk beside the TV.

She needs to get a hold of both of them and get out.

The light has faded outside the windows and The Arsehole is pacing again, the TV flickering in the corner with the sound muted down. He's taken his holster off, looped it over the back of the chair his jacket is on, but he's still wearing the gloves. He holds the handgun in his left hand as he paces, flexing the fingers of his right like he's trying to make a fist but can't do it. Every now and then he glares at the arm, bends it at the elbow and straightens it again. Geena tries to remember the things the old vet guy said, but can't.

It makes her nervous, his pacing. He doesn't appear to be tiring and she hasn't got a plan yet, not apart from knowing where the room key is. She's got the Alex Lloyd tune 'Lucky

Star' in her head, another one from Mum's playlist that feels like it sums up the shitshow of her and Charlie's lives right now, hanging in the balance. She's slept again, couldn't help herself, and dreamed about Charlie and Dad. One of those times Charlie was fighting at primary school and Dad caused a scene in the principal's office. It was always those two against the world. Charlie still hasn't called back.

Geena watches the cop a little longer and asks if she can use the bathroom and have a shower, and he surprises her with a yes.

He checks it out first, then takes the barrel of his gun and smashes the tiny useless bolt off the inside of the door, at which point her shower looks a lot less attractive. Still, maybe letting her get clean means he's not going to kill her today.

She gets into the bathroom and pushes the door closed with a rolled-up towel against the bottom of it. And she turns on the shower and goes up on tiptoe at the narrow flyscreened window. The view is of the quiet street and wheely bins and the Toyota in the small back car park, and a tiny sound comes out of her when she sees the midnight blue Commodore parked across the street.

The Commodore is Lee's, and the skin over her painful cheekbone tingles. Beautiful Lee has come to rescue her. He's not doing a whole lot of rescuing right now, it has to be said; he's listening to tunes inside his car. He's got the windows closed and his head is going up and down in the lemon-sherbet glow of the interior light. He'd better be paying attention. He's parked in front of a red door with a palm tree next to it. The sky above the palm tree is black and she can count three stars, one larger than the other two and glimmering.

*

Geena keeps her sundress and coral necklace on and washes everything under the shower. She's not getting undressed with The Arsehole the other side of the door. She comes out of there with her hair dripping down her back and does her best to act all soft and quiet and grateful, like he's done her this massive favour. Which he has, because now she knows Lee is out there.

The cop picked this room because it's closest to the street and his car, but that goes both ways. The covered walkway outside leads straight out the back from the motel door. His jacket is still on the chair, with the holster hanging down on one side.

He's intent on the TV screen, doing that thing with his fingers again. Geena studies the holster on the chair, trying to remember how it sits on his body, looped over his shoulder with the gun under his arm. Which arm, though? She's never been good with her left and right.

The holster is for a right-handed person, but he's holding the gun in his left. She's missed it, this whole time. He might not even be able to shoot with it. At the very least there's a better chance he'll miss.

She considers straight-up making a break for it, making what she can of the element of surprise, grabbing the key and running. She's trying to figure out how to improve on that when he goes to the bathroom. She doesn't even have to do anything.

He takes the gun in there and leaves the door wide open. He lifts the seat of the toilet.

'Hey, mate,' she says. 'I really don't need to see that, okay? You've got the gun. You've locked me in. I'm not gonna do anything.'

For a half a second there's this little boy vulnerability in his face that vanishes as quick as it came. He pushes the door closed until there's a foot-wide crack.

Which is likely the best chance she's going to get.

She flies to the desk, snatches up her phone with one hand and the key out of his pocket with the other. Back to the door with the key. He's still pissing. Her hands are shaking. She threads the key in and it rattles.

One turn and the door doesn't open. He's stopped pissing. She turns the key another turn. She presses down the handle.

And he hears her. He rips the bathroom door open and crashes against the doorframe. She pulls the room door open. His gun arm comes up.

His fingers brush her shoulder, hook the strap of her dress. She twists through the door, stomps it backwards with her bare foot. Her dress rips and she hears the door connect and crunch and bounce back. A snarl of pain. The kick reverbs through her leg as she takes off sprinting.

Out in the walkway. She skids left, nerves ringing. Her feet slap on warm brick and hot road. She bangs between the Toyota and the next car, cracking her elbow on a wing mirror. His footsteps sound behind her, hard and fast. Whistling breath. She knows he's got the gun up, doesn't know when he'll shoot.

Lee's Commodore is just across the street: the lemon-sherbet light and his music, thumping.

She gets both hands on the bonnet before The Arsehole grabs her. Her broken nails catch and scrape as he drags her backwards, and she kicks out hard and yells out Lee's name into the dark.

But Lee doesn't hear her. His head is back against the head-rest. Lee's fallen asleep.

*

The cop drags Geena back across the street with a choke arm around her neck crushing her windpipe. His arm is like steel rope and her nails do nothing. She can't twist her head to take a bite at him. He's got the gun jabbed into her throat with his left hand as if both arms were fully functional all along or all she's done is help him overcome the pain. She's warm and wet down the back of her dress and she doesn't know if it's water from the shower or it's blood, because she's pretty sure she broke his nose back there with that door.

She kicks and kicks and yells out Lee's name but it comes out a painful squeak. Lee lifts his head and swivels it around like he's caught the vibe, but he doesn't hear. The music in the car's too loud. You don't listen to loud tunes on a stakeout, bro. Even Geena knows that.

And then they're under the dark of the walkway, it's too late and she's stopped kicking. She thinks he might kill her now.

He drags her back through the door and drops her hard on the floor before her bed. She lands on her tailbone and lifts a hand to her throat, gasping. There's a tiny hope she was wrong about Lee, that he saw them, and any second now he's coming through the door with the cops. But The Arsehole is the cops, and he's bent over with the gun still in his hand and blood streaming off his face. He puts the back of the same hand to his upper lip, pulls it away and glowers at the blood there. Breathing deeper than he was, as if he's overcome that too.

'You. Are. Disposable. Have you not understood that?' Flecks of spit at the corners of his mouth and a muscle spasming at the angle of his jaw. 'A waste of conscious thought. As is your sister. And when I find her, because I *will* . . .' He flicks his blood off his hand like it disgusts him as much as she does. 'I will shoot her in the back of the head and then I will shoot you. And no one will come looking for you because no one will care.' The blood dripping from his chin makes a *tap, tap* as it falls to the carpet. 'You see what you make me do now? Look at this mess.'

The gun arm comes up and he cracks it across her cheek in the same spot, and this time she hears the bone break.

He leaves her on the bathroom floor, seeing stars and shivering, sucking down air. Her face hurts like fire and she feels her right eye swelling shut.

He was always left-handed, Geena. It's the right side of her face he's hit her across, the same as last time and the opposite from what she always got from Daryl. She's never been good with her left and right.

She should've gone in harder, run faster. She's let Charlie down. She's let Lee down. She's made things a hundred times worse.

She cries, of course she fucking cries. She's not a machine.

Sometime later, he opens the bathroom door and starts talking at her. She flinches and tries to crawl away but apparently he's not come to hit her again. He's got Geena's phone in his hand with the screen lit up, and he stands over her and holds it close until she sees the message on it and who it's from. And then he tells her what they're going to do next.

15

Charlie

The Pearl

We rock up to the caravan park in Broome just after eight at night. It's a rundown house on a red dirt block and the sign says THE PEARL: ROOMS, CHALETS, CAMPING, AIR-CONDITIONED. There's a tree in the front yard same as the ones all through town, a fat swollen trunk that looks like an old African woman with branches for hair.

Around the back is a beat-up white Merc and a full-on jungle of garden. I park and switch off the engine and Nao doesn't wake up. The heat and humidity's feral when I get out.

The Chinese kid in reception lets me pay cash for one night in a family chalet and doesn't ask for ID. He gives me a Wi-Fi password for the room and tells me there's a backpacker hostel near the cinema that's got computers. The LandCruiser's caked in red dirt halfway up the sides when I go back out. I don't reckon Nao needed to put that mud on the number plates. She's awake, stood outside the passenger door. 'What is this place?'

'Yeah, it's a shithole. Come on.' I take the holdall and the girl's studded handbag with her wallet and the rest of our cash in, and we head down the back through the garden.

The family chalet is a hut with a tin roof and veranda, two bedrooms and a kitchen. I take the bunk room and leave Nao the double, and I stick the bag of gold under the doona on the top bunk. The aircon sounds like a chainsaw when I stick it on but at least it works.

'I'm gunna go out to the internet place,' I say to Nao. 'Get that message to Geen.'

She's sat on the dirty cream couch, weird and quiet, like she's been the whole time since I spun us out in the car.

'You said you'd give us directions,' I say. 'To the place we gotta meet him. One of the pearl farms, you said.'

She blinks, gets a crinkled bit of paper out her pocket. I give her a pen out the girl's handbag and she writes on it and hands it over.

'There's a fair bit left of that cash. Want me to get us some dinner?' She shakes her head and nods like she's not even listening, like she's covering all her options in one go. Dunno what's going on – I'm the one should be freaking, not her. I get a glass of water out the tap, empty the glass out twice and wait for the water to run cool except it doesn't. I fill it and take it up to her. 'You orright?' I say.

'What?'

'You don't look orright. Drink this. It's feral hot here.'

She doesn't argue, does what I say and hands the empty glass back.

'You get whiplash or something, back there in the car?'

She says no, rubs both hands down her face and stares at me. She looks like she's gunna tell me something, and then she says, 'Thanks for being a friend, Charlie.'

That freaks me, my heart does this weird forward roll. 'No worries. Look, I'm gunna go.' I take the glass and rinse it out, and I grab the blingy handbag off the couch. 'The gold's in the bunk room. Top bunk.' Dunno what to do about the gun at the bottom of it. Not gunna look, is she?

She nods, hasn't moved. 'I'll guard it with my life.'

I get a bit lost in the garden outside the chalet, dunno what direction and I walk the wrong way. I turn a corner, come out between some ferns and fuck me:

The moon rising – blinding, fat on the horizon – dark blue sky, dark blue water. Like a fucken painting. Silver stripes under the moon like steps.

I go and get Nao. 'Not being funny, but you gotta see this.' I hope Geen's seen it too if she's here.

Nao comes out and stands next to me. 'The stairway to the moon,' she says.

'Yeah?'

It doesn't cheer her up, but. She stares at the water some more and goes back inside. I hope she's not getting sick.

I take the Landie and drive into town, past more fat trees and a sign to the cinema. There's people everywhere, coming outta pubs and caffs and late-opening shops. I get worried maybe I shoulda left the LandCruiser back at The Pearl, but it's Thursday night and it's dark so I keep on going. I don't see any cop cars.

The backpacker place is right where the kid said it'd be. I drive past it and park on a narrow side street, off the main drag where there's no streetlights. The backpackers is too bright – busy as – smells of perfume and suntan lotion. Japanese tourists, kids wearing bikini tops and boardies and Hawaiian shirts. They're missing the best thing, but, aren't they? The moon thing. A girl with a pommy accent wrinkles her nose at me and takes my five bucks for fifteen minutes of computer time. She shows me where they are – two screens in a cubbyhole off reception, no one else there.

I slide onto the wooden seat, half-on half-off it. Shoulda had a shower and washed my stuff, that's why the girl looked down her nose at me. Still took my money, but.

A shitload of noisy people come and go while I log onto Facebook. No TV screens in the place, so no me and Nao on the news, far as I can see. Everyone in a party mood and no one looking my way.

Geen hasn't updated her Facebook or Insta since last Friday lunchtime. I know she's in the dude's LandCruiser, but last Friday? Geen lives on those places. She's on there like fifty times a day updating stuff and posting pointless bullshit, even while she's at work. Why stop Friday?

And if she doesn't log back on, she's not gunna get my message.

Except the dude wants his gold back, so maybe he's letting her use her phone. I send the message, give the directions to the place Nao's written down. I tell Geen we'll head there tonight, we'll be up there by midnight to give him what he wants, we just want her back. I don't say we're staying at The Pearl.

What if she doesn't get the message? Nine minutes of computer time left.

I log off and waste the nine minutes, catch the stink of weed as I cross reception to the door. Happy people out with their mates, spending cash like they've got it. I trip over a girl's silver wheely case and flip her the finger when she says to watch myself. And then I'm out on the street, hot humid night and lights and traffic, walking fast.

I'm nearly at the side street where I've parked the Landie when I hear the footsteps behind. *Squeak, squeak*, like someone in sneakers trying to be quiet – it spooks me. Plus they're walking too fast to be quiet. There's no one up ahead and the street's getting darker. I walk faster and the footsteps speed up.

Fuck. Someone from the backpackers, seen me on TV? Some random who's gunna mug me for the bag?

I keep walking, my heart speeding, my thongs slapping the footpath between the *squeak, squeak* behind. I cross the side street and keep going straight. I see the moon, fat and silver, between two buildings.

The footsteps get closer, huffing breath over the squeaky shoes. I speed up, hold the girl's handbag tight to my side. The street ahead's empty and too dark. I wanna do a u-turn but I can't.

The footsteps change up as the person starts to run. I shoot forwards, my thongs tripping me. A shop on my right with a bright shiny window: *OPEN.* I duck right and bang through the door, skid towards the counter. A bell jangles. There's the rush of cold aircon on my sweat.

The woman behind the counter looks up and frowns. 'We're closing soon?' she says. 'Nine p.m.'

I nod but don't talk. I duck behind a display case – gold jewellery under glass, white sand and pearls – and turn to the window. Wait. Get my breath.

No one comes in after me.

The woman frowns deeper, watching me puffing. 'Fifteen minutes?' she says. She could be Nao's sister – dark hair, dark eyes – except she's skinny, her smooth hair scraped back, glasses with square gold frames.

'You're orright,' I say. I edge around the display case towards the window.

Empty footpath, streetlights, the moon across the street. A coupla cars drive by. The footsteps person is gone.

There was someone. No joke, there was someone. So where'd they go? Waiting around the corner for me to come back out, most likely.

'Ten minutes until we close?' the woman says. 'So, if you want to buy?'

It reminds me of Geen, the way she says everything like a question.

The whole shop smells like all the cash we never had. I check out the stuff in the display cases. The woman's gotta be kidding me, except she's not, is she? She's trying to get rid of me. I'm holding tight onto the girl's blingy bag and the rest of me looks like shit. She probably thinks I nicked it.

I did nick it.

The shop's all pearls and jewellery, gold and silver and other stuff, shiny as fuck. Big blown-up photos of shells and sand and ocean on the walls. Bet there's places like this in Surfers. Like the place Geen works, except better.

That's when I get why Geen's not been on Facebook or Instagram since Friday. How come she was weird all weekend, stressed out and smoking and trying to hide it. How come she got so mad when I took that bit of gold off Daryl.

They planned it. Together. Geen and Daryl nicked that safe with the gold in it.

Thinking it makes my head hot, my skin prickly where I've scratched it. She did it with Daryl and she didn't tell me. What's she gunna think when she finds out he's dead? And all 'cause I nicked that one bit. I grab a hold of it in my pocket, warm and smooth, the ridges where the letters are. It calms me down. Maybe we can keep this one. Maybe the dude won't notice, or we can tell him we lost it.

The woman's watching my every move like she knows what I'm thinking, like she knows I'm not worth shit and this bit of gold is all I've got in the world.

And then I'm up at the counter, five minutes till closing, showing it to her.

'I just wanna check it's genuine,' I say. 'How much it's worth and that.'

She frowns as she takes it off me, two lines on her smooth forehead. I see her eyes widen and check me out, back to the gold. She glances over her shoulder. There's a door there, into a back room. Shit, she knows something about it.

My breathing gets fast. I wanna get it back off her but I can't. I have to go along with the whole thing, nod in all the right spots like I'm paying attention. While the whole time, I'm thinking, *Fuck*, and, *Give me it back*, and *Get me outta here*.

She doesn't call anyone. Maybe I imagined her looking. Or

maybe she's got a button under the counter she's already pressed, like they do in banks. She gets an old-time set of scales out from under there and she weighs the bar. 'The weight is accurate,' she says. 'Dimensions, too, correct for the weight.' She glances at me and quickly away. 'The bar has a good lustre. It's poured, so the appearance is different.'

'Poured?' Fucksakes.

She blinks, clear dark eyes behind her glasses. 'Poured into a mould, not stamped. Not cut out of a sheet.'

Whatever that means. My fingers itch in my pocket. She's stopped telling me what the time is. My neck prickles and I look over my shoulder to the street. The sign on the door says CLOSED on the inside, OPEN on the outside.

'And there's a serial number,' she says, pointing. 'The number will match your paperwork.' She blinks again.

I swallow. 'Orright. Thanks.' I hold out my hand and see her hesitate.

She hands it over, I snatch it back and she flinches. I stuff it in my pocket and I see a back door out onto a side street. I've ripped it open when she says, 'You can check the price online. It changes all the time.'

I know what it's worth. It's worth eight grand. I only asked her to stop her looking at me that way, and now she's doing it ten times worse.

I get out in the heat and watch her lock both doors, go back behind the counter and pick up the phone. Who's she calling? Am I paranoid? Am I? I clock the sign above the door: SALTWATER GOLD AND PEARLS. I look both ways, hunch my shoulders up, wish I had a hoody. I head around the block towards the Landie, keeping off the main drag. My fingers curled around the gold in my pocket and my elbow clamped down on the handbag.

No one waiting to jump out from a lamppost, far as I can see. Only a Kombi van, further up, its windows dark.

Around the first corner I see the blue Commodore, kerb-crawler slow, coming straight for me. I know where I've seen it, 'cause of the bunch of antennas on the roof: behind the black LandCruiser in the car park outside Woolies in Port Hedland.

I shrink against a gate, watch the yellow headlights vacuum up the bitumen. What is he? A PI, an undercover cop? What was he doing following that LandCruiser? The dude inside's got dark blond hair, wearing aviator sunnies at night-time. He's looking left and right as he passes, searching . . . He looks right at me . . .

And keeps going.

Fuck this. I trip and skid around the corner to the LandCruiser and don't look back.

The kid from reception is watering the garden behind the car park when I get back, asks if I found the backpackers okay and I say yeah, thanks.

Nao's in the bathroom. I can hear the shower going. The full moon up in the middle of the window. I check on the gold and drink a glass of warm water out the tap. She comes out with a towel round her head and her dirty clothes back on. Shit, I forgot to get food.

I tell her sorry and ask if she wants anything out the LandCruiser, but she says she's not hungry. I go out there anyhow and find a tub of instant noodles in the back. The Chinese kid's hosing down the white Merc, washing the dust off it.

I get back inside and pour hot water on the noodles, ask Nao if she wants half.

She shakes her head.

'I sent that message,' I say. 'The directions you gave me. Before midnight, I said. How long to get there, d'ya reckon?'

'Thirty minutes or so.'

'I'm gunna eat this and get clean and we should head out.'

'I want to check the news. Ten p.m.'

As if it's gunna be good. 'Can you be ready when I'm out the shower?'

'Of course.'

Except when I come out the bathroom with my singlet and shorts and headphones back on, she's still on the couch in front of the small TV.

'Why d'ya need to see it?' I say. 'We already know we're on the news.'

'In case there's anything new. Just wait.' She's got it on a local channel, the remote in her hand, staring at adverts for camel treks and fishing.

'We need to go.' I get the holdall off the bunk, stuff my flanno shirt inside. The gun's still at the bottom of it. 'Someone followed me, on the footpath,' I say. 'Spooked me. I'm a bit antsy. That's why I went in that shop.' I check the moon in the window, a bit higher up. The shape of a palm tree stands out against the sky.

'What shop?'

'From that backpackers. I went in there, messaged Geen. Someone followed me after I came out so I went in a shop.'

She's not listening, watching the TV. Another advert, for a pearl farm tour.

'Geen hasn't logged on,' I say. 'I dunno if she's gunna get the message. What can we do, but? We gotta go.' I pick the girl's handbag up off the kitchen bench, see the Wi-Fi password the kid wrote out for me. 'Shit. Hold on.' I slide my phone out my pocket. Try to switch it on and expect nothing, same as last time, but the screen lights up. I put the passcode in.

'What the flaming hell is that?' Nao's staring at my phone.

'Forgot,' I say. 'Got Facebook on my phone. I can check if she got the message.'

'You threw it,' she says. 'Out the car window, day one. I saw you do it.'

She can freak all she wants. I don't give a shit, not now. 'Got my music on it. I didn't want to. I took the SIM card out.'

Her nostrils flare, each breath in and out. 'They can track it. The police. They could be tracking it now.'

'We're way past that, Nao. I'm only gunna check.' I put the password in and the Wi-Fi connects. 'Useless signal. Got a message! Fuck, it's a video.'

It loads on a close-up of Geen's face – crying, busted up. I feel faint, like I'm gunna spew. I sink down on the couch.

'Nao?'

'Shh!' She's not looking. She's watching the TV, elbows on her knees.

I play the video. Geen's face is bruised and swollen, one eye swelled shut. White tiles behind her head and blood and snot coming out her nose. 'Charlie Bear,' she says. 'I'm okay. Cross my heart it looks worse than it is. He wants to meet two hours further on from where you said. The Saltwater mine site. It's signposted. No police, no witnesses.' Her eyes dart to the side, scared. 'You need to do what the cop says for me, okay? For us. So don't—'

And my phone goes dead.

Fuck, no. I press the button, keep pressing. Nothing happens. Got no charger. 'Nao?' My guts like concrete. 'Nao!'

'Did you show that gold to someone? You'd better take a look at this. The gold's on the news.'

I hustle Nao out to the LandCruiser and stick her in the driver's seat with the bags. There's something different about the Landie and I see what it is: the kid's washed all the dirt off it, shiny clean WA number plates. Fuck.

Nao's staring at the steering wheel like she doesn't know what it's for. 'I don't think I . . . can you drive?'

'No I can't. You know the way.'

She gets it going. She looks both ways three times and pulls out the driveway of The Pearl, onto the dark street, checking the rearview the whole time.

'Can ya go a bit quicker?' All the windows up and the aircon on full. My feet back on the gold and my hand wrapped around my phone so hard it hurts.

'We don't want to be conspicuous.' She looks at me in the glow from the dash. 'How bad was it? Her face, in the video.'

Tears itch at me and I sniff them back. 'Bad. Keep going. Just get us there.'

And when we do, I'm gunna get the gun out the bag and shoot the bastard.

'What did she say?'

I take a breath, scrub at my eyes. 'No police, no witnesses. Get there and do the swap.'

We head back out the way we came in, a maze of streets and streetlights with fat trees sliding past. A few cars on the road and a handful of people on the footpath.

'He wants to meet at this place, further on up that pearl farm road. Saltwater something.'

'The Saltwater mine site? Oh God.' She looks crook, chewing her cheek.

'She called him *the cop*. That's what she said, in the video.'

Her eyes flick towards me and back to the road.

'Is it him?' I say.

'I don't know.' Her voice so low I can't hardly hear it.

'Someone working for him, you said.'

'I don't *know*, Charlie.' She checks the mirror. 'But yes, I think there's a good chance it's him.'

My hand's locked around my phone. I reckon she did know. She goes quiet and it's on her face. I try to remember what she said about him, the dead cop stepdad, back at the motel in Tom Price.

She turns left. 'Stick on the back streets,' I say. 'Kid at The Pearl washed the number plates.'

'Oh God. Why did you go into that shop?'

We come out the grid of streets to a roundabout. The cop shop's on the opposite corner. The lights on inside the building and two cruisers out front, one with its lights going, real slow. 'Shit, that was dark earlier,' I say. 'Could be normal, but. Thursday night.'

Nao pulls onto the roundabout. 'Charlie? There was another thing, on the news. They've found Daryl's body, back in the city.'

I stare at the side of her face, across at the cop shop. 'No way. They showed it?'

'A body in Claremont Lake, that's all. No details.'

'Got us on CCTV? Us with Daryl?' The words stick in my throat.

She grips the wheel, misses the exit. 'I don't know. They seem to think it's connected with organised crime.' She stays on the roundabout. 'She made a phone call, you said? The woman in the shop?'

'Yeah, she looked sus at me. Made the call when I left.' Dropkick, for showing it to her. We drive past the cop shop as the main door slides open. A cop in uniform steps out.

'So, she recognised the gold and called it in. The Saltwater mine – it's local. She must remember the story. They won't know it's us, not until they've checked the CCTV.' Nao goes back around. Two cops get in the second cruiser and it backs out into the street.

I grip my phone, the strap of my seatbelt. The cruiser turns the other way, back towards The Pearl.

'Bit over the top,' I say. 'Bit fast.'

'It's home grown,' Nao says. 'The story and the gold. They care about it.' She looks sideways at me, down at the phone in my hands. 'You weren't listening. You didn't hear the whole story.'

She makes the turn onto the street outta town. Floats a shaky hand up off the wheel and puts it back.

'The gold was stolen twelve years ago,' she says. 'From the Saltwater Gold Corporation up here.' She stops, takes a breath. 'It happened the same day my dad was killed. Three men were shot dead. The gold was never recovered.'

She slows for another roundabout, picks up speed again. The LandCruiser kicks forwards, presses me back in my seat. A truck passes in the opposite direction. 'My dad was one of those men, Charlie. It was his name on the news just now and I didn't know. My mum has lied about it my whole life and said it was a car accident. I don't even know what he was doing there that day.' She looks at me and down at the holdall. 'Warren killed my dad and he wants to meet us at the place where it happened.'

16

Nao

Armed and Dangerous

We stop for petrol before the turnoff onto the peninsula road at a low square building with rectangles of light spilling out. I indicate and turn in, past a pair of palm trees, and the headlights wash across a sign: DAVE BARRA CROCODILE PARK, five kilometres up the peninsula road. Charlie stares at the sign but says nothing. She's quiet apart from her breathing, her hands pressed tight around the phone in her lap.

I pull up to the pumps and turn off the ignition. The inside of me is numb but I focus on what we have to do: get Charlie's sister back. There's no way I can keep Charlie out of this now. But she'll have to stay calm.

She hovers while I fill the tank, fidgeting with her dead

phone. The night is hot and humid, full of insects and the smell of petrol. The full moon's at its highest with the only bank of cloud further north. Charlie's not happy about stopping – she's twitchy, her eyes darting between her phone and the high-way – but what can we do? We need the fuel. And there's no one else here.

'I don't think Warren's connected up here,' I say. 'He won't want the local police to find us either.'

She looks up from her phone. 'You don't know that.'

'No, but I wonder if that's why he suggested it, meeting us further out of town.'

'Remote,' she says.

'Yes.' As well as the scene of Warren's crime. I don't like it, that he's asked to meet us exactly there, but I'm not tell-ing her that.

The windscreen of the vehicle is spattered with dead insects: crickets and beetles and moths. We should clean those off. There are more of them, too: dark blurs bumping the lights above the pumps. One lands on the nozzle in my hand and takes off again.

The tank is taking ages to fill, stopping and starting like there's something wrong with the pump, and my hand is sweat-ing. Warren was the first responder, that's what Mum always said about the accident; that's how they met. But not even that part is true. Dad was already dead and Warren was in the other car, the car that hit us, on the run with the gold.

I think of everything that started that day and what else Mum's lie has enabled. But it's too much and my mind swerves away.

'How long did you know it was him?' Charlie says. A warning note in her voice.

'What do you mean?'

Her eyes are wet from crying but hard now. 'When did ya clock it? That it was your stepdad in the LandCruiser with Geen?'

I concentrate on the numbers ticking around. 'I didn't, not—'

'Bullshit. I can see it on your face.' Her voice is hoarse. 'How fucken long?'

I swallow. 'I didn't know for sure, but I thought . . . when you mentioned the driving gloves . . .'

'And you reckoned, what? It was okay not to tell me? You weren't gunna bother?'

'No, it wasn't that.'

'So what was it? What the fuck, Nao? Because I so wanna know why you don't tell me shit, why you think you know so much better—'

'Look, it's not that, I told you.' All the things I don't want to feel are underneath the numbness, threatening.

'Yeah, it is! All those times I asked ya not to bullshit me and you're still doing it. Like you reckon I can't handle knowing stuff, like you reckon I've got no brain—'

'I know you've got a brain—'

'Then stop acting like I don't! You need ta give me some credit, you need to—'

'It's not all about you, Charlie!' The tank stops filling with a clunk. I rip the nozzle out and she jumps backwards. 'Jesus, I was scared, okay? I was really really afraid and I didn't know what to do. I didn't want you to see that. I didn't think it would help.'

She sniffs. 'But we coulda—'

'What? We could have what? It wouldn't have made any

difference. Knowing it was him didn't change anything.' I slam the nozzle back. There's a tightness in my hands that's unfamiliar and I tuck them into my armpits. 'Do you think I don't know it's my fault he's here at all? That he's come after us?'

My voice cracks and we stand there, breathing hard. I screw the fuel cap back on. The man at the counter inside is watching us through the glass door.

'I'm sorry, okay?' I clear my throat. 'For not doing better. But we need to go. This is about your sister now. Getting her back safe.'

Charlie doesn't answer but she nods. I see her frown at the CCTV camera on the outside wall of the building; we've been in full view of it for far too long. She steps around me and leans into the car, pulls out the cash we need. 'Get back in,' she says. 'I'll do this. No use the both of us being on camera inside.'

I start the engine and the air-conditioning blows cool air. My heartrate settles but I still feel responsible, still don't know what we'll do when we get there. I'm staring at the dirty windscreen when Charlie slams into the car. 'Go! Didn't ya see them?'

'Who?' My head jerks up to the mirror. Nothing there.

'Those kids! Lock the doors!'

I rip my belt across and click it, lock the doors. 'What? I can't see what you're—' A face looms at my window and I flinch: an angry mouth, dreadlocks. He grapples at the handle, banging the glass with the flat of his hand. I fumble the handbrake off and see the green ute at the side of us. 'Jesus, Charlie. That's not—?' Another face at her window and more hands banging the windscreen.

'Drive!'

I shoot forwards, swerving out from the pumps. The tyres squeal as the bodies fall away.

'That dude Jez,' she says. 'The kids we nicked this off.'

The man from inside the building is silhouetted in the doorway as we hit the road.

'How is that possible?' I say.

'Musta followed us.' She's twisted around in her seat, getting her breath, watching out of the back window. The lights of the roadhouse drop back.

'What, all of them?'

'Both vehicles, the green ute and the Kombi. Can ya go a bit faster?'

Dark scrub flashes past. There's a dazzle of high beams in the rearview mirror and I press the accelerator. 'They're following us?'

'Reckon it was one of them followed me from the backpackers, before I lost 'em. Want their LandCruiser back.'

Another sign for the crocodile park and pearl farms. I slow and take the turn onto the peninsula road – dead straight, empty and dark. We pick up speed as the headlights turn behind us.

'Anyplace to lose 'em?' she says. 'Probably not as fast as we are.'

'It's one road the whole way. There's nothing else out here.'

Charlie swears. She's still kneeling in her seat, facing backwards, her tongue between her teeth. 'How long till we get to the spot?'

'A couple of hours, maybe a bit more.' What else did Sam say? The road surface is bad, so it's going to get worse. I glance at the clock: almost eleven p.m. We won't make midnight, but Warren changed the meeting place. 'You can't sit like that the whole way.'

There's a long curve to the right and the road straightens again. Charlie scratches her bare shoulder, still gripping her phone. 'No cops, no witnesses – that's what he said. We gotta get rid of them, Nao.'

I hear the catch in her voice. I press harder on the pedal and feel the kick in the engine as we jump forwards. We pull away from the first vehicle: the ute, its lights still on high beam.

One straight road, with Warren and Charlie's sister at the end of it. He could well have already killed her. I want to undo the thought but I can't. What's she worth to him? He's already killed for the gold – three men plus the truck driver. How many more? And I'm taking Charlie right to him.

I taste bile and swallow it, glancing at her as she clings to her seat with both hands. I wonder for the first time why Warren wants this ten kilos of gold so badly when he stole a hundred. It's evidence, isn't it, linking him to the crime. We should have handed it in as soon as we found it. We wouldn't be here if we had.

Headlights fill the mirror, they're all I can see. I imagine the scene from above, the three of us strung along the dark thread of road: the white four-wheel-drive, the green ute, the Kombi van with Jez's surfboards piled on top. I open both front windows and turn the air-conditioning off.

'Whatcha doing?'

'I need to listen to what's out there.'

'Get it to go quicker.'

The entrance to the crocodile park flashes past: a wide dirt driveway, silvered by the moon. We lose the bitumen. I feel the change in the surface to corrugations, a scatter of rocks flying up. I taste the dust and watch it plume in the lights behind, the ute following too close.

'You should sit down,' I say. 'Put your seatbelt on. We could hit something. I might have to turn off fast.'

She does it. Her phone is clamped in her hands, her head tilted up to the rearview mirror.

The pool of the headlights only highlights the darkness ahead and behind, the sense of empty country and racing scrub. I scan each side of the dirt road, looking for a turnoff, but there's nothing – no lights, no signs. I think of pulling over and giving them what they want. But we've a full tank of petrol and for all we know the police are back there looking for us.

'Can't fucken give up,' Charlie says.

'I'm not giving up.'

'There!' She points at the sign: CREEKBANK PEARL FARM. An opening on the left.

I don't slow enough for the turn. The vehicle bumps and slides as I swing the wheel, make the turn onto the rough track. Rocks kick up and ping against the sides.

The track is angled upwards: red dirt and potholes. I grasp the wheel against the juddering suspension. Charlie holds hard to the handle of the door, blinking against the dust. She's got the bag of gold up on her lap, hunched over it. I watch the headlights swing in behind us. 'This is crazy, Charlie. We can't outrun them, not out here.'

'Keep going. This car's better than theirs.'

There's the scrape of vegetation underneath us and something thumps against the front: a rabbit, and another one. The track forks and I swerve right.

'They're going to chase us down.' I say. 'We're heading for the ocean. There's nowhere to go.'

'What else are we gunna do? We gotta get to her!' Her voice is getting higher and faster.

We come to the crest of the rise and the track splits again. Over the top and the view opens out – scrub, beach, ocean, a maze-work of silver tracks. 'We might have to give it back to them,' I say.

'No way, what if they dump us out here and call the cops?'

'Is that so terrible? The police could help her. If we just—'

'No! They think we killed Daryl, plus that cop, plus that truckie. They think we're armed and dangerous and we nicked this gold.'

'We're not armed and dangerous.' We pick up speed, flying down the other side, rocks pinging. I see the stand of trees at the bottom of the slope as a cloud drifts across the moon.

'Head for those trees,' Charlie says.

'It's only a few trees,' I say. 'Not enough to—'

'Do it!' she screams. 'I told Geen we'd be there. He's gunna kill her. Keep going.'

The vehicles fan out behind: bouncing headlights, one set each side, trying to get around us. My blood's rushing too fast. Charlie's shoulders are hunched above the bag. She must be able to see this isn't going to work.

The Kombi van out to the right is zig-zagging crazily. What are they doing?

The trees come up fast, the ground dipping, the vehicle running away from me. We hit two more rabbits. 'Slow down!' Charlie says. 'Don't stack it.'

There's a bang as the Kombi hits something. One headlight winks out and the surfboards spill off the roof. The ute disappears into a dip on the left.

'Trees!' Charlie yells.

Branches snap across the windscreen, thudding the sides, *bang*, *scrape*, *crack*. I press the brake but we're already slowing, the ground bottoming out. 'I don't know what you think we can—'

'Stop!'

I slam the brake as a flare of high-beam lights floods the cab. Charlie throws up both hands and I do the same. A vehicle's stopped at an angle, dead ahead in the trees.

'What the fuck?' she says, eyes tight shut. 'How'd they get around us?'

'Is that them?'

There's the smell of exhaust, the sound of running feet and shouting. Arms reach through the open windows, pulling the doors open.

'Don't fight, Charlie,' I say. 'Give them what they want.' Someone pulls my seatbelt away and hauls me out by one arm. My feet get tangled so I fall on my knees. 'Ow,' I say. 'Okay, we're doing it. There's no need to—'

A girl's voice mutters, 'Bitch.' A fist punches the side of my head and then my face is in the dirt, with rocks under my knees and sharp fronds pricking my cheek. The doors slam, the white four-wheel-drive reverses away and the bright lights go out.

'Nao?'

'What?'

'You hit your head or something?'

'I don't think so. The lights blinded me.' There's an ache above my bruised eye but it's nothing.

'Come on.' I feel her hand on my back, groping for my arm. 'Gotta go.'

I blink and get one foot under me. Charlie tugs on my hand.

So dark I can't see her. Branches in my face. 'Where are they?'

'Shh. Gone. Come on.' She pulls me up and along and into a vehicle. 'Where's your bag?'

'Lost it. In the car. I don't know.'

'Shit.'

'It doesn't matter.'

She starts the engine, rolls forward and brakes. She keeps the lights off. I'm in the passenger seat, but not the four-wheel-drive. There's a smell of lemons. 'What is this?' I say.

She presses the pedal, the engine louder, crawling out from the trees, back up the slope we came down. The dark is like a blanket, with the track just visible in front.

'Dickheads,' she says. Her face pale in the dashboard lights. A yellow tree shape hangs from the rearview mirror.

'We're back in the green ute?'

She nods.

'The girl punched me,' I say. 'Jesus, Charlie, the gold!'

'What?'

'The bag! Do you have it?'

'Course.' She pats her hand and it's there between the seats. I breathe out.

'Okay.'

I open my window to the smell of ocean and scrub. We're halfway up the slope when we hear sirens, thin and whining, and she stops.

'Use the handbrake,' I say. 'Turn off the ignition.'

But she's already doing it. She keeps one hand on the brake. Red and blue lights appear at the top of the rise and she swears.

'Which way did the others go?'

'That way.' She grips the wheel. 'Back out the track.' We

watch the cruiser glide across the top, take the left-hand fork and disappear.

'Let's wait,' I say. 'Roll back to the trees. Keep the lights off.'

She does it, and there are no more police lights, no engine sound up on the track. But I check the dashboard and wonder if Charlie's noticed the light there. That we're almost out of petrol and we don't have any money.

'Hear anything?' Charlie whispers.

'No.'

'Me neither. Reckon they're out there still?'

'I don't think we should move yet, if that's what you mean.'

We sit in the dark and listen. Parked in a gully off the side of the road, a hundred metres down a track marked *Salt Bay Pearls*, where Charlie moved us to when the police cruiser didn't come back. The vehicle sounds we heard when we first got in here have died away.

There's no breeze in the gully – it's the densest patch of bush we could find, filled with paperbarks – and the only sounds are crickets and frogs. The faint settling of moonlight on everything and a smell of eucalyptus that takes me back to Aunty's hidden backyard garden. I wipe the sweat from my forehead with the back of my hand.

'Midnight, I put in the message,' Charlie says.

'We weren't going to make that, anyway.'

'Reckon he'll wait?'

'He wants his gold, Charlie. He won't want anyone else to know about it.' I can't tell her my worst fears for her sister. All we can do is get there and see.

She bites her thumbnail. 'Your head orright?'

'It's nothing. A bruise. It wasn't a hard punch.'

'We got any water?'

I rummage on the back seat. 'Just this.' It's one of the bottles I filled at the motel in Tom Price. Dented and dusty with around two hundred mils in the bottom of it, warm. Better than nothing, which is what they've left us with. I take a drink and pass her the bottle.

'Reckon they spat in it? Quite pissed off with us, weren't they?' She takes a sip, makes a face and looks down at the steering wheel. 'Gotta be a way to get fuel. Another vehicle. Siphon it off, what d'ya reckon?' She seems very calm.

'That would be an excellent idea,' I say. 'If we could find one.'

She cracks the door open, tilts her head and listens but there's nothing. 'I'm gunna do a reccie.'

'Don't let anyone see you.'

It's thirty minutes until I hear the crunch of her feet coming back.

'There's an office,' she says. 'Open seven in the morning. Nothin' else. No cars.' She sits on the bonnet on the driver's side, talking through the open window. 'There's a bathroom window, only a bit of flyscreen. I reckon I can get in it.'

I clunk my door open. 'Is there a phone in there?'

'Probably. Who we gunna call, but?'

'What happened to that bit of paper I gave you? With the directions on it?' I go and sit up next to her.

She pulls the mashed and sweaty bit of paper out of a pocket and passes it over. I check Sam's number is still on it. 'That the kid who gave you a lift?' she says.

'He didn't like leaving us, the other night. He lives in

Broome. He's only got to bring us some petrol.' And right now, he's all we've got.

She jumps down. 'Let's go. I'll have to do it. You won't get in the window.'

'Not *now*. It's the middle of the night,' I say. 'We want him to say yes. We'll go at first light, before the office opens.'

I see her brace to argue but she doesn't. 'First thing, yeah?'

'First thing.' I sip the water and offer her some more. She drinks and hands it back.

She goes and digs in the passenger door of the ute, brings back the Cherry Ripe. 'Go ya halves?'

We share it, chocolate melting over our fingers. We should have saved it, I think, after it's gone. I drop the wrapper in the window and I stand on the track opposite, listening to the sounds of the scrub. I remember the snake back at Aunty's place, the cockatoos on her roof. I remember running away from home, through Karrakatta cemetery, towards Charlie's house.

If I had to run into anyone that night, I'm glad it was her. I'm not sure she'd think that herself, though. Not now.

'Whatcha doing?'

'Thinking. I don't know.'

''Bout what?'

'That if I'd let you call the police like you wanted to, after Daryl, none of this would have happened.'

She shrugs. 'Nah. Anyhow, I reckon it was Geen started it.'

'What?'

She kicks her heels against the ute, looks at her feet. 'I reckon she planned it. With Daryl. To take that safe.'

'Why would you think that?'

'Dunno. Probably did it for me. Dropkick.'

'It's going to be okay.'

'You don't know that.' She wipes her eye. 'That kid we're gunna call. Did you tell him what's going on?'

'Of course not.'

'You reckon he knows, but? That we're wanted all over the state? That we're armed and dangerous?'

'We're not, Charlie. We didn't shoot anyone. I don't know why you keep saying that.'

She opens her mouth and shuts it. Frowns and licks her lip.

'What?' I say.

She slides off the bonnet and goes and pulls the bag of gold out from the ute. She gets it up onto the bonnet, unzips the holdall and reaches inside. She digs to the bottom and takes a moment to meet my eye. 'Promise you won't be angry?' she says.

'Why? I don't know if I can—'

And she pulls out a handgun. Matt black in the moonlight, like it's sucked up all the light.

'Where did you get that?'

'You're angry,' she says.

Oh God. The dead police officer, the gun spinning out of his hand on the highway.

'You picked it *up*? Are you telling me that's been in there the whole time?'

'Armed and fucken dangerous,' she says, and I don't like the way she weighs it in her hand. I don't like the way I want to hold it. I want her to zip it back inside.

17

Geena

Run To Paradise

The Arsehole has put Geena back in the boot. That everyday car-boot carpet smell will never be the same again. She's on her side like before with her jacket under her head and her legs cramped up, and she can feel the long handle of the shovel across her back. She grips her half-empty bottle of water and she can't see her hand in front of her face.

She watches Charlie jump on her bed with her headphones on, too big above her sharp collarbones and narrow shoulders. Charlie's twelve years old again and listening to that playlist of Mum's. She's still inseparable from Saskia and Mum is alive in the next room.

It's calming, imagining this. Geena counts each time Charlie goes up and comes down again, in synch with her heartbeat against the vibrations of the Toyota. She watches Charlie's unco-ordinated skinny arms jerk up and float down, her legs and her head and her hair kicking out one way and then the other like she thinks she's being funny or cool, although she never really got the chance to be either of those things.

Geena thinks about the formative effects of heartbreak on Charlie's life, how it seems to find her at every turn and could be about to get a whole lot worse. The song she's listening to is 'Run to Paradise' and Geena wishes they could.

She's scared to touch her cheekbone in case it's all wrong, though her face is mostly numb. There's another loose tooth, her eye is still swelled shut and she's pretty sure she needs the hospital. But he gave her two painkillers and a bag of ice before they recorded the video message.

She couldn't explain it to him right. That stealing his safe was her idea and had nothing to do with Charlie. That Geena planned it and if anyone needs to get hurt it should be her. But he wasn't listening and he doesn't care.

All he did was tell her the police are out looking for Charlie and Naomi, the girl from outside the motel, and the white LandCruiser they've stolen. The girl is his stepdaughter, a law student; he told her that, too, like he held Geena personally responsible for her being involved at all. She and Charlie are wanted state-wide in connection with a series of crimes and if Geena ever wants to see Charlie alive again they all need to do exactly what he says.

Lee wasn't parked out back of the motel when the cop marched her out there, either. She doesn't know what that means; if the cop got him moved on or it's something worse.

Each one of them is up shit creek, basically, not to mention the last bit of news the cop enjoyed telling her. That they've identified a dead body pulled out of Claremont Lake as Daryl's, and they're treating his death as suspicious.

So, Daryl is dead and not coming back. This is less of a surprise than it might have been, knowing Daryl's mates and how events have played out so far. And however hard she tries, Geena can't seem to feel a whole lot about it either way.

Far worse is knowing Charlie has watched the video message and she's going to do exactly what the cop wants. That this is all Geena's fault and there's nothing she can do to stop it.

She must've fallen asleep, what with the painkillers and the sleep deprivation and the rocking of the car, because she wakes up in a cold sweat as the vibrations change: bigger, less regular. They're driving on a dirt road, straight, no slowing or turning. She has no clue how long they've been driving; it could be ten minutes or three hours. The air is stale and her face is aching, so she tries not to breathe too deep.

The vibrations thicken, the car slowing down, and her skin tenses. She doesn't want to get there yet. She's not ready. But the Toyota takes a curve and then another one, and it speeds up over the corrugations again.

Charlie said in her Facebook message that she and the girl have the gold and want to do an exchange. But Geena hopes the cops are looking real good for them and get to them first. Because the downside of The Arsehole having no cop mates up here? He's got a fair bit to lose.

Geena doesn't imagine for one second that he's planning to exchange her for that gold the girls have got. She doesn't know about the stepdaughter, but Charlie and Geena? She's one hundred per cent certain that after everything they've been through, this is going to end with a bullet in the head and a grave out in the desert someplace. She wonders if he'll get them to dig it themselves and if she could swing that shovel at his head.

He was pale and sweating as he bundled her in this time, his breathing once again shallow. She doesn't think he was faking it, but she remembers the change in him, back inside the room. The colour in his face, the sinewy strength in his arms. The effects of adrenaline. It's not lost on her that she brought that on all by herself, and the same could happen the next time.

From what she can see, the only way out is they have to kill him. And they'll likely only get one shot at it.

FRIDAY

18

Charlie

Dead Or In Jail

We head down the track to the pearl farm office soon as it gets light. Layers of pink cloud in the sky and still cool from overnight, even with my flanno shirt back on over my singlet. The holdall drags on my shoulder 'cause of the broken handle.

I get Nao to hold the bag and I push the flyscreen in at the dunny window. It clatters down inside but there's no one there to hear it. Nao gives me a leg up and I climb down onto the vanity unit and through the office to the glass sliding door at the front. No alarm or nothing. It's a shit office, like those extra classrooms at school. There's a row of cactus plants along the edge of the one desk.

I unlock the glass door and slide it open. She looks past me but doesn't shift. 'Not like we're robbing it,' I say. 'It's life and death. Phone's on the desk. I'm gunna wait outside.'

She leaves the holdall on the dirt. I slide the door shut after her and watch her make the call. The sky getting lighter the whole time and a bunch of noisy pink and grey galahs on the roof. Nao's nervous, big eyes, chewing her cheek while the phone rings. I can tell when he answers 'cause she twitches, like she gets an electric shock off the phone. She's got the horn for this Sam kid. She makes like she hasn't but she has.

There's a line of bull ants headed for the bag and I shift it out the way. I pulled the gun out the bottom again last night while Nao was asleep in the ute and put it back before she woke up. It's heavy for the size of it, kind of plasticky, not what you'd expect. Not what it looks like when people shoot guns on TV. I dunno how hard you have to press it, how hard it is to keep the thing steady. Wish I knew how to shoot it so it'd work the exact first time.

I get to thinking about Sass, how she changed after Mum died, kept her distance and couldn't stop me fighting no more, couldn't calm me down. She got scared of me, didn't she? And I reckon she was right to be.

Nao's still talking. I bang on the glass and tell her to hurry the fuck up. She nods.

The sun comes up and disappears into thick cloud as we walk back. I get in the driver's seat of the ute and sit with my arm on the open window, the sun warm on it from behind the cloud. There's no breeze still, even with all the windows down. The flies and sandflies are little bastards so I take my shirt off and wrap it over my mouth and my nose.

The kid takes ages. It gets hotter and the smell of the

paperbarks comes in at the windows. The sandflies stop biting. I'm antsy about Geen, thirsty and pissed off that all the water's gone. 'Is he definitely coming?'

She nods. 'He said yes.'

'You tell him anything?'

'I told you I wouldn't.'

She's antsy too, it's coming off her. Keeps chucking looks at the holdall under her feet.

'You reckon we should get it out?' I say.

She shifts her eyes off the bag. 'What?'

'The gun. Get it out and have a practice with it?'

'No. Definitely not.' She crosses her arms and stares straight ahead out the windscreen.

'But what if we—'

'No. Leave it. You should never have picked it up.'

She feels bad, I get that. About Geen, about her stepdad. Hardly her fault, but, is it? Nao was in the wrong spot at the wrong time with a prick for a stepdad. Not even her real dad. I feel bad, the same as she does. Worse. If I hadn't killed Dickhead Daryl we woulda never taken the ute, never found the gold, never done the lot of it. If it's anyone's fault it's mine.

Plus Nao's still here, isn't she? She hasn't bailed out on me. Lots of times she coulda done a runner and she didn't. Except what if that's not enough?

I don't want Geen to die, not if that bastard's the last person she's ever gunna see. I think about shooting him in the head and solving all of our problems in one go. Not as if another dead dude's gunna make the difference, is it? Not for me. I'll most likely land up dead or in jail either way, same as Dad.

I haven't told Nao everything, either. Not like I hated Dad, is it? He was funny. He stuck up for me. He said it was me and him against the bullshit.

We were mates, until he fucked up and killed Mum. Makes it worse.

The kid rocks up an hour later. Feels longer, but. He parks his beat-up red ute, rap music hurting my brain until he shuts it off and gets out, leaves his two dogs tied up in the tray. He's wearing a faded Triple J T-shirt, jeans and boots covered in dust. He nods at me, says hi and I say hi back. He stands there looking scared of me – wavy lines across his forehead like corrugations on a dirt road – and I dunno what Nao's told him about me.

He puts fuel in the green ute from a jerrycan and Nao leaves the gold in the footwell while she talks to him. Dunno if he notices the change of vehicle. If he does he keeps it to himself. He gives Nao a bottle of water and she drinks some and brings me some, nice and cold. 'Thanks.' I wipe the top of the bottle with my shirt and hand it back. While they're facing the other way I get the gun out the holdall and stick it in the waistband of my shorts at the back. I tie the flanno around my waist so Nao can't see it. No point freaking her and it feels safer, having it in there.

Sam starts up his ute, turns it around and Nao climbs back in the passenger seat next to me. No one else has come down the track so far and it's past seven a.m. We better not pass anyone on the way.

'He's going to show us the way back to the main road,' she says. 'Make sure we're okay.'

'We are okay. We know the way back to the road. He better piss off when we get there.'

'He will.'

He doesn't. He stops well back from the turn and gets out. I pull in behind him, yank on the handbrake and keep my hand on it. Watch as he walks back through the dust he's kicked up and stops at Nao's window. He's got the hots for her, or he thinks I'm a psycho, or both.

'You want to follow me back to town?' he says.

Nao says, 'Um—' and I punch her in the arm.

He looks at me and then her. 'You're going up to that mine site,' he says. 'Where the gold was stolen from. The place you asked me about.'

Fucksakes.

'We have to meet someone,' she says.

'We're late,' I say.

He squints one eye, looks down at his boots and back up. 'I'm not happy, eh? I wasn't happy the other night, leaving you there on the highway, and I'm not happy now. There's things going off, in town, in the news.'

'We're fine, Sam,' Nao says. 'We can explain later, but right now—'

'There's nothing up there. Nothing except the waterhole. It's all closed up.' The corrugations on his head are working overtime. 'We'll go another time. I can show you, both of you, we can make a trip out of it, but not now. It's going off, like I said — this stolen gold bullion thing, the truck driver that got shot. Now's not the time to be heading out of town, especially not there.' He glances back at his dogs, panting at him from the tray of his ute, straining at the ropes he's got them tied up by.

Nao's got her mouth open, looking a bit desperate. I stick the ute in park, open my door and get out. Nao says, 'Charlie.'

I go around to him. The gun sticking into me at the back. I put a hand on it under my shirt. I can feel the aggro building 'cause I'm antsy about Geen and he's in the way. Except I'm remembering what Nao said about us keeping our heads, how she said it like she reckoned I might be able to. Got my hands in fists but I'm breathing slow, like that paper bag's still on my face back in the bathroom at home. I'm trying, like there's another version of myself I didn't know about. 'Leave it, mate,' I say, real quiet. 'Orright? We don't need anyone's help. Not being funny. Get back in your car and go.'

He looks at Nao in the green ute, her hand on the top of the door.

And he recognises us. I see it happen. His forehead smooths out and his mouth opens. 'Shit,' he says.

And then a couple more things happen.

The blue Commodore goes past on the road in a tunnel of dust, third time I've seen it. Doesn't clock us set back from the road or he's going too fast. 'See that?' I say to Nao.

I pull the gun out and show it to Sam, hold it out with both hands. My hands shake but I'm not aggro. I'm not. I'm only showing it to him. Except he doesn't have the same reaction the girl in the LandCruiser did.

He faints.

And his foot kicks out as he falls and gets me in the shin. 'Ow!' I jump back and the gun goes off. *Bang.* It kicks back and my arms fly up and I drop it. 'Sam's leg jerks like I've hit him and he groans.

'Charlie!' Nao shoves her door open, practically falls out on top of him. 'I can't believe you did that.'

There's a red mess at the toe of his boot. Blood in the dirt, his leg twitching like fuck.

'Didn't mean to! Honest.'

She's kneeling near his head, not touching him. 'You had your finger on the trigger.'

'Couldn't get a hold of it otherwise. Only way I could. Should be a safety thing on it.'

Sam growls like one of his dogs. I can smell the blood. The dogs are yapping the shit out of it, going mental, flipping this way and that on their ropes.

'Least he was unconscious already,' I say.

'That's hardly the point.'

He scrabbles his arms in the dirt. Tries to push himself up, groans, drops back again. I pick the gun up off the ground and pull on Nao's arm. 'Come on.'

She staggers up and steps on his hand. He yells and she says sorry. 'Charlie, we can't leave him.'

'Yeah, we can. He's got water. He's got his ute and his dogs and a phone.'

'We can't.'

'We can. Fucksakes. It's Geen. It's your stepdad. It's only his foot.'

We leave him. We get him into his ute, driver's side, and leave him there with the dogs still yapping. We get outta there fast.

It's his left foot. He's got water. He'll be okay.

We get back in and I drive, going the same direction the blue Commodore did. The windows down, hot air blasting and a trail of dust behind us. I've got the gun down between my seat and the door where Nao can't see it.

'How far?' I shout over engine noise.

'An hour and a half maybe,' she says. 'There should be a sign.'

Nao's pissed off at me, pissed off about the gun. I'm not too happy with her, either, am I? Sam knew about the mine. She told him about it. Sooner or later he's gunna call the cops.

A bit over an hour along, there's a turn off right. A blue sign says MINE SITE with an arrow to a tall arched gate across the track, metal rusted to orange: SALTWATER GOLD CORPOR-ATION. I slow the ute, glance at Nao and we take the turn, a dirt track inland under the gate and on through green scrub.

The track's rough and I take it slow, the tyres crunching. The road dips down and the ground gets higher out to our left like we're headed into a valley. The breeze through the windows dies to nothing.

There's fuck-all when we get there except a clearing, a high wire fence and more rusted signs – *fuck off* and *keep out* type signs. Metal sheds and machinery behind a big set of double gates, padlocked shut. The track carries on around the outside of the fence in both directions.

I stop by the gates and keep my foot on the brake. No other vehicle, far as I can see. Nao's frozen, her hands wrapped around the strap of her seatbelt, staring at the fence. Dirt and dust streaked up her arms and across her face. The bandage on her hand crusty and brown.

'You orright?' I say.

She nods but doesn't shift. She's got goosebumps up both of her arms.

Freaked out about seeing him, isn't she?

'I can do it,' I say. 'Only needs one of us. You don't even have to talk to him. You can stay in the car.'

'We don't even know that he's here.'

'He is. Saw the blue Commodore, remember?'

She blinks. 'Who is that?'

'Dunno. Seen it around. Could be an undercover cop. Gotta be careful.'

There's tyre marks in the soft dirt, along the line of the fence to the left. I follow them, hearing every crack and scrape of the tyres. I keep the fence on our right, the gun down between me and the door. The trees and scrub crowd closer as we head out of the clearing, the ridge still there to the left of us above the tops of the trees. After a few hundred metres the track does a circle and doubles back on itself. The fence keeps going and disappears.

'Dead end.' I stop the ute.

A heap of big rocks and a stand of trees dead ahead, next to a flat stretch of water. The ridge and straight-up walls of a gorge further back like the water's coming out the mouth of it. The heat and humidity's full-on and the cloudy light makes everything stand out bright.

'The waterhole,' says Nao.

She puts a hand on my arm and I see it: the black LandCruiser parked at one end of the rocks, on this side of the water. It's backed up under the trees with the front end facing out towards us. I'm relieved for about a half a second until I remember Geen's face in the video.

The windows are tinted dark so I can't see nothing inside. My heart's going mental and there's no sign of him or Geen. She's gotta be in there.

I slide a hand down next to my seat, scrape my fingers down the handle of the gun. I can't see the Commodore. Where did it go? That Sam's gunna call the cops. 'Come on,' I say. 'Dunno how long we've got.'

'We're not going to do anything stupid,' Nao says.

Like she's trying to convince herself.

19

Nao

Warren

Charlie shuts the engine off and the sounds wash in – cicadas, frogs, crickets – a waterfall of noise. The place stretching out behind the black four-wheel-drive is exactly as it is in the photo. The dark pool with steps and slabs of red rock climbing to the ridge behind. The tumble of rocks this side where the ground slopes down to the water. Eucalypts and ferns and grasses ringing the edge of it.

'I don't even know why Dad was here,' I say. 'The day he was killed.'

I should sense it, that Dad was here and he died here, but there's nothing apart from the familiar feeling of his absence. I'm still numb from the news last night, scared of the trap we've

295

walked into: what Warren plans to do and might already have done, how we're going to make it out alive.

Aunty knew, didn't she? She suspected the truth about Warren and Dad and didn't tell me. She wanted to keep me safe, but here I am.

Charlie's eyes skip to my face and away. 'We gunna do this, yeah? Give me the bag.'

'I want to take it.'

I heft the bag and we step out of the ute, leaving both doors open as if we've discussed this. As if we've agreed to leave it that way for our getaway, an insane movie idea. I don't know what time it is. I've lost my sunglasses and Aunty's hat. I notice the light and put a hand up against it. The sun is trying to burn its way through the cloud.

Charlie hitches up her shorts at the back. Her shirt is tied around her waist in a bulky knot. She's lost weight, we both have. She was skinny enough at the start.

Warren's vehicle is backed down the slope with the front part raised up and the water behind it. There's an arm of rock extending out into the water like a natural jetty and three square slabs further out from it, a metre or two between each like a giant's pathway into the gorge. The yawning stretch of water beyond is wider than it looked in the photo.

I run my eyes over the four-wheel-drive – no movement, no shadows from the overhanging gum leaves. Is he inside? I wonder why he's parked it there, in that particular spot. The paintwork and windows look like the gun did when Charlie first pulled it out, dense black and reflecting nothing.

We start towards it. My sprained ankle has stopped hurting and I have to look down to check my feet are moving. The smell is wet rocks from the waterhole, sharp green from the trees and the scrub. A mineral taste in my mouth. The bag in my hands is heavier than it's been at any time.

The rock walls of the gorge seem to shimmer as we move closer, distorting the air above the ridge like a heat mirage until I see it's a cloud of black cockatoos, forming and reforming. The bird sounds are layered in among the other sounds: the scrape of small feet out in the scrub, the clatter of insects.

We're halfway to the vehicle when he calls out from behind us. 'Naomi. Stop there, please.' The words are like a push in the back, and I trip. More red-tails explode out of the trees and Charlie flinches.

I step in front of Charlie as I turn, and he's there, emerging from the trees beside the ute where he was waiting for us. The cut on my hand throbs, remembering. The hair at the nape of my neck, too. His nose is swollen like he's broken it, with a black rim under each eye. He's wearing a black cap and the reactor sunglasses so I can't see his eyes. A stained dressing protrudes from the grimy neck of his shirt.

None of these things reassure me as he limps towards us. He has a handgun, exactly like the one Charlie took from the dead police officer, held low in his left hand, and his right arm hangs awkwardly from the shoulder, not moving apart from the flexing and extending of his gloved fingers. Like he's fighting a battle with pain or trying to make it function.

He stops a few paces off and I see his breathing, fast and shallow, the grey pallor of his skin. But I feel his eyes from behind the reactor lenses and my cells wash with adrenaline just the same. I did this. I did these things to him.

I keep my eye on the gun in his hand and keep my body

between him and Charlie. I can't see him staying patient with her for long.

Charlie has half of her top lip raised, radiating hate like something wild. I understand I've not seen the worst of her and I want to tell her to keep it back, to suck it up inside. She's got one arm under her shirt behind her back, and the panic in me ramps up as I realise she's got the gun there. She thinks she's going to shoot him with it. 'Charlie?' My voice cracks on her name.

'Where's Geen?' She steps out past me to face him: her chin lifted, one dirty foot in front of the other one, pointed at him. One hand bunched in a fist and the other moving under her shirt like she's scratching an itch.

He barely looks at her. 'The bullion,' he says. 'Naomi, open the bag.'

Charlie says, 'We're not giving it to ya until we know she's okay.'

'Charlie.' I gulp and swallow. 'It's fine.' I step between them and try to unzip the bag with one hand while I hold it with the other but I can't. I kneel down in the dirt, keep a watch on him, wipe the sweat that's dripping into my eyes. I unzip the bag and hold it open. 'It's all in there,' I say to him. 'We haven't touched it.'

'Except to remove the GPS unit,' he says. One end of his mouth kinks into an almost-smile. There was a time he used to charm with that smile and I thought it was real. But we are long past all of that. 'Bring the bag to me.'

I stand up to do it but Charlie says, 'No way, mate,' and grabs the handle to hold me back.

'Naomi,' he says. 'To me.' I sway and take a step. It's impossible not to do what he wants.

Charlie moves in closer and takes the weight of the bag. 'We need to give it to him,' I whisper.

'No. Don't let him get to ya.'

Warren says, 'Naomi!' but I let go and let her take it.

She kneels and unzips it in one motion, lifts a handful of the heavy bars out, inside their cloth bags. Another handful. 'There's a hundred,' she says. 'Same as there was at the start.' She tips one out and shows him, dull gold in the strange light. Puts it back and shows him three more, her hands quick and steady. 'You're not getting it until we've got Geen.' She zips the bag closed and stands with a foot either side of it, arms crossed like a comic book character.

Warren's jaw is locked tight and Charlie stands there like she doesn't get it. I wait for him to lunge at the bag, to shoot her in the face or the leg, to shoot both of us. He lifts the gun and steps forward, stronger than he looked a second ago. My gut lurches and I make a grab for her. I'm not going to be quick enough.

But he turns his smile on me as if he knows I'm thinking all these things, and he swings his gun arm to point at his vehicle. 'Let's go and look, shall we?' he says.

Warren makes us walk ahead of him. Charlie takes the bag, the handle looped over one shoulder. I keep between them, terrified he'll see the shape of the gun under her shirt and shoot her in the back.

But he has barely looked at her, as though he's already decided she's not worth his time.

Instead, I feel Warren's eyes in the centre of my back like all my worst nightmares come at once. I think of Dad, and whether he was afraid in the moments before he died or didn't see it coming. My heart is beating so hard I can't think straight.

Charlie watches the four-wheel-drive. She stumbles as we get close and one of her thongs slips sideways in the dirt. I want to tell her not to trust Warren but she must know this. He says, 'Stop there, both of you.' Her fists tighten but she does.

We stand a few metres off from the front of the vehicle, the ground sloping towards the water and the natural jetty. He's parked on a dirt ramp, the only clear access to the waterhole, the rest ringed with scrubby gums and slabs of rock. There's no sound or movement from the four-wheel-drive, no sign of life at all and I'm not getting a good feeling from it, from that or the water behind. I watch Charlie's pinched face when she turns to him, her tense shoulders rising and falling, and I think she feels it too.

She licks her bottom lip. 'What have you done with her? Geen!' She turns back to the vehicle. 'You in there, Geen? You orright? Where is she?'

Warren steps around me. 'Naomi, tell this person what will happen if she doesn't behave.' He aims the gun casually at the lower half of her body and I remember the bloodied toe of Sam's boot.

'Charlie ...' I blink the sweat out of my eyes and edge between them again but he moves to where he can see her. 'We did what you said,' I say to him. 'No police. We haven't told anyone.'

'I believe someone has,' he says. 'Been careless, at any rate.' He sneers at Charlie and she gives it back, tensing the knuckles of her right hand. But he lowers the gun to his side and angles his head, listening. He nods. No distant engine sound, above the other sounds. No rescue party.

The sound of the place rises and falls like something breathing. The sun has broken through the cloud. 'Please,' I say. 'We can leave before anyone knows we're here.'

'Yeah,' Charlie says. 'Soon as we get Geen, you get the gold. Not that ya fucken deserve it.'

His gun arm twitches. She can't talk to him like this.

'The girl is in the back of the vehicle,' he says.

She starts towards it. I go to follow her, a beat too late. 'Not you, Naomi,' Warren says. 'You wait with the bag.' He gestures at Charlie with the gun. 'Leave it.' She glares at him but she does. She presses it against me and our eyes meet. I see how scared she is underneath the attitude, how much she's bluffing, before she turns away.

She doesn't look back. She gets to the front of the car and picks her way towards the back of it, down the slope. 'That's it,' he says to her. 'Around to the rear door. Right around.' There's barely any space between the rocks and the car, and a metal stud on her shorts scrapes against the side of it. There's a sound like she's keying the paintwork but Warren doesn't bat an eye.

'This has gone too far, Naomi.' I frown at him but he's watching Charlie's back. He's further in front now, nearer to Charlie and the water, and I didn't see him move. He's in between the two of us and I get a thrill of fear.

'Let them go,' I say. 'You've got me here. You don't need them.'

But he goes on as if he hasn't heard me. 'The older girl plotted this. The sister. She stole my safe. Her and her thug, now deceased.' His eyes flicker towards me. 'You needn't have got involved with these people.'

These people? I hold the bag tighter against me. He hasn't said a word about me trying to kill him. Surely that's what this is about.

Charlie presses between the rear side panel and the rocks, the water tilting behind her. She lifts one foot and then the next, one hand on the roof to steady herself. I don't know how I let this happen – Charlie and her sister on one side of him and me on the other. It's like looking down a telescope from the wrong end.

'Charlie?' My voice catches. 'Come back. I don't know how deep that water is. Please, Warren,' I say. 'Take the gold. Let me swap with them.'

But he talks over me, the same way he always does. 'You have no idea the lengths I've gone to,' he says. 'I've tidied countless loose ends. Removed witnesses, destroyed property. You've left a trail four lanes wide, littered with dead men.'

No. That was you. I step wide, trying to keep sight of Charlie as she moves, but Warren does the same. He's still in between us with the gun down at his left side. The bag drags on my arms. 'You burned Charlie's house,' I say.

'I'd tracked the last known location of your phone to the lake. I'd found the thug's body. I couldn't have you implicated.' His words wash back towards me but his gaze is fixed on Charlie.

She disappears around the back of the vehicle and I hear her try the handle. 'Can't open it,' she says. 'Locked.'

'It's not locked,' Warren says. 'Try again. Put some effort into it. Don't you want to see your sister?'

It's like one of those dreams where I can't move my feet. The still water. The shimmer of birds circling higher over the ridge. I think of Sam, seeing my connection to this country when he'd never even met me, and Warren, always in the way. I think of Dad again, dying here. How shadowy he has always been to me and how unfair that is.

Charlie would do something. She wouldn't just stand here, holding onto the bag. 'Charlie,' I say. 'Don't open it.' But I see the rear door float upwards and confusion drift across her face.

'Be quiet, Naomi! This no longer concerns you.' He needs to shut up.

He raises the gun and I see his plan too late. To kill them both and put them in the water.

'Nao?' Her voice bends in the air as Warren sights along the gun. I'm not having it. I'm not losing Charlie the same way as Dad.

I yell, 'Charlie, get down!' and I charge at him.

Charlie swings wildly, her elbows like wings, trying to pull the gun out from the back of her shorts. I smash the bag into Warren's back – I aim it high on his injured side – and he steps and staggers forwards.

He shoots, and Charlie falls. I run at her as she does, up and over the rocks, and when I get there I see that the back of the vehicle is empty.

20

Geena

Charlie Bear

The Arsehole lets Geena out of the boot for a pee in the early morning daylight. Her head is banging from the tail end of sleep and those pills he gave her, and she gets a look at the place and no more – the place they arrived at in the early hours where Charlie and Naomi are going to meet him with his gold. He's got the Toyota parked on a slope next to a big waterhole and doesn't let her go far. She can smell the water and there's a racket of about a million frogs bouncing back at her. Likely bloody cane toads in there too. Geena's legs have got no juice in them for running or swimming for it, not that she'd want to get in there. She's out of strength or opportunities to kick him where it hurts, basically, or do anything other than exactly what he tells her to.

She splashes handfuls of water on her face, though, and the cool is beautiful. Some of the swelling's gone down and her eye has opened up to a watery blur. She asks him for more to drink before he shuts her back in the boot but he doesn't answer. She sees the way his eyes go dead at the question before he bangs the door back down on her. He doesn't mean for her to come out of this.

She's got around two hundred mil left of the water he gave her back at the motel. It's hot in the boot but she hasn't suffocated yet. It's not over until it's over. But that only makes her think of Mum.

His feet crunch away from the car until there's nothing except the white noise of the frogs. She thinks of her idea last night to kill him and she tries to keep the faith, because what is he? One oldish guy, not well in body and mind. Armed with one handgun with how many bullets in it? Against the three of them, including Naomi, the stepdaughter. And what have they got going for them? The water. They can put him in it, as long as he doesn't put them in it first. They only need to be smart, and not panic.

The panic comes anyway. It crawls in slowly, with each breath in and out, like it's taken a while to find her. Because she remembers how it woke him up, her smashing that door into him and breaking his nose. It's not over until it's over goes both ways. And where's he gone? Where are the girls? Are they still coming?

She thinks of Mum again, and Dad. Before Mum died the way she did, Dad could do no wrong in Charlie's eyes. They stood up for each other. Fought each other's battles. They were out of the same mould.

But after? Charlie wouldn't talk about Dad or visit him, wouldn't acknowledge she even had a father. It half-killed Charlie, doing that, Geena knows it did.

If Geena makes it through this, if they both do, she's going to get Charlie there and she's going to bloody well get the two of them to sort their shit out. This whole mess is entirely Geena's fault. She can do this one thing.

She's trying to remember what Dad's face looks like when she hears a car engine. It stops as soon as she registers it and she wonders if she's magicked it up, or if it's the girls. Do they know The Arsehole is out there waiting?

She hears the crunch of footsteps, slower than before. Only one set – it's not the girls, it's the cop coming back. The tread sounds different, like he's limping or hesitating or carrying something heavy, and the dread sucks at her, like someone's pulled the plug on the waterhole out there. This is it. He's got the gold from Charlie and he's shot her and dumped her already and he's come back for Geena and the shovel. She can see that crook arm at his side, imagine the crabbing sideways walk as he carries the holdall with his gold in it.

A door opens at the front of the car and the weight shifts as he climbs in. There's a moment where he does nothing and she holds her breath and waits, and then a scraping, huffing sound on the other side of the seats near Geena's head. The seat starts to move and fear rockets through her. He's putting the seats down. He's got Charlie with him and she's already dead. He's going to pile Charlie's body in next to her and drive them away.

And then Lee's voice says, 'Geena? Babe? Give the seat a push from your side?'

*

Between them they get one seat down and she squints as the light floods in. Lee's hassled face stares through the gap: his designer stubble going to seed and his aviators on crooked.

She grabs his hand in a death grip; after her failed escape attempt at the motel she thought she'd never see him again. 'I thought you were him, come back to kill me. I thought Charlie was dead meat.' Her heart is wobbling like a spinning top in her chest. 'Have you seen him? Did he see you?'

'Not seen him, no. I parked back out on the track.'

'What about Charlie? You seen two girls?'

He shakes his head. His eyes are wide, running over her bruises and down at the shovel and back up.

'We need to get out, Lee. He could be back anytime. We need to get to her before he does.'

He clunks the door open and she squirms over the shovel and out, into the light and the frog sounds, the hot damp air, getting the blood flowing back into her arms and legs. Lee touches her shoulder but pulls back like he's worried he'll break her. 'Babe. Your face.' She knows it looks bad: her fucked-over cheekbone and stained sundress, her Coral Sunrise nails ripped and broken.

She tries to smile but it hurts. 'It looks worse than it is. You should see the other guy.' But she goosepimples up when she sees the water again. How close to the edge of it The Arsehole has parked.

'Can you walk?' Lee whispers.

'I'm fine, Lee. That shovel in the back. Can you bring it?'

They can bash him with it. It's better than nothing. She hustles Lee ahead of her into the shade – head-high boulders, wattles and paperbarks. They turn and watch the Toyota from between two rocks, close enough to see inside when The Arsehole comes back to it.

'You followed us,' she says. 'You came the whole way up here.'

'It's a bloody big distance, Geena. It's a lot of fuel. Four full tanks.' He looks so serious in the dappled light, the worry rippling his forehead and creasing the outer corners of his eyes. She can't believe he's come through for her, how much she's underestimated him.

'What are we going to do?' she says. 'Which way did he go? How do we find the girls?'

'Daryl's dead, Geena.'

'I know.'

'You do?'

'The Arsehole told me. It was on the news.'

'Oh, yeah. Right.' He frowns. 'I saw him. At your place.'

'Daryl?'

'*Him*. The man who took you. I got him on my phone.' He talks in a harsh whisper, pulls his phone out of his jeans pocket. 'Video.'

'When was this?'

'Monday night, in and out the back of your place. Burning it.'

'He *what?*'

'Shit, you didn't know that.'

'I didn't know that.' Except maybe she did. The petrol smell when he got back in the Toyota Monday night. She presses a hand to the centre of her chest. Hell, they've got nothing now. She has to get to Charlie.

'Why would he burn our place?' she says. 'Just to get back at us?'

'Don't know, babe. But I got him on video, I told you. Evidence. We can show it to the cops.'

She looks at him, all happy-bunny with himself. 'We can't show the cops, Lee. Of course we can't. We stole that safe from him!'

'Oh. Yeah.'

'He's a cop, too, himself, did you know that?'

His mouth open. The happy-bunny expression extinguished. 'You mean, we stole that safe off a—'

'Shh,' she says. 'I didn't know, either. Engine. It's them.'

Geena and Lee watch the girls get out of Daryl's green ute, across the clearing from the Toyota, back near the wire fence. They leave both doors open and walk side by side down towards the water, to where she and Lee are hidden. The tall girl, Naomi, is carrying the bag with the gold.

Geena's choked at the sight of Charlie; she can't believe it's her out there and she's in one piece. She wants to yell out to her but she grips Lee's forearm with her nails instead. The Arsehole could be anywhere. 'We need a plan, Lee.'

It is her, the girl Geena saw outside the motel. She's a head taller than Charlie, straight-backed and striking. With dark eyes and the ghost of a bruise around one of them, her hair yellow-blonde now and cut short against her skin. No shoes and owning it, like she never needed any.

They're both owning it, aren't they? They've come all this way together. The two of them throw long shadows as they walk, as the sun burns through the thinning cloud. Charlie's got a suntan Geena's never seen on her. A length in her stride she's never seen before either.

They're halfway to the Toyota when The Arsehole steps out from the trees behind them. He says something that stops them dead and Naomi moves to put herself between him and Charlie. He's got the gun in his hand and Geena thinks she might faint. She looks at the shovel leant against the rock in front of her. What the hell use is that going to be? What's the use in Lee pulling her out of the car if they can't do anything? The cop will shoot them all.

But Naomi's his stepdaughter. That's got to count for something. He's talking to the two of them. Charlie unzips the holdall and shows him the gold.

Our gold, Geena thinks, even after everything. He burned their bloody house down. He doesn't deserve it back.

Things happen fast. They walk closer and Charlie yells Geena's name. Lee has to wrap both arms around her to stop her racing out there. Charlie talks back to the cop with her hands in fists. 'Suck it up, can't she?' Geena hisses.

The Arsehole gets between the girls with the gun and Naomi takes the holdall.

'What's happening? I don't like this, Lee. We gotta do something.'

The Arsehole says to Naomi, 'The girl plotted this. The sister. She stole my safe.' He looks at Charlie with the same disgusted stare. She's at the back of the Toyota and she's opening up the boot, and Geena sees her face as she clocks on that it's empty.

The Arsehole raises the gun. Naomi yells at Charlie and runs at him.

Charlie's head snaps around as they hear the shot.

And then Geena's free of Lee and she's running. She can taste the blood on the air and see the spray of it, see Charlie twisting as she falls towards the water. She looks like a damn gymnast, a perfect ten. Charlie's dirty brown singlet balloons out behind as she goes under.

Lee shouts, 'I'm on it, babe.' They dive in side by side and he's a second behind her.

Rosalie Primary School fifty-metre freestyle champion four years in a row, Lee gets to Charlie first. He's got her in a surf-lifesaving headlock when Geena breaks the surface. The water is winter-cold and has sucked all the air out of her. 'Charlie? Is she breathing?'

'Don't know, babe. Give us a second.'

Blood in the water. Charlie's eyelids are fluttering, her arms and legs drifting like wood.

'Get her up on that last rock.' It's not fifty metres, it's more like fifteen, but they put as much distance between them and the cop as they can. Geena levers herself onto the slab of rock, the furthest out. She can't see The Arsehole, knows he's back behind them with the gun.

She gets on her hands and knees. Her heart is body-slamming her from the inside. She plucks at Charlie's singlet, gets a hand under her neck as Lee pushes from below. They heave her up onto the rock, but Charlie's too still, too pale, and the front of her shoulder and chest are slick with red. They've not come all this way for her to die. They have not.

'Charlie Bear? Can you hear me? Get her headphones off, Lee.' They're still around her neck.

'Use my shirt, babe.' Lee gets up beside her, rips the shirt off and she balls it up. She presses it to Charlie's shoulder, knowing there's big stuff under there, blood vessels and nerves and who knows what else.

'I can't see her breathing, Lee! Hold this. Put pressure on it.' She checks Charlie's airway, remembers the moves from high school lifesaving. She can't see anything wrong and doesn't know if she's doing it right. Charlie's lips are pale blue.

Geena angles herself to start CPR and gets a glimpse of The Arsehole, back on dry land beside his Toyota. He's gripping that right arm and fighting for breath, the gun drooping and the girl Naomi backing away with the bag of gold in her arms; she thumped him pretty good with that bag. Geena feels for a moment his gaze on her and Lee and the glaring question in it, *Where did you two come from?*

Naomi turns and runs from him along the jetty of rock towards them, and Geena hears the sounds her feet make as she puts her hands to Charlie's chest and makes the first compression, the slapping of wet stone where the water's washed across it.

Charlie's lips part and she hauls in a breath.

21

Charlie

The Gun

Hot pain in my chest. Hurts to breathe. Ringing in my head and the smell of wet.

Geen's voice. 'She's alive. She's breathing. Lee, help me.'

Someone rolls me on my side. There's wet rock under me. Clammy. I cough up a shitload of water.

'Geen?'

'Don't talk, Charlie. Keep that pressure on, Lee. The bullet went right through. It's bleeding worse at the front.'

He shot me? What the fuck?

'She needs to keep calm.'

I open my eyes but the sun's too bright and I shut them again. I catch sight of Nao's face and Geen's busted-up one, both here with me. The gun still down the back of my shorts, pressing into my back, except my arm's stuck and I can't get to it.

Where is he? I peel my eyes open again. 'Geen?' I say, too quiet. 'Nao. Take it.'

Nao's blank face. She doesn't get it.

'Nao.' Louder. 'Take it!'

The bastard's voice. 'Stand back from there, Naomi.'

'Nao, fucksakes, the gun!' I say.

Her eyes widen – she gets it. I feel her pull it out, the slap of her foot on rock as she steps away. See her arm swing round, the cut-out shape of the gun against the sun.

'No, Warren,' she says. 'You get back.'

The bastard and Nao are facing-off like movie cowboys. The dude called Lee is on his feet and dripping water, both hands up in front of him.

Geen's got my head in her lap, one hand on my forehead, the other one pressing hard against my chest. My breathing not right. 'Charlie,' she keeps saying. 'Charlie. He could have killed you.'

He might still.

'Naomi. Put the gun down. Step aside,' the bastard says, stood on water.

Except I look again and he's not. He's on a flat bit of rock, the black LandCruiser back behind him on dry land. There's one big rock in between him and us, a wide step from each one to the next. Me and Geen and Lee and Nao are on the last one, out in the middle. The gorge open at our backs, water the whole way around us and fucken deep, 'cause I never hit the bottom of it before Lee hauled me out.

'No, Warren,' Nao says. She's between him and the rest of us with the holdall clamped to her side. She's not letting it go. I can see the one handle caught over her shoulder, stretched too far like it's gunna break. Her two hands pinched around the gun.

'You have no idea what you're doing with that. Calm down.' He's chewing on his teeth and puffing with the effort, his face grey and sweaty. He's lost his hat and sunnies, his right arm's hanging straight like it's fucked and there's blood on the bandage at his neck. He's still too close, but: four, five metres, tops. Close enough to shoot us. Four bodies in the water and he won't even need to dig a hole.

'No. I will not calm down.' Can't see Nao's face. Is she gunna shoot him?

Shit, she's gunna shoot him. 'Don't, Nao,' I say. 'Not worth it. Remember what you said? We only need to keep our heads, and you were right. Give him it. Give him the gold.'

'Be quiet, Charlie. He changed the rules when he shot you.' She swings her head and I see her properly, her arms out straight with the gun. The sweaty side of her face, her wild eye. 'My dad died for this gold.' Her voice rough. 'I'm not having you die too.'

Lee chucks a look at Geen, drops a hand down behind him and she grabs it.

'Collateral damage, Naomi,' Warren says. 'Your father intervened in something he should not have. I had no idea who he was.'

'No, but you knew who *we* were, Mum and I, when you ran us off the highway on your way from killing him. Reckless, speeding, not paying attention. How did you guess? The name? The car registration? The picture on Mum's phone?'

'I couldn't possibly have known.'

'But you figured it out, fast, didn't you? You needed to keep her close. You had to cover up the accident. Mum told me you were first on the scene, that you helped us, but you were the one that *hit us*. How did you get her to lie?'

'She needed me, Naomi. You both needed me, as you well know, after your father was gone.'

'Bullshit!' The word cracks out, makes me jump. The stepdad doesn't blink.

'And there was the money,' he says. 'For the material things you had to have, the music lessons, the expensive education, pointless as that clearly has been. Money you have never once questioned.'

Nao goes quiet. Rubs the sweat out her eyes with the inside of her arm.

He squints past her at us, still puffing. 'Put the gun down and we can talk.' Softer. Trying it on. I don't trust it.

Neither does Geen. She shifts us backwards. 'Ow, Geen!'

'So you can shoot us, you mean?' Nao says. 'Me and my friends? You erased my dad my whole life. You don't get to erase me too.'

'Drop the weapon.' The hard back in his voice. 'These people are not your friends.'

'Put your gun down first,' she says to him. 'I will if you will.'

Geen yanks me back to the edge of the rock. 'Geen! Shit.' She hisses sorry, her breath hot on my skin. Lee moves in front of us, his arms up like he reckons he can take the dude. Course he can't take the dude.

'I want what belongs to me, Naomi.' A blood vessel squirms on his head like that snake back on the highway. 'If you don't give it to me, I will take it.'

'Try that and I will pull this trigger. We've already shot one man today.' She flicks a sideways look at me. 'You okay, Charlie?'

'Been better. Still alive.'

She keeps talking at him, quieter. 'It wasn't an accident, Sunday night. Do you know that?'

'Don't, Nao,' I say. 'Don't wind him up,' but it's like she can't hear me.

'What are you saying?'

'You heard me, Warren,' she says. 'It wasn't an accident, trying to kill you. I thought it was but now I know better. I should have finished the job.'

He goes real still. Geen's breathing is ragged in my ear.

'I've done all this for you, Naomi, cleaned up this mess at great personal cost so you can come home, and this is how you thank me?'

The holdall slips down Nao's arm and she grabs it back up, gets both hands back on the gun. 'It's not so I can come home,' she says. 'Blaming me is a lie, it's what you've done for years and you can stop it right now. All those news reports, the Corruption and Crime Commission investigation? I worked that out. It's your mess you've been trying to clear up, not mine. You've done it for yourself.'

And the bastard swings his arm and shoots Lee in the head.

Lee is fucked, the back of his head all over the rock. A dark slick of it on the water and I can smell the blood. He's fallen on his side, facing away towards the ridge, one white arm under the surface like a fish. Another dead dude, the fourth one this week. *Don't think about it.* Geen's mouth is open, staring at him. Her chest going in and out. The sound of the shot still ringing.

Geen dips her fingertips in the blood and holds them up. I get up on my knees; hurts like a bitch except I can breathe a bit better. I grab a hold of her arm and pull her away. 'No, Geen.' She won't stop staring at him. There's a black knot of flies and I dunno how they got on there so quick. The buzzing makes me wanna spew. 'Geena.'

I glance at Nao. Her eyes are flat with how screwed we are. The stepdad's one rock closer, only one more step between him and us and I didn't see him make his move. Water washes over the rock, the ripples spreading out from Lee as the bastard bends down and yanks the bottom of his suit pants straight.

Nao sticks her hands up. 'I'll put it down if you do the same. But only if you stay where you are.'

He narrows his eyes. Tilts his head. 'Of course.'

'Don't trust him, Nao.' My body shiny with blood and I'm shivering. I dropped the shirt Geen had against my shoulder, can't see it.

Nao bends and puts the gun down on the rock at her feet. The bastard does the same.

He smiles. 'Seeing sense.' The smile drops when he looks down, but. He sees the deep oily water between him and his gold, the long step onto slippery rock. Nao sees it too.

She swings the holdall off her shoulder, holding it away from her with both arms, out above the surface. 'One step closer, Warren, and this is going in.'

His face twitches and he swipes his good arm across it. Gritting his teeth at the pain. 'Naomi,' he says. 'Be realistic.'

'You got a mobile phone with you?' she says. 'We need to call an ambulance, for Charlie.'

'No signal,' he says.

Geen leans into me. Her heart going flat-out through the front of her dress. 'He's not gonna call an ambulance,' she says. 'He's got that shovel. He's only gonna kill us.'

Nao shifts her feet, frowns. 'What shovel?'

'In the back of the Toyota.' Geen's staring at the flies walking up and down Lee's body. The bloody bits of his hair on the water.

'Don't look, Geen.' I turn her head away.

The whole place wobbles in the heat except the inside of me is cold. The sound of everything louder – cicadas, frogs, the flies – and only a metre of water between Nao and him. The shadow of the bag skimming the surface.

'No closer,' Nao says. 'Not unless you want to go in after it.'

'Give it to him,' I say to her. 'He can ... have it.' I'm getting outta breath.

She shakes her head. 'No. He's going to help you.' She scans the far bank. 'Leave now, Warren. Drive until you have a signal. Call the Flying Doctor for Charlie. Do what you want after that, I don't care. If you still want this you can come back for it.'

His eyes are locked onto the holdall, his breathing fast and shallow. 'I will do no such thing.' He takes a step nearer the edge, the rock wet under his leather shoes. He slips and recovers, kicks out. His gun clatters off the rock and it's gone.

There's a white splash, the other side of the waterhole. I see Nao clock it. 'Leave now,' she says. 'Last chance.'

The gun on the rock at her feet and he sees it.

I dunno what Nao's thinking, what she's gunna do.

I hear the engine sound. Distant, quiet at first, can't tell if it's real against the buzz of the rest. But Nao hears it and so does the stepdad. I watch his chest move quicker, the tight angle of his neck.

'That'll be the local police, Warren,' Nao says. 'Looks like you're out of time, to recover the rest of it, the other ninety kilos. I imagine that's what the shovel is for.'

Dunno what she means. He does, but, and he's this close to losing it. He bends down to the leg of his pants again, scratching an itch. Except when he straightens up there's another gun in his hand. 'Give the bag to me. I will count to five.'

Bastard had it strapped to his leg.

The engine sound gets louder. A cloud of dust, moving above the trees.

'Naomi. I won't ask again. Hand it over or I shoot.' He leans and reaches for the holdall, too far and he gives up. He's puffing harder, more blood at the neck of his shirt. Nao doesn't shift. She won't give it to him.

'The girl will be first.' He swings his arm, aims at my heart. His arm shaking but I reckon he can take the shot.

'Nao?' My lips feel funny. 'Give it to him.'

I see her face change when she knows we've lost. She drops to her knees, dumps the bag down on the rock. Everything gone still as she looks up at him.

Maybe he'll take the gold and go. Maybe the cops'll get here in time.

'Leave Charlie and her sister,' she says. 'I'll come back with you. We can still call an ambulance.'

His arm steadier now. 'Too late for that, Naomi,' he says.

The gun cracks. Geen cries out and slams a hand to my chest.

I can't feel nothing. I see the bastard's eyes lock on Nao, wide open in surprise.

A red stain spreading across his shirt. Nao holding the gun out in front of her.

Fuck. Didn't see her pick it up. The gun she had down at her feet.

Her hands shake and she drops it. It bounces off the rock and goes in. *Plunk.* The bastard goes down slower. He sinks and his knees bend, the right leg slipping out from under him as he falls. A dull crack as his head hits the rock. Blood pooling under his head and his arms jerk once before he's still.

Nao says, 'Charlie?' There's no sound except the three of us breathing, Geen shivering against me. Then the flies come back, and the engine noise.

Nao says, 'Charlie? I didn't know I was going to do that.'

'S'orright. It's gunna be fine.' Except I'm getting colder, we gotta be quick. I slide Geen's arms from around me and crawl over to the bag. Look at the cloud of dust across the clearing.

'They're almost here.' Nao's shaking hard. Her breath pushing in and out.

'Both those guns go in the water? Plus the extra one?'

She nods.

I grab up the holdall, the dead dog weight of it. One arm still works. I make the step to where the bastard lies still. 'Know what we gotta do, yeah?'

Nao shakes her head.

I start pulling bars out the bag. I stuff three in his pants pocket. 'Geen? Get here and help me.'

She does it. We empty the bag out. 'All of them, orright? We never had it.' In all his pockets. Down his shirt, tucked in tight, underneath the blood. I rip the one out my pocket, don't even blink. The bag goes in under his shirt too.

We roll him, Geen and me. Straight over and in; he doesn't make a sound.

There's no trace after he's gone except ripples, bigger than before, pushing up over the edges of the rock. Washing away the blood. 'We say he did a runner with it,' I say. 'Shot Lee and took off.'

Nao's frozen, swaying on her feet. 'Charlie, you're really bleeding.'

'Yeah.' My head light like I'm gunna faint. My arms heavy.

The cops roll up across the clearing as Geen sticks her arms back around me, the front part of me slippery with blood. I sink down into her and see the thing move under the water. A dark stripe, long as the ute. A flash of pale belly.

'Stay well back from the edge,' Nao says. 'That's a saltwater crocodile.'

Geen and Nao get either side of me, get me up and walk me from one rock to the next, real slow because my legs won't work. Looking out for the croc except we don't see it.

Two cops are stood there, shocked and waiting by their LandCruiser. A set of handcuffs bright in the sun.

'Nao?' I say.

'Shh. Don't talk, Charlie.'

'It was all me, yeah? All of it. You didn't do nothing.'

'No, Charlie.'

'You wanted to go to the cops. That's what I'll tell them.'

'No. That's not right.'

We get to the cops and it kicks off. Nao and Geen start talking at the same time and I dunno if they're doing it right. One cop's going on about an arrest warrant while Nao argues back, saying they need the Flying Doctor for me, plus there's a dead body out on the rock and a big croc in the water.

And then I'm laying down in the dirt not feeling good and Geen's stroking my forehead. The flies are buzzing and tickling and it's too bright. I squint at Lee's body out there, pale like the underneath of the croc. The water flat and dark and deep and the bastard at the bottom. He better be gone forever.

One cop brings a set of handcuffs and wants to put them on me. Nao argues some more, yells at him and stamps her foot, saying what the hell is he thinking and can't he see I'm injured bad? So he puts one on each of us instead, her left hand to my right. Fucksakes, it's not like I'm going anyplace.

Nao's nervous, talking more than I've heard her all week, all this stuff about the law and she better not drop herself in it. She's telling the cops about the shovel and her dad and saying she knows where the rest of the gold is, the other ninety kilos, and my brain hurts trying to figure out everything she means.

Someone puts a blanket over me, one of those reflecting ones that feels like it does fuck-all. Nao's saying the Flying Doctor's coming and Geen's telling me it's gunna be okay, except I'm shaking hard and I can't breathe too good and I'm so cold.

And then it's like the sun going down and I can't hear the flies or the crinkle of the blanket. I can't feel Geen's hand on my head no more and it goes quiet.

SATURDAY

Nine months later

22

Nao

Country

Geena turns onto a long avenue of eucalypts, I don't know what kind, and we pass from bright winter sunlight into shade. It seems appropriate and I get a shot in the arm of nervousness. We haven't talked on the drive down but what is there to say? We did all that, back then.

The place looks like what you might expect. The car park is a quarter full and Geena says we're early, shutting off the ignition. She sits, scrolling on her phone, maybe so she doesn't have to talk to me or maybe she's being considerate so I don't have to talk to her either, I can't tell. She carries the shadow of everything that happened, you can see it on her. And she's got to be nervous too.

We're parked in the sun and it's warm on my face through the glass. There's nothing to see out there except the building and car park, the banksia bushland at the back of it that gives the place its name. The kind of winter clouds that move fast and high up so their shadows run across the country like an army. I watch them flowing over the grey roof of the building like someone has speeded up time.

Geena would know, about the eucalypts. She's good with plants, isn't she?

I steal glances at the line of her jaw, her tongue in the gap between her teeth and her speedy fingers on her phone, all of which remind me of Charlie. I try not to think about all the things it's impossible not to think about, but that never works and today of all days I just give in to it.

I remember Geena's face when she first talked about Warren, her wide eyes and the fear like a shutter coming down. 'The Arsehole', she called him. How I felt I had to apologise to her and how she told me to stop. We were sitting in another vehicle in another car park that day, the first chance we got to speak to each other after Warren had killed her friend.

'It wasn't down to us; it was all down to him,' she said. 'They've got it in for him, anyhow. Anti-corruption. I gave the sarge this name. Brunno. Brunswick?'

She expected me to recognise it, the name of Warren's contact via the burner phone she said he had, and I felt sick. No, I didn't recognise it but how would she have known that? I hadn't even spoken to Mum by then.

Geena said the Brunno name was the game-changer, that and everything she could tell the police – first in Broome and then the anti-corruption mob, as she called them, down in

Perth – about the burner phone, where they'd stopped and who'd helped Warren along the way. The timeline of events including Daryl and Lee's theft of his safe plus the footage Lee had on his phone of Warren setting fire to Charlie's house.

Nine months on and Warren remains a person of interest in a series of criminal cases and they haven't found his body. This feels more miraculous with each day that passes, especially considering Daryl didn't stay down in that lake for even a week.

The Deputy State Coroner pronounced Daryl's death unlawful homicide with insufficient evidence to determine the person or persons responsible. Warren had destroyed the scene and the body had been submerged long enough during that week of warm spring weather that nothing more than the likely cause of death could be determined.

I wonder if Geena guessed the truth and whether she and Charlie went into it. I'll probably never know.

'How much longer?' I ask, and she jumps.

She rolls her eyes, a hand to the centre of her chest. 'Shit, my nerves are shot. Fifteen minutes, if they're on time. Let's have a ciggie.'

We get out and she offers me her pack and we light up, leaning on the side of the car facing away from the entrance. I imagine Charlie's reaction to this while I trace the outline of what's in my skirt pocket. This at least makes me smile, despite everything.

Geena's testimony did a lot to keep the focus on Warren, but so did mine.

The shovel he brought with him all the way from the city wasn't for digging Charlie and Geena's graves, but for digging up his treasure. Ninety kilograms of gold in unrefined eighteen-kilogram bars that he'd buried on site, too conspicuous or too heavy to take with him at the time of the theft. Enough of a haul and buried shallow enough for a team to find with metal detectors, stashed in the scrub right next to where he'd parked by the waterhole. Warren's retirement fund, now given back to the traditional owners of the country and the mine.

The small bars was where Warren screwed up – one hundred commemorative bars of a hundred grams each to be gifted to investors to celebrate the first twenty-five years of the mine's output. Distinctive, unique and local, he should have buried them too or better still never taken any of it in the first place.

Mum told me we'd been making trips out to the waterhole with Dad since before I was born, none of which I remember. She and I were on our way to meet him there that day but she'd had problems with the car the day before and we were running hours behind. Dad waited for us, we didn't show up, he heard shots at the mine and went to investigate.

Aunty says the photo was the country's way of calling me back. The pull I felt from the gold too, maybe; it never stopped being a part of the place, after all. I know there's more to the story, about our family and the country, and that Aunty will tell me more when the time is right. For now, she's been teaching me about *liyan*. She says it's a kind of intuition all Kimberley people have, that it guides our sense of wellbeing, our sense of belonging and connectedness. It makes me think of that feeling of safety I could never quite get a hold of, and when I told her I wasn't sure I had it she said I did. She said I'd been listening to it the entire time.

My memories of Dad are coming back too, now that Warren is gone.

I'm still not ready to forgive Mum for the years of what she admits is denial, and I'm not sure she's forgiven herself either, but I guess it's early days.

Did they believe us, that Warren had done a runner with the ten kilos of gold? He'd abandoned his vehicle but it was entirely feasible he'd had help, and our stories were vaguely consistent. We were traumatised. A man was dead. We'd been out on that rock in the sun next to Lee's body. And Geena was right: they wanted to believe us; they wanted Warren behind bars.

It feels right that the gold is holding him down there in the dark, whatever is left of him by now.

However hard I try I can't remember the moment I picked up the gun. I don't remember the sound of it going off or what it felt like in my hand. There is only before – Warren flinging his gun arm at Charlie, the spearhead of fear – and after, his knees sinking and the blood blooming across the front of him and the sound of the gun hitting the rock as I dropped it.

Did I plan to kill him? I'll probably never know that either.

'Okay,' Geena says, and it's my turn to jump. 'Action stations.'

She crushes her cigarette under the toe of her boot and checks her hair and her face in the wing mirror. She smiles when she sees me do the same.

'Dipshits,' she says. 'But it's a big day. Should have brought balloons or something.'

'Is she into balloons?'

She flicks her hair back over one shoulder. 'Jeez, I doubt it.'

I hold back and tell her to go ahead, the nerves floating up inside me like bubbles in water. I watch as she approaches the entrance, the white glare of sun off the glass.

After various mitigating circumstances were taken into

account, including her recovery from gunshot wounds inflicted by a serving police officer, Charlie was sentenced to six months in juvenile detention for the aggravated theft of the four-wheel-drive. This was reduced to four months for her surprisingly (according to Geena) good behaviour and because she turns eighteen today. A state-wide initiative to keep youth offenders out of adult prison.

She took the rap for me just like she wanted to and I'm still not sure how I feel about that.

23

Charlie

Gold Coast

Geen's sent me some winter clothes and I put them on and wait in my room – jeans and sneakers and a new shirt, nice and cosy. I keep thinking they're gunna change their minds and keep me in here, that it's a joke or a mistake. I'm waiting for one of the officers or my youth worker to come in and tell me.

Except they haven't. Not yet.

I got a new set of headphones off Geen too, which they let me have 'cause it's my birthday and I'm getting out. Been listening to Mum's playlist again, the one Dad made me from prison with all her favourite stuff on. From what I can tell, he's added some new tunes he must think I'm gunna like. I even added a couple of extra ones myself, like that country song Nao was singing along to when we drove into Port Hedland.

Maybe I can start visiting Dad when I get out. Not sure. I know Geen wants me to.

Geen says we're never gunna know exactly how Mum died because Dad won't talk about it, and maybe Mum and Dad were an accident waiting to happen. After she said that I tried to tell her about Daryl except she wouldn't let me.

They never done me for killing Daryl, did they? Couldn't believe that. It just goes to show, you never know what's gunna happen until it happens. They never caught us on camera driving out to Claremont Lake, 'cause Nao stuck on the back streets. Weren't any forensics on the ute either, 'cause of us driving it through a cyclone.

I reckon we were luckier than what we realised.

Even that Sam told his mum and dad he shot himself in the foot out spotlighting rabbits, according to what one of the nurses at the hospital in Broome told me while I was in there. I reckon Sam only did it because of having the hots for Nao. I bet he asked her out, too, after. But would she have said yes?

They come and get me out my room. It's not like the movies with all the locks and gates opening and shutting behind ya. Juvie feels more like school, which is okay I guess. I caught up on some schoolwork in here and Geen is bloody rapt.

My shoulder hurts like a bastard today, 'cause of the cold weather. The doc says it's gunna stop doing that, that I'm young and in a year I won't even know the bones got messed up and I almost died from a collapsed lung and bleeding and all the rest. It's bright out for a winter day and I can't see Geen's face properly as I head out the doors. Got all my old stuff in a placcy bag and I'm gunna chuck that straight in the bin, soon as.

Geen's emotional, isn't she? Fair enough. I hug her back but I dunno if I'm in the mood for it. 'I'm orright, Geen. I'm okay.' She looks good except I can smell cigarette smoke and I tell her off for it and she rolls her eyes.

It's only when we get past the other cars I see it. Daryl's green ute.

'That a joke?' I say.

'He left it to me,' she says. 'It was in his will. Can you believe that?'

I can't, not fully, except it's not the green ute I'm staring at, it's Nao. She's leant up against it and she's got this smile on and a brand-new cowboy hat, better than that one of her aunty's. I wanna run up to her but I don't.

Nao looks like a queen again, tall with her hair longer and dark now, almost back to how I remember her from that first night except she's wearing shoes and she's not freaked out like she was then. No black eye, no cut on her hand. Her hair all shiny and fanned out around her shoulders and not stuck in that plait.

She presses her lips like she's not sure, except she's smiling at the same time.

I never let her visit me, did I? Never put her on the list and I dunno if she's pissed off at me about that or not. I didn't want her to have to. I knew she felt weird about it, me taking the rap for everything, even though we only got to talk that one time.

It was fair enough, I reckon. One thing I could do right. She saved me from the bastard, didn't she? She never gave up on me, either. I remembered that the whole four months I was in there. I thought about her every time I needed to keep calm.

Geen hangs back and lets me go up to Nao on my own. I'm

still not sure if she's mad at me but she pushes herself off the ute and stands there chewing her cheek. I've got my hands in my pockets except I want to hug her. So I do and she hugs me back.

'Happy Birthday, Charlie.'

'Didn't know if you'd be here.'

She lets go and has a look at me. 'Oh, I was always going to be here. You look good. I like the hair.' She frowns at the doors I just came out of. 'Listen, I hope it wasn't—'

'It was orright, Nao. Bit like school, except not as bad.'

She only half smiles, so I tell her I'm doing okay, that I'm gunna finish high school. 'Still got to sit the exams, but.' I glance behind at Geen. She's staring hard at her fingernails like she's trying not to listen. 'How about you?' I say to Nao. 'Gunna go back to uni?'

She says yeah, she is. 'I need to do a few things first. I got you something, too.' And she pulls this shiny thing out her pocket and hands it over.

It's a Cherry Ripe, two bars in the one pack. She tells me I can share it but only if I want, and I smile and say thanks. And then she checks the car park in both directions, the same as she was always checking the rearview mirror, and she gets another thing out her pocket and holds it out.

No way. It's one of the gold bars, the same as the one I nicked off Daryl. 'Is that for real?'

She nods and I take it, holding it close so no one can see apart from the two of us. It's heavy and small, the exact same as before. 'For real,' she says.

'Where did you get it? How?'

'I guess I picked it up.' She's squinting in the sun and not looking at me straight on. There's a dimple in her cheek I never noticed before.

My heart feels weird, happy and fast at the same time. I run my thumb across the gold and it's warm like how I remember it, like the whole of that week is inside this one thing. 'Probably can't sell it, can we?'

'That might depend,' she says. 'On where you want to go with it.' She looks past me at Geen. 'What do you think, Geena?'

'Oh, I think the Gold Coast, for sure. What do you reckon, Nao? Have we got a full tank of fuel in that ute?'

'I think we might.'

Are they fucking with me? Except I clock the back of the ute piled up with stuff. Nao catches me looking and smiles some more. I've never seen her smile so much in one go. It's the best birthday I've ever had.

Nao walks around the ute and climbs in on the driver's side, and Geen hops in the back seat. 'Charlie, you ride shotgun,' she says.

I get in the passenger side and do my seatbelt as Nao revs the engine and sticks it in drive. She catches my eye before we take off, one eyebrow and the corner of her mouth turned up like it's gunna stay that way forever. 'You know that's just a figure of speech, right?'

Mum's Playlist

Reckless (Don't Be So)	Australian Crawl
Say Goodbye	Hunters & Collectors
Dumb Things	Paul Kelly
Teenage Crime	Adrian Lux
Away, Away	Weddings Parties Anything
Confide in Me	Kylie Minogue
Pleasure and Pain	Divinyls
Mace Spray	The Jezabels
Rattlesnakes	Lloyd Cole and the Commotions
Alone with You	Sunnyboys
Weir	Killing Heidi
Two of Us On The Run	Lucius
The Captain	Kasey Chambers
Under the Milky Way	The Church
Diamonds	Rihanna
Runaway Train	Kasey Chambers
When It Don't Come Easy	Patty Griffin
Wide Open Road	The Triffids

Lucky Star	Alex Lloyd
Bring Yourself Home to Me	Jimmy Little
Run to Paradise	Choirboys
Like Cockatoos	The Cure
Charlie	Mallrat
Yandool	Stiff Gins
Thank You (for Loving Me at My Worst)	The Whitlams
For Real	Mallrat

Author's Note

The road trip Charlie and Nao make in *No Country for Girls* is one I've made myself several times. The story takes place in a real setting but, as I couldn't get back home to research the road trip, I worked from memories, photos, journeys in Google Street View, and the impressions of family members who were either working as fly-in-fly-out contractors or on road trips themselves during the travel-restricted year that 2020 turned out to be.

Writing this on a thirty-degree evening in January 2022, at last back in Western Australia after three years away, it is strange and wonderful to be seeing, hearing and smelling things I have put into the book, and that have been waiting for me here all along.

I have taken quite a few liberties with geography and geology, either to serve the story or because I wanted to keep to a particular memory; locals may notice that all is not quite as it appears. Bardi Jawi country up on the Dampier Peninsula is somewhere that has had a pull for me for many years, and is a trip I was planning before the pandemic hit. The setting of those sections of the novel, including the Saltwater Gold mine site, is entirely fictional.

Both Nao and Charlie have big backstories related to their families and I knew I didn't want everything resolved at the end for them both. In Nao's case, her Aboriginal family were affected by the Stolen Generations and this meant, even without the events that take place during her lifetime, it wasn't going to be straightforward for her to find her way back to her dad's country and extended family. In a sense, Nao's dad was still finding his way back to these things himself.

There are many resources online and in books and film about the Stolen Generations, the forcible removal of First Nations children in Australia from their families. I recommend *Growing Up Aboriginal in Australia*, edited by Anita Heiss, an anthology of fifty-one diverse voices and stories about childhood, family and country that contains many first-hand accounts of the effects of this policy and which I found so helpful in writing Nao's story.

For the writers reading this who are yet to be published – I didn't plan to submit this novel to agents because I thought I'd messed it up. Please keep doing whatever you need to do to get the good stuff of your imaginations out into the world. Don't stop now.

Acknowledgements

I wrote *No Country for Girls* as an experiment, not imagining in a million years that it would be published. I would not be here writing this if not for the great number of people who have helped me at every stage.

Thank you to my agent, Euan Thorneycroft, for getting in touch before 'big things happened', for your enthusiasm and hard work for the book and your unwavering support. And to Jessica Lee and the rest of the team at A. M. Heath for keeping me up to date with all the things I'd never thought about and for your brilliant work behind the scenes.

Thank you, Cal Kenny, my editor at Sphere, for taking a chance on me and the girls and changing all our lives. You've been incredible with these characters. Thanks for every single thing you have done for me and the novel over the past year and a half, and for never failing to be upbeat about whatever was happening.

Thanks too to Ed Wood and the Sphere editors and judges of the UEA Little, Brown Award way back in 2020 for awarding me the prize and being in my corner ever since. To Vanessa Neuling for the light touch of your copy-edit while at the same time not missing a trick. And to Thalia Proctor, Tom Webster and everyone else at Sphere who helped turn what felt like a never-ending work in progress into an actual book.

Thank you to Bekki Guyatt and the Studio of Ideas team for so exceeding my expectations with the stunning hardback and bound proof covers. To Aimee Kitson and Frankie Banks for marketing and publicity, Lucy Hine in international sales and everyone else who has championed the book at Little, Brown.

Thank you too to Jonathan Kinnersley at The Agency for your great work on the novel's behalf.

To my tutors on the UEA Crime Fiction course, Henry Sutton, Tom Benn, Julia Crouch and Nathan Ashman, thank you for your insightful feedback and for encouraging me to let rip. Nao and Charlie are grateful to you for that too. Thank you to all the UEA crime writers for blazing a trail, and to my fellow students and early readers in the 2020 cohort – Denise Bennett, Bridget Burgoyne, Jennifer Debley, Lucy Dixon, Mark Hankin, Helen Jones, Lin Le Versha, Lissa Pelzer, Amanda Rigali, Mandy Slater, Paul Stone, Martin Ungless and Lucy Wood – for cheering me on, making me laugh each time I wanted to cry, and having my back. This book would not exist without you.

Thank you to the following authors for their support over the last year: Sophie Hannah, Lizzie Pook, Tracy Darnton, Tamsin Cooke, Christina Vinall, Anita Loughrey, Cath Howe and all my other writer friends. Every interaction has helped get me here, and many have stopped me giving up when I wanted to.

On the subject of not giving up, Jo Franklin, Alli Jeronimus, Tasha Kavanagh and Jen Miles, I would have done a thousand times without you. Thanks for your confidence in me and the girls when I couldn't find it myself.

And to the 2022 debuts group on Twitter, thank you for the solidarity and kindness, for apparently never sleeping and for asking and answering every publishing-related question under the sun. It's a privilege to be among you and I can't wait to see what you all do next.

Thank you, Jo Hine and El Styles, my early West Australian readers, for spotting the things I needed you to spot. To Jane Stephens, thanks for the many lockdown beers and for putting me right on injuries and medical procedures. And to Mark Styles, Alex Castle, Claire Kaylock and Mike Batt for geological, law school and road trip advice respectively.

I'm grateful to Katrina Williams and John Albert for answering my questions about Nao and Sam's characters and your own experiences of country and culture, for both changing my perspective and giving me the confidence to keep doing what I was doing.

To Edie Wright, thank you for your insightful sensitivity read and for encouraging me to put things in I'd have otherwise left out.

There were many other people I consulted about aspects of the country, journey, characters and plot of *No Country for Girls*. Everyone I've asked anything of in relation to the book, thank you. Any mistakes or liberties are entirely mine, or are there because the girls wanted to do things their way.

To my UK friends, thanks for the lockdown walks and Zoom chats, to Chris for wine, bread and pizzas, and to pretty well everyone for giving me space when I needed it but always being there when I came back to you. To my WA family for sending pictures and videos from your road trip adventures, telling me what things sounded and smelled like, and for being on the end of the phone when I struggled with being so far away, which was a fair bit of the time. Mum, Dad and Annie, Miri, Mark, Pip and Mike, Alex, El and Mel, Tim and Phoebe. Thank you.

Last of all, thank you for reading *No Country for Girls*. I hope you had as much fun reading it as I had writing it, and that there are many more adventures to come.